# THE ORPHAN TRAIN SAGA

## ENDURANCE · BOOK 7

*Enjoy the Journey*

# SHERRY A. BURTON

Dorry Press

# Also by Sherry A. Burton

*The Orphan Train Saga*
*Discovery (book one)*
*Shameless (book two)*
*Treachery (book three)*
*Guardian (book four)*
*Loyal (book five)*
*Patience (book six)*
*Endurance (book seven)*

**Orphan Train Extras**
*Ezra's Story*

**Jerry McNeal Series**
*Always Faithful (book one)*
*Ghostly Guidance (book two)*
*Rambling Spirit (book three)*
*Chosen Path (book four)*
*Port Hope (book five)*
*Cold Case (book six)*
*Wicked Winds (book seven)*
*Mystic Angel (book eight)*
*Uncanny Coincidence (book nine)*
*Chesapeake Chaos (book ten)*
*Village Shenanigans (book eleven)*
*Special Delivery (book twelve)*
*Spirit of Deadwood (a full-length Jerry McNeal novel, book thirteen)*
*Star Treatment (book fourteen)*
*Merry Me (book fifteen)*
*Hidden Treasures (book sixteen)*
*Company Business (book seventeen)*
*Dearly Departed (book eighteen)*
*Family Ties (book nineteen)*

***Clean and Cozy Jerry McNeal Series Collection***
***(Compilations of the standalone Jerry McNeal series)***
*The Jerry McNeal Clean and Cozy Edition Volume one (books
1-3)*
*The Jerry McNeal Clean and Cozy Edition Volume two (books
4-6)*
*The Jerry McNeal Clean and Cozy Edition Volume three
(books 7-9)*
*The Jerry McNeal Clean and Cozy Edition Volume four (books
10-12)*
*The Jerry McNeal Clean and Cozy Edition Volume four (books
13-15)*
*The Jerry McNeal Clean and Cozy Edition Volume four (books
16-18)*

***Romance Books (****not clean*** *—sex and language)*
*Tears of Betrayal*
*Love in the Bluegrass*
*Somewhere In My Dreams*
*The King of My Heart*

***Romance Books*** *(clean)*
*Seems Like Yesterday*

*"Whispers of the Past" (a short story)*

***Psychological Thrillers***
***Storm Series***
*Surviving the Storm (book one, contains Sex, Language, and
Violence)*
*Sinister Winds (book two, contains Language and Violence)*

# Endurance

*Book 7 in The Orphan Train Saga*

Written by Sherry A. Burton

*A special thanks to*

My editor, Beth, for allowing me to keep my voice.
My cover artist, Laura Prevost, for the amazing cover.
My proofreader, Latisha Rich, for that extra set of eyes.
To my amazing team of beta readers, thank you for helping take a final look.
To my husband, aka the Roadie, thank you for everything you do to help me stay in the writing chair.

*Dedication*

*To the children who found it necessary to do the unthinkable to survive, and to those who made it their mission to help them. Remember, without a past, there is no future.*

*~ Sherry A. Burton*

# Chapter One

*Fall 2018*

Dorthia rested her hands on the arms of her wheelchair, searching the sky as if the passing clouds somehow offered clarity of a time long ago. "I was an old woman at the age of seventeen when I found myself in a company of orphans on a train heading west. At least it felt that way, as I'd already lived a long-tormented life by the time that came to pass. While I held no hope of finding a family at my advanced age, I knew I would not return to the asylum, as they would be releasing me back onto the streets of New York City as soon as I reached my eighteenth year. I had suffered those streets once; I had no intention of doing so again. My plan was simple: I would enjoy the change of scenery until such time I would simply slip away unnoticed."

"You've told this story before."

Pulled from the moment, Dorthia looked at Emily Chase, the young woman who'd interrupted her. "Of course. People are always curious when they hear I rode the orphan train. I thought that was why you are here."

Emily lowered her pen and studied her through deep brown eyes. "You promised to keep this professional. I don't know you, nor you me. I am hearing your story for the first time. I know you rode an orphan train, which intrigues me, but it isn't the only reason I'm here. While I appreciate the highlights, I was hoping for a little more."

Dorthia gripped the arms of her wheelchair as she stared up at the young woman. "More?"

Emily nodded. "Yes. If I'm going to write this book, I need to know your whole story. We can start with how you ended up on the streets in the first place. That is, if you can remember."

"You know there is nothing wrong with my memory." Realizing Emily was staying in character, Dorthia wagged a slender finger at the woman. "While my body has let me down, I assure you, my mind is as sharp as a tack."

Emily pursed her lips as she tapped her pen and looked over her notes. "I've read that some of the children who rode the trains weren't actually orphans. Was that the case with you?"

"My mother died in childbirth. My father was killed in Germany in 1914. That was when I ended up on the streets."

Emily scribbled on the pad before launching her next question. "You didn't have any family that would take you in?"

"I had plenty of family," Dorthia told her. "I just didn't know how to contact them."

"Surely the authorities could have helped you find them."

Dorthia shrugged. "The language barrier was too great."

Emily looked at her notes once more. "Language barrier? You were seven years old. Why weren't you fluent in German?"

"My father didn't feel it necessary to teach me, as we were only supposed to be over there for a short time."

Emily paused her pencil. "You weren't born there?"

Dorthia shook her head. "No. Father and I traveled there in the winter of '14—that's 1914. Father was an engineer. He went to Berlin to consult on a bridge project."

Emily blinked her surprise. "World War I started in 1914. I can't believe he took you along."

"We arrived in early March, and it wasn't as if he knew there was going to be a war. Besides, it wasn't unusual for me to go on trips with him. Only this time, he said he had a bad feeling and wanted to leave me at home. I had my father wrapped around my finger and convinced him he was only worried because Miss Pauline, my governess, had taken ill and would not be making the voyage with us." Dorthia brought her hands to her face in prayer form, rubbing her palms together as if trying to erase the past. "I've often regretted not having listened to him. Who knows how different things might have been had I stayed. Then again, I may never have known the truth of how my father died."

"How did he die?"

Dorthia stared past the woman. "He was murdered." As she spoke, the past came rushing back, and she was a little girl again, full of innocence and hope…

***

Dorthia stood in front of the Brandenburg Gate, staring up at the five arches, listening as her father relayed all the artistic information about the gate, including the man responsible for its design and the date of completion. That was the way with her father, as the man could look at almost any building and most structures and tell their history. He was so good that Dorthia often wondered if he kept each detail written on an invisible map inside his brain.

She didn't have the heart to tell him she didn't care about the construction when those details seemed to give him such joy. While he seemed truly fascinated by the enormous pillared gate before them, the only thing that caught her eye was the chariot on top of the structure. The truth of the matter was that the gate didn't look like any gate she'd ever seen, as there were no doors to close to keep out unwanted guests. No, to her, it just looked like an unfinished building to which they'd forgotten to add walls. She was more interested in the Reichstag building they'd seen earlier and the people coming and going from what looked to be a castle rising into the sky.

Dorthia humored him by half listening to him talk about the gate while her mind focused on a woman standing off to the left of the structure. Dressed in a tattered coat which flapped open in the wind and worn boots, the woman stood in the snow. Mindless of the chill, she dipped her hand into her pocket, then, pulling it free, she tossed seeds to the pigeons who eagerly swooped to get their share. While Dorthia had seen people feed birds, they were usually women in long dresses and men in suits—people of means who could afford to give away food. She tugged on her father's arm to get his attention, then pointed at the woman. "Father, why is the woman feeding the birds if she's poor?"

Her father looked where she was pointing, then took hold of her arm. "Don't point, Dorthia. It isn't polite." He placed her hand in his and began walking in the opposite direction as if wishing to shield her from such unpleasantness.

"You didn't answer my question," she said when they stopped to look at the gate once more.

Her father glanced at the woman. "Why do you think she's poor?"

Dorthia stared at her father, mouth agape. "Why, because she'd dressed in rags, of course. Look at her coat; it doesn't have a single button to protect her from the cold."

"Not everyone is as fortunate as we are, Dorthia. Perhaps her good dress is on the line drying in the sun." That was another thing about her father, the man never missed an opportunity to teach her a lesson.

"If she only has one good dress, why is she using her money to feed the birds and not buy buttons for her coat?"

Her father laughed an easy laugh. "I wouldn't presume to know."

Dorthia sighed. "How can you know so much about buildings but so little about people?"

Her father chuckled. "Because, as an engineer, it is my job to know about structures."

"I don't care about a silly old gate. I prefer buildings, but not really. I merely want to know about the people who live in them." Dorthia realized what she'd said and clapped her free hand over her mouth. "I'm sorry, Father, I didn't mean it."

"Of course you meant it or you wouldn't have said it," he said, patting her gloved hand. "There's no need to lie, Dorthia. You don't understand buildings any more than I understand the people who live inside of them."

Dorthia blinked her surprise. "You're not mad?"

He kept her hand tucked in the crook of his arm as they stood and looked up at the gate once more. "Of course not. You understand the fundamentals of what it takes to create such breathtaking structures; that's all I ever wanted. You are not supposed to know how to build them. You're supposed to know how to decorate them. Someday, you'll marry a man who will build you a castle, and it will be your job to fill it with things that will make you smile just to look upon them."

Dorthia gulped. "You mean I'll live in a house as big as the Reichstag?"

Her father laughed, his warm breath sending a white puff into the freezing air. "No, I don't suppose you will, but there is an English phrase that says that a man's home is his castle, and if that is the case, you'll be the queen."

"A queen? Will I get to wear a crown?"

Her father kissed the back of her gloved hand. "I shall purchase it for you myself as a wedding present."

Dorthia giggled, stopping when she saw a man with a crooked smile watching them. Leaning against the wall of one of the openings, he stared at them so intensely, it gave her a chill. She was about to mention it when her father pulled the gold chain that lifted his watch from his coat pocket.

He opened the lid to check the time. "It is nearly lunchtime. We shall go get some soup to help warm our bellies. Before we go, do you remember why the chariot is called a quadriga?"

"Because there are four horses abreast pulling it," Dorthia said, quoting what she had recalled from her father's earlier lesson. "The cross was added after Prussia's victory over France."

He beamed his approval. "And here I thought you weren't listening."

"I always listen. I just don't always hear." She looked for the man who'd unnerved her, relieved to no longer see him standing there.

"That's because your mind is carefree enough to allow you to float away," her father said, drawing her attention. "The trick of it is to not get swept out to sea in the process."

Dorthia recalled the voyage over from America and the swirling seas that sometimes tossed the ship so fiercely, they had to remain in their cabin for fear of falling over the side. She gulped. "I do not ever wish to be swept out to sea."

"You remind me so much of your mother at times," he said,

then looked away as if the memory was too much to bear.

"I wish I could remember her," Dorthia replied.

He whipped his head around and kept his tone light. "Impossible; she died bringing you into the world. Lucky me, as I get to have you all to myself."

Though he laughed at the supposed joke, she could feel the pain in his words. Dorthia worked to gather the courage to ask the question that had haunted her of late—to ask if he was mad at her for killing her mother. Though she'd often lain in bed at night wondering, she'd never brought herself to ask, as she didn't want to know the answer. She opened her mouth to ask when the birds took flight, drawing her attention to the woman once more. "Do you think she has a home?"

"You have a good heart, my dear." Her father dipped his hand into his pocket, drew out a silver coin, and placed it into her palm.

The coin felt warm in her hand. "What's this for?"

He glanced at the woman who'd been feeding the birds, then looked at Dorthia and smiled a kind smile. "I fear if you don't run and give it to the woman, you'll not be able to enjoy your day without worry."

"Oh, Father, you know me so well." Dorthia clutched the coin. "What if she's too proud to take it?"

Her father contemplated this for a moment. "If she balks at your charity, tell her to use it to feed the birds."

The excitement Dorthia felt as she ran to give the woman the coin was palpable. The look on the woman's face when she handed it to her reflected her joy.

Tears welled in the woman's eyes as she moved the coat aside and quickly stowed the coin in the pocket of her skirt. "*Danke schön.*"

"You're welcome." Remembering herself, Dorthia answered in German. "*Bitte.*"

Dorthia turned, eager to tell her father of their exchange, then slowed at seeing him speaking with the man whom she'd seen watching them only moments before. Her father's stance was guarded, showing he wasn't enjoying the conversation. He saw her coming and held up a hand to stop her.

The man turned, looked in her direction, and smiled the

same crooked smile.

Her father took hold of the man's arm. "Dorthia, run and don't look back!"

She hesitated and watched in horror as the man hit her father. Her father doubled his fist and answered with a punch of his own. This went on for several seconds until the man thrust his hand once more, sending her father to the ground.

The man stood over him, wielding a knife in one hand and her father's pocket watch in the other.

"FATHER!" Dorthia shrieked. Though she willed her legs to move, they didn't respond. She stood, watching helplessly as the man slipped the watch into his pocket and bent to rummage in her father's pockets.

The man stood and saw her watching. As he stepped toward her, his lips curved into the same crooked smile.

The woman who'd been feeding the birds moved in front of her. Wielding a small knife of her own, the woman raised it in her fist while yelling something Dorthia didn't understand.

The man spat, then turned, disappearing into the gathering crowd.

Dorthia ran to her father's aid, but it was too late, as there was no life left in the man's eyes. She wasn't sure when she'd started running or how long she'd been doing so. Her only thought was to get as far away from her father's lifeless body as possible.

# Chapter Two

"You returned to America after your father's death?" Emily asked when Dorthia failed to continue.

Dorthia picked at the fabric of her dress. "Yes, but not right away."

Emily flipped the page, looking over her notes once more. "That's right, you said you lived on the streets. You mean you never returned to claim your father's body?"

Dorthia laughed a haunting laugh. "That would have been the practical thing to do, would it not?"

"I'm not judging. I'm just asking the questions my readers will want to know," Emily said. "Why didn't you? Did you not think the authorities would send you home?"

"Maybe, maybe not. And what if they did?" Dorthia asked bitterly. "I was an orphan. Kids living on the street were a dime a dozen. People didn't care about them other than scorning them for stealing enough food to keep them alive."

Emily leaned forward in her chair. "Please, I am only trying to understand. It sounds as if your father was well-to-do. Didn't you have any other family?"

"Sure I did, but Father and I lived in Boston. Father's kin

lived in Chicago, and I'd only met them a time or two. Once, when I was five, we took a train to Chicago to visit them. Before you ask the question that's begging to be asked, my father's name was John Smith. Do you know how many people with the last name of Smith lived in Chicago in nineteen twenty?"

"It was freezing. You didn't speak the language. How on earth did you survive?" Emily asked.

"I did what all the other children did to survive. I became a thief. Unlike the others who lived on the streets, I could never remember a time when I was hungry. Oh, sure, I'd felt a pang telling me it was time to eat, but I'm talking about true hunger, where your stomach gnaws at itself, and your head swirls as if you are on an ocean cruise during high waves. That was new to me, and I didn't like it at all. I was still in shock from seeing my father killed and hadn't eaten." She closed her eyes, recalling the days after her father died.

***

Dorthia aimlessly wandered the streets in a blind stupor, replaying the moments of her father's demise in her head. While her father had warned her there were bad people in the world, this was her first encounter with someone who was truly evil. A watch, a lousy gold watch. It wasn't even a good piece—in fact, the watch had no sentimental value at all, as her father always made sure to leave those pieces at home whenever he traveled for precisely that purpose. If the thief had asked, her father would have readily given it to him and wished the man a good day. But no, the man had to take everything, including the life it was attached to. Picturing her father's face when he'd yelled for her to run brought forth a fresh set of tears. It was the first time she could remember willfully disobeying the man, and that, too, weighed on her mind. She was a good daughter, and good daughters listened to their fathers. Only if she had, she might never have known what happened to him that day, and not knowing why he, too, had abandoned her would have surely driven her mad.

Dorthia pushed her hat back and angrily wiped her tears away. She was cold, hungry, and weary, and had no idea where she was supposed to go. Seeing a group of well-dressed men and women, she approached. "Please, I need help."

Instead of taking her into their fold, they looked upon her as if she were nothing before turning their backs on her. She ached to tell them she wasn't an urchin, only she didn't know the language and couldn't summon the words. As she stood there watching them walk away, she realized she was wrong: her father was dead, and her mother long gone. Though she might be dressed better than most children she'd seen living on the streets, not having a home to return to or any money with which to ensure she didn't starve, a street urchin was precisely what she was.

An orphan.

As that realization came to her, a new onslaught of tears streamed down her face. How she still had tears left to spill, she didn't know. It occurred to her sometime later that she was ambling around like a marble in a box without direction, and if she didn't find somewhere to spend the night, she would not have to worry about tomorrow, as she would likely freeze.

As if the universe heard her plea for help, she stumbled upon a vent along the street with steam funneling up from below into the branches of a thick, leafless bush. As luck would have it, the area beneath the tangle of branches was bare and made somewhat of an upside-down nest that blocked the snow. Dorthia pushed the limbs aside and slipped in through the branches and, for the first time since watching her father be murdered, felt safe from the world. She sat huddled on the frozen ground using her heavy coat to block out the winter chill as a small stream of steam whiffed inside the bowed branches, creating a welcomed warmth. Exhausted and overwhelmed by the day's events, Dorthia closed her eyes.

***

She woke after a restless night where images of her father being stabbed filled her dreams. The hollowness in her heart weighed heavy, and a part of her wanted nothing more than to remain huddled under the bush until, at last, she either succumbed to the fog that seemed to have settled in her brain or lay there in hopes that someone would discover her. Having lived in Boston, she'd seen policemen snatch up orphaned children who lived on the streets and watched as they were dragged away, kicking and screaming to be let go, which they never were. She'd once asked her father where they were taking the children. He'd told her they would most likely go to an asylum or prison, depending on what they'd done. She'd begged him to help, but her father had hung his head, telling her there were too many. When she'd pressed the matter of what would happen to them in the asylums and prisons, he'd simply changed the subject, as if wishing to protect her from the horrors the children faced. That fear of what would happen if she were, in fact, discovered kept her from seeking out a policeman and begging for help.

Instead, she emerged from her hiding place, searching until she'd finally returned to Brandenburg Gate. She didn't know what invisible force pulled her in that direction, other than a childish sense of hope that she would arrive and discover her father waiting for her, and this all to be just another terrible nightmare. Only he wasn't there, nor was the bloodstain marking the spot where he'd met his demise. She found the lack of evidence both comforting and nauseating because at least a stain would let her know she hadn't imagined the whole thing.

A flutter of movement caught her eye. She looked to see a flock of pigeons settling high on top of the gate and knew they'd come in hopes of getting a meal. As the pigeons cooed their greeting, she became exceedingly aware of her own hunger and wondered if any of them would get fed this day. Though she didn't have anything to offer the birds, she liked hearing their coos, as their presence not only kept her from feeling alone but also reminded her of her father's last act of kindness.

She stood with her back to a wall where she could feel the sun on her face, and watched the birds. After a few moments, she grew weary and sank to the ground. Wrapping her arms around her knees, she used her coat to warm her legs. She'd been sitting there for some time when several pigeons took flight, hovering several moments before coming to roost once more on a nearby roof. Dorthia shielded her eyes against the sun as she looked to see what had frightened the birds. Her heart skipped as she saw the bird lady making her way toward the gate.

Dressed in the same tattered outfit as the previous day, the woman spoke in soft tones that belied the harshness of the language she spoke. Though Dorthia could only understand a few of the words, she found them comforting. The pigeons must have felt the same way as, one by one, they took flight, gliding down to the street to feed on the seeds she scattered. If the woman remembered her, she did not let on. Not being able to communicate with the lady, Dorthia remained in place, wishing for a moment that she was a bird so that she, too, could get fed.

Laughter drew her attention away from the birds as she looked to see a group of five children, three boys and two girls, all of whom appeared to be close to her in age, making their way toward the city. She surmised by their ill-fitting clothes and dirty faces that they were street children and, for the first time, felt a kinship with the urchins.

Having nothing better to do, Dorthia followed, listening to their chatter, wishing she could decipher their words as they spoke amongst themselves. Though she couldn't understand what they were saying, it was clear they moved with a purpose. They must have noticed her, as every now and then, one of the kids would pivot as if checking to see if she was still following.

They turned down a street, then another, until, at last, they reached an outdoor market. Instantly, the smell of cooked sausage and other mouthwatering delights filled the air. For a moment, she was home on the streets of Boston, visiting the market not far from the two-story apartment where she and her father lived.

*Used to live,* Dorthia reminded herself. *You have no home now.*

One of the boys broke from the group and stood in front of her, scowling. He held his hand up and said a whole string of things she didn't understand.

Dorthia shook her head.

The boy's scowl deepened as he repeated his words. This time, one phrase stood out. *"Gen sie weg."*

Dorthia narrowed her eyes. "No, I won't go away!"

The boy blinked his surprise, his eyes widening as he looked her over. "American?"

Dorthia nodded. As she did, her stomach rumbled loud enough to be heard.

The boy left without comment.

Dorthia followed, stopping when he met up with the others, who all turned and looked at her as if she had two heads. They mumbled amongst themselves before heading off once more. Curious to see what they were up to, she followed as the group moved through the crowd, then stared in rapt fascination as one of the boys broke from the group and moved alongside a woman who was picking through a wagon full of fabric. Just as he reached the woman, two girls from the group began to squabble. They must have done this on purpose, as their ruckus drew the woman's attention long enough for the boy to dip his hand into the pocket of her skirt. He saw Dorthia watching and winked as he pulled the woman's coin purse free and emptied the contents into his own pocket. He glanced at her once more while he replaced the empty coin purse and walked away without the woman catching him.

Anger boiled inside as she recalled the man with the crooked smile. *They are but thieves, just like the man who killed my father. No, not quite; at least the boy didn't kill the woman.* Bile rose in her throat. Had her stomach not been empty, she would have released its contents. The boy's arrogance enraged her. She moved closer, intending to out him and insist he return the money to its rightful owner.

The boy must have known her intentions, as he moved to cut her off. "*Nein.*" His voice was low and threatening.

She narrowed her eyes at him and attempted to push past.

"Nein," he repeated, grabbing hold of her arm.

She kicked him in the shin with the toe of her shoe as she jerked her arm free.

Instead of turning angry, the boy grinned and pressed a coin into her hand.

She stared at the coin without blinking and held her tongue as the boy disappeared into the crowd.

Screams pierced the air as the woman realized her coin purse had been emptied.

Dorthia gulped, a pang of guilt washing over her as she slid the pilfered coin into her own pocket. Had things been different, she would have quickly done the right thing and returned the coin to the woman. Instead, she gave the lady a wide berth and made her way to the sausages she'd smelled when first arriving in the market.

Standing beside a small, boxed cart with large, spoked wheels, the vendor looked at her expectantly.

"*Wurstichen.*" Dorthia held up the coin, praying it would be enough.

"*Ja,*" the man said, plucking the coin from her hand. He reached into the box, drew out a sausage and slapped it on a round bun, adding a heaping pile of sauerkraut before she could stop him.

Not knowing how to tell him to remove it and being entirely too hungry to care that she wasn't a fan of the fermented cabbage, Dorthia sank her teeth into the first meal since the morning prior and found the pungent cabbage to be surprisingly enjoyable. What she didn't enjoy was the juices from the cabbage. Each time she took a bite, they flowed down her chin and along her arms, dripping inside her coat and reaching both elbows. She tried to remember her manners and slow her eating, but hunger overrode her social upbringing, and she scarfed down the meal so quickly that she finished with a loud belch.

Appalled by her lack of manners, she slapped her hand over her mouth as the heat rose up her face. It occurred to her that her father had been dead but a day, and she was already acting like one of the street urchins they passed when walking through the city. She thought of the children she'd followed, wondering how they came to be living on the street and why the boy had given her the coin when she'd treated him so poorly. While she wished to know the answer, it would probably remain a mystery, given her limited grasp of the German language. That thought stayed with her as she walked through the market, listening to the locals chat amongst themselves.

Now that she had food in her stomach, her thoughts grew clearer, and a sudden sense of panic washed over her. Thinking he'd always be around to translate, her father hadn't taught her more than a fistful of words in German. Most of those were simple phrases so she would appear polite. She couldn't live under the bush forever, and it wouldn't be long before the clothes and shoes she had on were too small. It was her own fault as she'd insisted on bringing both the emerald green dress and ill-fitting shoes, telling her father she would outgrow them both before they returned home. She thought of the clothes she'd brought with her, clothes that her father had sent to be pressed the moment they'd checked into their hotel so she would look nice whenever they had their evening meal.

The hotel!

There was a man there who spoke English. Her heart began to race. Her father had told her he'd paid for the month – the amount of time he expected them to stay. If she could find the hotel, perhaps she could convince him to allow her to stay there until the money ran out.

***

Dorthia spent the better part of the day searching for the hotel. With each wrong turn, she grew increasingly angry she hadn't paid more attention to her father when he'd commented on the architecture of the building or pointed out a landmark. She turned down a street and grew excited when one of the buildings looked familiar—a fleeting sense of joy, as the only reason she recognized it was because she was now passing it for the third time. She turned back the way she'd just come. Reaching the end of the street, she realized she'd retraced her path so much, she hadn't a clue as to how to get back to the market, much less find the bush she'd been sleeping under. She thought perhaps that if she could make her way to Brandenburg Gate, she would be able to reorient herself. She hurried to catch a man who was walking down the street. "Excuse me," she said in German, "Brandenburger Tor?"

The man looked her over, then spoke as he pointed.

"*Vielen Dank*," she said, thanking the man before hurrying off the way he'd signaled. Though she had no clue what he'd said, he had at least pointed her in the right direction. She asked for directions four additional times, and it had grown dark by the time she reached the gate, then finally managed to make her way back to the safety of the bush. Though the street was quiet, she stood watching and listening for several moments before pushing aside the limbs and ducking inside the cluster of roots.

Dorthia pulled her knees to her chest and thought about the day's events and how she'd disrespected her father's memory by not returning the coin the boy had given her. She further wondered if the woman would have allowed her to keep the coin if she'd had the words to tell her she was hungry and knew the answer to be no. People didn't care about kids; if they did, there wouldn't be so many of them running about the streets. It suddenly occurred to her she should have stayed to face her father's killer, as he probably would have taken her life as well. While she had no desire to die, she had even less desire to live the life she was now destined to live. Just the thought of living her life begging for scraps of food in a country whose language she barely understood brought on a new onslaught of tears; this time, she allowed them to run their course.

# Chapter Three

The second night was easier only because Dorthia was too tired to care. She opened her eyes the next morning, surprised to see the sun already high in the sky. Worried about being discovered, she peeked to make sure no one was near before cautiously making her way out into the open. She considered making another attempt at finding the hotel; however, she moved in the direction of Brandenburg Gate instead. Though the place made her skin crawl with terrifying memories, it also offered her comfort, as she knew she could find her way without getting lost. To her surprise, the boy who'd given her the coin was there when she arrived. Leaning against the wall where she'd sat when she first saw him and his friends, he looked up, smiling as if he'd been waiting for her.

Dorthia hesitated, recalling the last time a stranger had smiled at her like that. Swallowing the bile that threatened, she studied the boy from a distance. Standing half a foot shorter than her, barefoot, with grime-stained, ill-fitting clothes, he didn't look very threatening. Curious as to what he wanted, Dorthia took a cautious step forward.

The boy's smile widened, but he didn't break his stance.

Instead, he continued to lean against the wall as if knowing any sudden move would send her fleeing in the opposite direction.

She counted the steps it took to reach him—twenty-two. While she wanted to ask what he wanted, she didn't know how, so she waited for him to make the next move.

He pointed to his chest. "Baylor."

She repeated the gesture. "Dorthia."

"American?"

She started to tell him they'd already established that point. Instead, she merely nodded.

He looked to see if anyone was watching, then reached into his pocket and pulled a bracelet free. He took hold of her hand without asking permission and placed the bracelet on her wrist. Dorthia frowned at the bauble, wondering why he'd given her the gift. She started to ask when he moved past her, brushing against her ever so lightly. She looked down, and to her surprise, the bracelet was gone.

He stopped a few feet away, grinning as he held the bracelet up for her to see.

Dorthia narrowed her eyes. She did not like this game.

Baylor moved forward and slipped the bracelet onto her arm once more. This time, he removed it, letting her watch the process as he did. It dawned on her this was some kind of lesson. Her mouth went dry as she realized he was teaching her how to steal. She recalled the boy she'd seen being hauled out of the marketplace kicking and screaming. She peered at Baylor, wondering how to break through the language barrier to tell him she didn't wish to go to prison.

As if sensing her hesitation, Baylor slipped the bracelet into his pocket. When he withdrew his hand, he wielded a shiny silver coin just like the one he'd given her the previous day.

Dorthia's mouth watered as she recalled the sausage she'd spent it on. If she knew how to get the coins herself, she'd never have to be hungry again. *Forgive me, Father*, she thought, and nodded her head.

***

"I'm sorry, I don't mean to interrupt your thoughts, but you grew quiet. Are you okay?" Emily asked.

"Just remembering."

Emily handed her a tissue. "Do you want to stop?"

"No." Dorthia dabbed at her eyes. "It's just that I've often wondered what became of the boy, what with the war and all."

"He taught you to steal?"

Dorthia smiled. "He did."

"He liked you?"

"He liked what I represented."

"Which was?"

"America. Had my father taught me more German, I don't think Baylor would have paid me any mind. As it was, it was he who taught me how to dip pockets and he who indirectly helped me find my way back to America."

"Helped how?" Emily asked.

Dorthia stared out the window. As she spoke, the memories came flooding back.

***

Dorthia pulled the threadbare blanket close to ward off the morning chill. Though it added an extra layer, the cloth was so tattered that it provided little warmth. She'd taken it from a clothesline, not caring that the person who hung it there might need it. She'd done a lot she wasn't proud of since her father had died, and unless something changed, she feared she would do plenty more. She stretched, grimacing as her toes dug into the ends of her shoes. Her father had spoken highly of the workmanship of German cobblers and had her fitted for a new pair of shoes on their last morning together. Her father had paid the man extra to have them delivered to the hotel and promised she'd be wearing them by the end of the week. A promise—like so many others—that remained unfulfilled.

She coughed, her breath coming out in a cloud of steam. She'd tried to keep track of her time in Germany and had long ago grown tired of counting the days. While she didn't know what day it was, she knew it was cold. Surely spring couldn't be too far away. If she had to endure many more frigid days, she was likely to freeze to death in her sleep, and they'd find her body under the bushes come spring. Instead of being upset by knowing her demise was forthcoming, a welcome calmness washed over her. A sense of relief that was short-lived when her stomach rumbled, reminding her that if she didn't get to the market to pilfer a coin, she would starve to death long before the snow melted. She folded her blanket, pushing it close to the base of the bush before making her way out of the tunnel of limbs and hurrying to the market.

The street was filled with both vendors and shoppers. While some of the vendors were content waiting for someone to approach and purchase their wares, others stood on wooden boxes barking comments to draw people near.

Dorthia followed a slew of shoppers as they funneled close to one such man. She was too short to see what he was selling, but that was okay. She wasn't there to buy; she was there to pilfer the pocket of someone so caught up in what the man was selling that they wouldn't notice a small hand dipping into their coat pocket to relieve them of a coin or two. It hadn't taken her long to learn to dip pockets. If her father had been alive, he might have even called her a natural and told her she had a knack for such things. Then again, if he were alive, she wouldn't have had to learn the skill in the first place.

Pilfering the pockets of coats was easy – as long as the person she was stealing from had indeed put their coins into their outer pocket. Even those who were cautious eventually let their guard down. Sometimes, it was only for a moment or two. A person would pay for their purchase and slip their change into their outer pocket just long enough for them to exit the crowd and properly stow their money. Those were the easiest marks, as they were so focused on what they'd just bought that they didn't pay as close attention to what was going on around them.

Baylor had shown her how to trail behind, then blend into the crowd and wait for the right moment. Blending in was easier in the beginning, as no one paid attention to a child who was properly dressed. Now, instead of fitting in with her store-bought clothes, she reeked of the unwashed, and her once pristine clothing hung on her like a rag. Her lip trembled as she recalled the first time she'd seen the dress in the department store window and begged her father to buy it and the emerald green hat that matched so she could wear it to church on Sunday morning. She'd walked up the cathedral steps feeling like a fine lady with her hand tucked into the crook of her father's arm. He'd patted her hand and told her she was the most beautiful girl in the church that day.

Dorthia held up her hand, recalling the warmth of his touch. The dirt under her fingernails jolted her back to reality. There was nothing beautiful about her now. Her arms were covered with scrapes, her skin streaked with dirt, and her toes were covered with scabs from having them rub against her shoes while running away from near encounters. She was a beggar and a thief. Her father would not think her beautiful. He would consider her a wayward soul to be looked upon with pity.

Thinking of her father's disapproval dissolved her momentum, and she slunk from the crowd empty-handed. What did it matter if she starved to death now or months from now? Dying was dying. She may as well succumb to death and get it over with.

A shrill shriek pierced the air as a man's voice rang out. "*Stoppen Sie, Dieb.*"

*Thief?* Dorthia turned as an excited murmur swept through the crowd and swallowed as Baylor pushed his way free. He saw her and smiled.

The smile was short-lived as a man grabbed hold of the boy's arm, triumphantly lifting it into the air. "Dieb!"

Rage filled every inch of Dorthia's body as she recognized the man. She stepped forward without stopping to consider the consequences and pointed a finger. "No, *he's* the thief! He killed my father!"

No one moved.

She firmed her chin and spoke in German. "Dieb!"

"Ja!" The man bobbed his head, lifting Baylor's arm higher.

Baylor frowned, obviously upset that she'd ratted him out.

"Nein!" Dorthia said. She moved closer and pointed to the man with the crooked smile. "Dieb."

The thief faltered, staring at her as if trying to recall where he knew her from.

A police officer pushed his way through the throng of bystanders who'd all turned when Dorthia had confronted the man. Seeing the constable, the thief pushed Baylor into the officer's hands and said a string of things she didn't understand aside from the final word, which was once again the German word for thief.

"Nien!" Dorthia spat, pointing at the man who'd killed her father. "Dieb!"

The officer looked the man up and down. "Dieb?"

Dorthia held firm to her conviction. "Ja, Deib!"

The thief took a step back. Two men who'd been watching the exchange blocked his way.

The police officer passed Baylor off to another man as he faced the thief and said something in German.

The man shook his head and started to walk away.

Seeing his opportunity, Baylor stepped backward and disappeared into the crowd unnoticed.

The police officer firmed his tone, and the two men who'd been blocking the thief's way took hold of his arms.

Dorthia held her breath as the police officer searched the man's pockets, a small part of her hoping the search would produce her father's pocket watch. Disappointment rushed over her as the officer pulled his hand free, producing a gold necklace that he dangled in front of the thief's face.

An elderly woman wearing a heavy coat stepped forward. She peered closely at the necklace before kicking the thief in the shin and snatching it from the officer's hand.

The officer handcuffed the man and then motioned for the woman to follow as he led the thief away.

As the crowd dispersed, a thin woman with two wide-eyed girls at her side stood watching her. One of the girls was a head shorter than her. Dorthia knew that didn't necessarily mean the girl was younger, as she was often suspected of being older than her years. Her father had told her it was because she was not only tall for her age but also had a better vocabulary than most girls her age.

After a moment, the woman started in her direction with the children in tow. Stopping directly in front of Dorthia, she looked her up and down. "You are American, yes?"

Excitement surged through Dorthia's veins. While the woman had a thick German accent, it was the first time she'd heard anyone speaking her language since her father had died. She bobbed her head. "Yes!"

"That man killed your papa?"

"Yes." This time, the word came out in a whisper.

"Where's your mother?"

"Dead," Dorthia replied.

The woman looked at her daughters, then studied her once more. "Come," she said, leading the girls away.

Dorthia heaved a heavy sigh and longed to follow as the trio walked away.

After several steps, the woman stopped, looked over her shoulder, and crooked her finger. "Come."

Dorthia raced after the woman and fell into step behind as she and the girls began walking once more. It didn't dawn on her to ask where they were going, nor did she care. It was the first time since her father died that she dared to hope she wouldn't follow him to his grave.

# Chapter Four

Dorthia followed in complete silence for three blocks until, at last, the woman led her into an ornate building, where they climbed two flights of stairs and used her key to enter an apartment. With tall ceilings and white walls, the space was modest compared to the brownstone Dorthia shared with her father in Boston, but it was clean and warm and far superior to the bush she'd been living under since her father died. She suspected the family had some money, as the apartment was not a single-room dwelling like she'd seen in some of the photos her father had shared with her when telling her of the differences between German and American living. There were also long, colorful drapes hanging over the floor-to-ceiling windows and woven rugs lining the floor. Given the family's apparent good fortune, Dorthia dared to hope that the woman had taken pity on her and brought her home to offer her a meal before sending her on her way once more.

The woman shrugged out of her coat and motioned for the girls to do the same. "What is your name, girl?"

"Dorthia. Dorthia Jean Smith." Dorthia stood by the door, waiting to see what would happen next.

"My name is Liselotte Robberts; these are my daughters, Anneliese," she said, nodding to the taller of the two girls, "and Leni." She indicated the smaller of the two. The woman said something to Leni that sent the girl hurrying down the hall. She turned to the taller girl and spoke to her in German.

Anneliese glanced at Dorthia, then scowled at her mother. "Nien!"

The woman's hand was swift as she repeated her earlier words. Tears sprang to Anneliese's eyes. She clutched the side of her face, stomping off without another word.

Dorthia wondered at their relationship. Though her father had scolded her from time to time, he'd never gotten angry enough to strike her.

Ignoring the girl's attitude, Mrs. Robberts turned her attention to Dorthia. Her gaze trailed over the length of her, and for a moment, Dorthia thought she was going to tell her to leave. Instead, the lady forced a smile. "Come with me."

Dorthia followed, stopping when the woman pushed open the door to a water closet. Leni sat on the side of a cast-iron tub, trailing her fingers under a thin stream of water that worked to fill the plugged tub. Dorthia gazed at the tub with such a longing that she emitted a soft sob. While she had managed to dip her hands in a random bucket or horse trough a time or two, she hadn't had a bath or washed her hair since her father died.

The woman moved aside and waved a hand toward the tub. "You wash now."

"The bath is for me?" Dorthia gasped.

"You'll not sleep here unless you're clean."

"Sleep here? You wish for me to stay?" She was trembling, and her words sounded shaky to her own ears.

"You prefer to sleep on the street?"

"NO!" Remembering her manners, Dorthia checked her enthusiasm. "No, ma'am, I do not wish to ever sleep on the street again."

Mrs. Robberts motioned toward the girl. "That's enough water, Leni."

"Yes, Momma," Leni said, then hurried to twist the knobs.

Anneliese appeared in the doorway, a frown tugging at her face as she handed her mother a stack of neatly folded dark brown and cream checkered fabric. She slid a glance to Dorthia, then left the room without uttering a word.

Mrs. Robberts set the stack on a ledge next to the toilet, then pulled a towel and washcloth from the standing cabinet. "Don't just stand there. Get in before the water turns cold."

Dorthia hesitated. While she was eager to get into the tub, she wasn't thrilled about getting undressed in front of strangers.

"You've not got anything I haven't seen before," the woman said curtly. "Besides, you're going to need my help. I doubt your head has seen a brush in some time. How long has it been since you've washed?"

"I do not know. Not since my father…" Dorthia's voice trailed off.

"When was that?"

"March thirteenth. I know this because it was the day after we arrived in Berlin." Dorthia swallowed, looking at the pile of rags that was all that was left of the once beautiful dress.

Mrs. Robberts' eyes grew round. "You've been living on the streets ever since?"

"I have."

"Where do you sleep?"

"Wherever I can." Dorthia decided not to tell the exact location in case the woman failed to keep her promise of allowing her to stay. She changed the subject as she began to undress. "You speak English very well."

"My husband comes from America. He taught us his language and insists we speak English whenever we are in the house."

"Your daughters did not learn it from birth?" Dorthia asked.

A sadness touched the woman's eyes. "The girls are mine. Stephen is not their father."

"You live in Germany, so why is it important that they speak English?"

"My husband wishes to take us to America when his job is done."

Dorthia lowered into the tub with a splash. "You're going to America?"

"Ja," the woman said, forgetting herself. "In a few weeks. My husband began teaching us his language two years since, saying it would be easier for us if we knew the words. He is right, no?"

"Your husband is right. It is scary when you don't know the language. I wish my father had taught me more German before we came." A thought occurred to her. "Perhaps now we can help each other."

Ignoring the comment, the woman reached behind her and plucked a soft, bristled brush from the edge of the tub. She then retrieved a bar of strong-smelling soap from the ledge, which she dunked into the water before running it across the bristles. She handed that brush to Dorthia, then started brushing through her hair with a different one. "Did that man at the market really kill your papa, or were you just trying to save the boy?"

"It's true," Dorthia said, using the brush to scrub her torso. "Sadly, he'll not be charged with killing him."

"He'll go to prison all the same," the woman assured her.

"He will?" Dorthia didn't even try to hide her excitement.

"Ja. Same for you if you get caught with your hand in someone else's pocket."

Dorthia started to tell the woman she wasn't a thief but decided against it, feeling the woman was too smart to be duped. "Is that why you brought me here?"

Mrs. Robberts slid a glance at her youngest daughter. "I brought you here because my husband would wish it to be."

"Because I am American? Ow," Dorthia said as the woman worked her way through a tangle.

Leni snickered, then quieted once more when the woman fussed at her in German.

"Because you can help tell our daughters about life in America. How old are you?" the woman asked.

"Seven."

Leni's eyes grew wide as she looked at her mother. "She is the same age as Anneliese. How can that be?"

Mrs. Robberts frowned. "You look much older."

A slight panic rose in Dorthia's chest. "Does that mean I cannot stay?"

"You'll stay," the woman said, recovering. "You'll take Anneliese's room. She will move into her sister's room."

Though this announcement didn't seem to bother Leni,

Dorthia wasn't so sure Anneliese would be as agreeable. The girl hadn't been pleased about giving up her dress; she probably wouldn't be thrilled to learn she'd be losing her room as well. While there had been a time when getting a room all to herself would have seemed right, Dorthia had been sleeping under the bush so long that anything would be an improvement. "No, I can't take her room. A blanket in the corner will be just fine."

"You'll take the room." The woman's tone left no room for discussion. "Leni, go tell Anneliese to take her belongings to your room."

The young girl ran off as if eager to tell her sister of the news.

Dorthia looked at the discolored water and the dark ring that was forming along the sides of the tub. "Ms. Pauline would not be happy to see me this dirty."

The woman cocked an eyebrow. "Ms. Pauline?"

"My governess."

"Governess? I do not know this word."

"She watches over me when my father can't."

"She is a relative?"

"No, just someone my father hired to watch over me. She was supposed to come with us on the trip, but she got sick at the last minute. Father was going to leave me home too, but I begged him to let me come. I wish he hadn't been so eager to see me happy."

"This Ms. Pauline, you do not know how to contact her?"

Dorthia shook her head. "I do not."

"Perhaps you could be a governess for my daughters."

Dorthia laughed off the comment. "I'm not old enough to be a governess. Besides, Leni said I am the same age as Anneliese."

"This is true, but you look and act much older. You must have good wits to have survived living on the streets for so long. My girls will need someone to watch over them on the ship when I cannot. You could help keep them safe and show them how to behave like Americans."

On the ship? A surge of excitement raced through her as she knew at that moment that she'd agree to almost anything if it meant going back to America. "You mean you'd take me to

America with you?"

"Yes," the woman said as the brush caught another tangle. "That is if Mr. Robberts agrees."

"Do you think he will like me?" Dorthia asked hopefully. Mrs. Robberts was quiet for so long that Dorthia didn't think the woman was going to answer.

"Yes, I suppose my husband will like you just fine. I think that will do it," she said as she pulled the hairbrush through Dorthia's hair and didn't meet any resistance. "I think you are capable of taking it from here. I'm going to start supper. Make sure to run some clean water and rinse it from the spigot when you are finished washing."

Dorthia couldn't believe her good fortune. Not only was she getting clean, she'd soon be wearing a clean dress and have food in her belly before going to sleep in a real bed. If the woman noticed Dorthia's look of surprise, she did not comment.

Instead, she reached into the cupboard and pulled out a small jar. "Use this salve on those bites when you are finished bathing. It will keep them from itching and help your skin heal."

"Yes, ma'am," Dorthia said, bobbing her head. "And, Mrs. Robberts, I thank you for taking me in."

"You have no cause to thank me. I'm a mother. I do what I must do."

Dorthia sighed and hid it with a splash of dunking her head into the water as a sudden sense of longing for a mother she'd never known washed over her. She kept from letting her feelings be known as the woman left the room.

The water was cold to the touch by the time Dorthia forced herself to climb out of the tub. She tugged the plug free to allow the water to drain and frowned at seeing the dirt ring. She looked in the cabinet, hoping to find something to clean it with. Not finding anything, she rubbed the washcloth over the soap and used that to clean the ring. When she'd finished, she soaped the rag once more and ran the ends into itself to clean the dirt from the rag. Satisfied with the cleanliness of the rag, she rinsed it and draped it over the spigot to dry.

Next, she unfolded the clothing and got dressed. While she and Anneliese might have been the same age, they were not the same size. The dress fit tight and was shorter than seemed fitting for a girl of her age. Still, it was all she had, so she decided to make do.

Leni was sitting on the floor outside the door when, at last, she finished. Upon seeing her, the girl scrambled to her feet. "Momma told me to show you to your room."

Dorthia lowered her voice to keep from being overheard. "Is your sister mad?"

Leni cocked her head and frowned at her. "My sister is quite sane, thank you."

Dorthia smiled. "No, not mad as in loony. I'm asking if she is angry at me for taking her room."

"Oh," Leni said, returning her smile. "She'll be fine."

"I hope she knows I did not ask for this," Dorthia replied. A wonderful smell drifted through the hallway, reminding her how hungry she was. "That smells so good."

"Ja, Momma is making cheese spaetzle and potato dumplings." Leni stopped in front of a closed door. "This is your room. Momma says to tell you to hurry. Papa will be home soon."

Dorthia opened the door. The room was just that—a room. Anneliese had been thorough in cleaning out her belongings. The only thing left was a bed and a dresser with a round mirror attached. She walked to the dresser and pulled open the drawer. Empty. As was the next and the one after that. It occurred to her that she now owned nothing. Even the clothes on her back, as ill-fitting as they were, belonged to someone else. She walked to the bed and sat on the edge to gather her thoughts and give thanks for her sudden good fortune. Not only did she now have a roof over her head, but she had the promise of being fed. And, if all went well, she would be returning to America soon. While she had no hope of returning home, she would at least be able to speak to those she encountered and understand what they were saying in return. She looked toward the ceiling. "I'm going to be okay, Father."

The door creaked open. Anneliese poked her head inside the room, looked her over and frowned. "You should not be dawdling. Papa is home and waiting to meet you."

"I'm sorry I took your room," Dorthia said, pushing from the bed.

"We are leaving for America soon. I will not miss it," Anneliese replied curtly. The girl looked her up and down. "That dress is too small for you."

Dorthia pulled at the fabric. "I know. Thank you for letting me use it."

"Come, Papa does not like to be kept waiting."

"I hope your father likes me."

Anneliese stiffened and lowered her voice to a firm whisper. "Mr. Robberts is not my father. My father is dead. He was a good man."

"My father is dead too," Dorthia said softly. "I miss him very much."

Anneliese eased her tone. "Your father was an American. No?"

Dorthia bobbed her head. "Yes."

"You were not scared of him?"

Dorthia shook her head. "Of course not. He loved me very much."

"He treated you well?"

Dorthia smiled. "When he was alive, my father never let anything bad happen to me."

"I will say a prayer for you tonight," Anneliese said firmly.

"Thank you. I will add you to my prayers too."

"There is no need. My prayers have already been answered," Anneliese whispered.

As they entered the hallway, a man's voice, speaking fluent English, flooded her senses. Tears pooled in her eyes, and for the briefest of moments she was standing in her Boston apartment. *No, it can't be. I watched my father die.* She stopped to regain her composure and hurried to brush the tears away with the backs of her hands.

Anneliese turned to see what was keeping her. "You're crying."

Dorthia batted the tears once more. "It's been so long since I've heard proper English."

Anneliese wrinkled her brow. "Do I not speak proper English?"

"You speak the right words the wrong way," Dorthia told her.

"I don't understand."

"It's like when I say a word in German. I can speak the words, but it doesn't sound the same as when you or your mother say them."

Anneliese nodded her understanding, then added, "I know what it is like to miss someone." As they entered the kitchen area, Anneliese hurried to help her mother set the table.

Stephen Robberts sat at the table, drinking from a handleless mug. Wearing a dark suit and sporting a neatly trimmed beard, he peered at her over the cup and then lowered it to the table. "My wife said you are an American." The table was set with five place settings. Mr. Robberts motioned for Dorthia to be seated across from him.

Dorthia nodded, then remembered her words. "I am."

"My wife said she took you in because your father was killed? You're sure your father is dead?"

"Yes, sir. A man stabbed him with a knife and stole his watch."

"You saw it happen?"

A shiver traveled through her as Dorthia recalled the incident. "I did."

"Where is your mother?"

"My mother died giving birth to me." Telling this wasn't nearly as painful, as she'd never known her mother.

"What of your other family?"

"There are some in Chicago, but I do not know how to reach them."

"Chicago? Is that where you lived before coming to Germany?"

Dorthia shook her head. "No, sir, my father and I lived in Boston. We had a grand apartment there with windows overlooking the harbor."

"Your father was wealthy?"

"We were never hungry," Dorthia assured him.

"What brought you to Germany?"

"Why a ship, of course. Unless you mean Berlin, and we came here by train."

The edges of the man's mouth lifted ever so slightly. "What I meant was, did you come to sightsee or visit?"

"Father is an engineer. The German government asked him to come help with a bridge." She sighed. "Was an engineer…we were only supposed to be here a month."

"Did you not tell the authorities what happened?"

"No, sir. I cannot speak the language and did not think they would take the word of a child on any account. My mother was already dead, and my father had just been killed. I know what they do to orphans, so I ran."

"You did not stop to think the authorities might be able to help you get back to America?"

Dorthia shook her head. "I was frightened. I guess I didn't stop to think about anything."

Mrs. Robberts used mittens to pull a dish from the oven, then brought it to the table and set it in the middle on a folded cloth. Anneliese busied herself by pouring milk from a pitcher into each glass.

Dorthia's mouth watered as the girl filled each glass three-quarters of the way full.

"Anneliese," Mr. Robberts called as she started to leave. "I doubt our guest has had milk in some time. Give her some more."

Anneliese nodded and poured the milk to the brim of Dorthia's glass.

While Dorthia wanted nothing more than to pick up the glass and drain its contents, she wanted to make a good impression. Leaving the glass in place, she sat on her hands to avoid temptation.

"My wife made cheese spaetzle as she knows it's my favorite dish." He lifted the lid, exposing bubbling yellow cheese. "I expect you like mac and cheese?"

Dorthia worked to quell her excitement at recognizing the dish. "Oh, yes, sir."

Mrs. Robberts and both girls took their places at the table, each passing a plate for Mr. Robberts to fill. "Pass your plate, Dorthia," she said, holding out a hand.

Dorthia did as told, her stomach rumbling as Mr. Robberts doled out two heaping spoons of the bubbling delight before passing the plate back. She waited for everyone to begin eating before taking a bite, then forced herself to chew slowly, sighing as the rich, gooey delicacy slid down her throat. She smiled at Mrs. Robberts. "This is so good."

Mr. Robberts beamed his approval. "You'll not find a better cook in all of Germany than my wife."

"It's the best I've had since coming to Germany," Dorthia agreed. "The food at the hotel was good, but I haven't eaten anything but the occasional sausage since Father was killed."

Mr. Robberts pointed his fork at her. "That's right. You've been living on the street. Tell me, girl, where is it you've been getting your money to pay for those sausages?"

Dorthia wished she'd had the chance to finish her meal before he asked, as he would surely tell her to leave the moment she told him the truth. "My name is Dorthia, not girl. I stole the money to pay for them."

Leni gasped, and her mother shushed her.

"Your father taught you to steal?"

"Of course not!" Dorthia said heatedly.

"Someone must have shown you, or you would have been caught," Mr. Robberts pressed.

Dorthia lowered her eyes. "There was a boy."

"A boy?"

"Yes, Baylor. He took pity on me and showed me how to dip my hands into pockets without getting caught."

"And what did you give this boy in return?"

"Nothing."

The man leaned forward in his chair. "Not even so much as a kiss?"

Dorthia shook her head. "Of course not! I'm but a girl. No one has touched me."

This seemed to please the man as he smiled.

Mrs. Robberts, on the other hand, refused to look in her direction, leading her to wonder if she'd spoken out of turn.

***

Dorthia turned from the window. "I wondered at the touch of sadness within the woman's eyes. I found out a couple of nights later."

"You're saying he…"

"He was a touchy man."

"You were a child. Did the wife not care about her

husband's actions?" Emily asked.

"Of course she did. I did not realize it at the time, but Liselotte took me in to keep her daughters safe."

"She knew, and she was still willing to go to America with him?"

Dorthia laughed. "You ask that like you think she had a choice."

"Didn't she?"

"It was 1914. Women did not have rights."

"You could have told someone."

Dorthia wheeled her chair around. "Who would you have had me tell? The wife? She already knew. The police? What would they have done but lock me away? No, the damage was already done. I decided to bide my time. We would be leaving in a matter of weeks after all."

"You weren't afraid they'd leave you behind?"

Dorthia smiled. "The wife said if the husband liked me, he would take me to America. He liked me very well."

A blush crept up Emily's face.

Dorthia laughed. "I was seven years old and living in a country where I didn't speak the language and had just been told there was a chance I could return to America. By that point, I would have done just about anything short of murder to get back here. If that confession shocks you, then you'd better find someone else to conduct the interview or put on your big girl panties, as I assure you, I've had to endure much more than that during my life."

The blush brightened. "I'm sorry, I didn't mean…It's just that you were so young."

"Age was just a number. The whole innocence of childhood was stripped from me the day I watched that man murder my father."

"Do you have any regrets about running away that day?"

"I've asked myself that question a million times over, wondering if it would have changed things had I stayed."

"And?"

"My dear husband said it best when at last we spoke of it. He said it was best for me not to dwell on the what-ifs, as there was no way of knowing what the true outcome would be."

"Your husband sounds like a wise man."

"My husband was a very fine man. Do you wish to know of him?"

Emily smiled. "Yes, but we'll get there in time. If you don't mind, I'd like to hear about your journey back to America and what happened once you got here."

# Chapter Five

"It turned out that Mr. Robberts was an extremely resourceful man and, after questioning me at great length, was able to find the hotel where Father and I stayed. While the establishment had not held our room, they had held Father's and my belongings. He chose not to claim my father's belongings but retrieved mine. Along with having clothing that fit, I also had my papers, which would allow me to go back to America with ease. All Mr. Robberts had to do was tell them my father had died and he was taking me home to my family. Of course, that part was a lie, but who was I to correct him? Even though I was the same age as her oldest daughter, Mrs. Robberts insisted that her husband hire me as a governess to her girls. I think perhaps doing so helped ease her guilt. Anyway, he agreed and promised to pay me ten cents a day on top of my travel costs."

"Ten cents a day?"

Dorthia nodded. "Plus travel. It was rather generous of him."

"Did you go through Ellis Island?" Emily asked.

"No, there was no need. Mr. Robberts was an American

citizen. He and Liselotte were legally married, so she and the girls were allowed to enter without inspection." Dorthia turned her wheelchair toward the window, staring out the window as she spoke. "The train ride to Bremen, Germany set the pace. The seats were adequate, but nothing like the luxury class when I traveled with Father. It was the same with the ship, which happened to be the same one Father and I had arrived on only a few short months before."

"Do you recall the name of the ship?"

"The S. S. *Susquehanna*. I read later they used it as a troop ship during the Great War, but when we traveled, she was fitted with berths and staterooms. Father and I had a nice stateroom with a separate bunkroom for me. The Robberts family and I traveled as a group, sharing one modest room. The girl who I was on the trip over would have deplored those arrangements, but I'd changed…"

***

The ship was tied to the pier as if waiting for them to arrive, docked in the same place as she'd last seen it. For a moment, Dorthia wondered if it had been there the entire time. Of course, she knew that wasn't the case, but it still felt like an old friend patiently waiting to take her home.

Only she had no home to go to.

Dorthia pushed that thought aside. She was going to America; for now, that was enough. And get there she would, if only she could get on the ship. It felt as if she'd been waiting for an eternity. Then again, she wasn't with her father, who seemed to be able to breeze his way through any line with ease. Though she'd led a good life, she hadn't realized how privileged she'd been until she'd lost the safety net her father had cast around her. That net was long gone, and as she waited in line with the others, she fought to keep her fears at bay.

The skies were ominous, as if speaking to the long voyage ahead, and seagulls floated near, screeching for her to hurry as if they, too, feared something would prevent her from boarding.

"This is so very exciting!" Leni's eyes were wide as she spoke.

Anneliese's face held a more subdued expression, leaving it difficult to tell if she was excited or scared. Liselotte, however, seemed utterly terrified, her long, slender fingers clutching at her bag as tears trickled down both cheeks.

Dorthia searched her mind for something that would comfort the woman. "Don't be afraid, Mrs. Liselotte. I know the ship looks daunting, but the *Susquehanna* is the same one that carried my father and me across the waves. I can assure you it is quite safe. Father said she—he said all ships were ladies—was built in 1899. She's been on many voyages and hasn't sunk yet. That must mean she's a lucky ship and more than sturdy enough to carry us to America."

A rosy blush brightened the woman's cheeks as she hastened to bat away the tears.

Mr. Robberts stepped up beside them. "Don't you worry yourself, Dorthia. Unlike the two of us, my family is hesitant about leaving Germany. Isn't that right, my dear?"

Liselotte gave the slightest of nods.

Mr. Robberts beamed his approval, his smile widening when the line moved forward. He pulled their boarding papers from his pocket and showed them to the ship's representative. Dorthia recognized the man as Mr. Pennington, a tall, kind-eyed gentleman who'd greeted her and her father when they first boarded the ship in Boston a few months ago. She had been fascinated by listening to the conversation between him and her father when he'd joined them for lunch on the third day of the cruise. Unlike some of the men her father would speak with, Mr. Pennington had actually included her in the conversation from time to time. He'd also appointed his nephew, a young man named Tomas, as her and her father's personal aide during the passage over.

Pennington looked them over and stopped upon recognizing her. "Why, good afternoon, Miss Dorthia. It's good to have you traveling with us once more. Will your father not be joining us this trip?"

Mr. Robberts cleared his throat to get the man's attention. "I'm afraid the young lady's father met his demise while visiting Berlin. I'm taking the girl back to the States, where I'll return her to her family."

Pennington frowned. "My sincerest apologies, Miss Dorthia. If there is anything you need during your return trip home, please let me know." He looked at the papers once more, the crease in his brow deepening as he stepped aside to allow them entry. "Welcome on board the *Susquehanna*. You'll find a map of the ship on the table over there that you can use to find your cabin."

Had Mr. Robberts booked them in a stateroom, someone would have shown them directly to their cabin and even offered to carry their bags for them. But since he had not, they were siphoned into yet another line waiting for passengers to clear the way while Mr. Robberts examined the map. As she stood waiting, she caught sight of Tomas. A few years older than her with blue eyes and a carefree smile, he saw her staring at him and hurried over.

He looked her over and smiled a wide grin. "Dorthia! Shall I show you and your father to your stateroom?"

"I'm not traveling with Father," she said, trying to hide her pain. "Mr. Robberts is trying to find our cabin."

Tomas glanced at Robberts and was met with a scowl from the older man. Tomas ignored the look and reached out his hand. "If you'll show me your boarding pass, I'll take you there myself."

Mr. Robberts thrust the paper into the boy's hand as he hoisted his bags to his shoulder and motioned for Liselotte and the girls to do the same.

Tomas smiled at Dorthia. "May I carry your bag?"

Dorthia started to hand it over.

"The girl can carry her own bag." Mr. Robberts' tone was curt. "You can take one of mine."

Tomas started to respond, then took the bag. Walking without further comment, he led them down a long passageway, two sets of stairs, and an equally long hallway before stopping at a cabin door. He used a key to open the door and waited while the Robberts family went inside. Dorthia felt him watching her as she took in the small cabin. With four single cots bolted one on top of the other on two of the steel walls, the simple cabin was nothing like the ornate, polished wood-walled two-room stateroom she'd shared with her father. Why, there wasn't even a porthole with which to get a tiptoe view of the water. She noted the lack of rugs—another luxury allotted the staterooms—and hoped the floors were somewhat clean, as she didn't expect any of the four cots to be offered to her. Then again, with her and the family all sleeping in the same room, she doubted she would have to worry about nightly visits from unwelcome guests. The realization gave her a newfound excitement for the journey to New York, and she offered Tomas a brilliant smile. "Thank you for showing us to our room."

The boy's brows knitted together. "You're happy with the room?"

Dorthia bobbed her head. "It's perfect."

Mr. Robberts moved in between them, reaching for the bag Tomas was still holding. "That will be all, boy."

Tomas craned his neck and spoke to Dorthia as he relinquished the bag. "I'll see you around."

Before Dorthia could respond, Mr. Robberts closed the door in the boy's face. "You'll not be seeing that boy," he said firmly.

That Mr. Robberts thought he had any say in who she did or did not converse with shocked her. "Excuse me?"

"You heard me. I saw the way that boy looked at you. Boys like that are nothing but trouble."

Why of all the nerve. "Tomas is more of a gentleman than you are!" The words were out before she could stop them. She gasped when Mr. Robberts' hand connected with her cheek.

Dorthia was incensed. Never in all her seven years had anyone raised a hand to her. She tried unsuccessfully to quell her tears as she pressed her palm to the side of her face to ease the pain. "How dare you strike me!"

Mr. Robberts narrowed his eyes at her. When he spoke, his words were slow and deliberate. "The ship has yet to set sail. I paid for your voyage and can easily tell them I've changed my mind about sponsoring you."

Dorthia glanced at Liselotte. The woman's wide-eyed expression told her she believed her husband's words, a truth further illustrated as she wrapped her arms protectively around each of her daughters. Instantly, Dorthia's heart ached to have a mother who would protect her.

The boat blared three long whistles, letting the passengers know it was ready for departure.

"You promised we could watch the ship depart." Leni's

voice was hesitant.

Mr. Robberts whipped his head around as if he'd forgotten they were standing there. "Yes," he said, recovering. "Liselotte, take the girls topside. I'll be along directly. I want to have a word with Dorthia first."

Dorthia gulped and shot a pleading look to Liselotte.

"Perhaps you should come. The ship will be out to sea soon, and you don't want to be caught unaware."

Mr. Robberts considered this for a moment before nodding his head.

Liselotte's shoulders relaxed as she released her grip on her daughters.

Once free of her mother's embrace, Anneliese moved beside her and looped her arm through Dorthia's. "You've been on the ship before. You can lead the way. Hurry," she whispered before Robberts could object.

Though this area of the ship wasn't familiar, Dorthia did recall the route they'd taken when going to their room. That, along with the steady stream of passengers heading in the same direction, let her know they were going the right way. The going was quick, with everyone hurrying topside to see the ship away from the pier. As she walked, Dorthia recalled what Mr. Robberts had said about changing his mind about paying for her journey. Not wishing to be sent back, she decided to bide her time until they were well out to sea. Once far away from land, she'd retrieve her papers and hide on the ship until they reached America. While she doubted Mr. Robberts would be able to convince the captain to turn the ship around, she decided not to take that chance. He wouldn't be able to send her back if he couldn't find her. They reached the stairs, and it took everything she had not to use this opportunity to disappear into the crowd—that and the fact that Anneliese still held on to her arm as if afraid of losing her way.

The ship was already away from the pier when they reached the main deck. The crowd hurried to the side of the ship, all eager to get one last glimpse of what they were leaving behind.

Mr. Robberts moved to his wife's side as Liselotte's silent tears turned into sorrowful sobs. "There, there, Liss. There's no reason to cry. I promise you will love America just as much as

I do."

Undeterred by her mother's grief, Leni wormed her way through the crowd.

Dorthia and Anneliese followed and soon found themselves standing against the rail. As Dorthia looked to the shore, she found it difficult to control her emotions. While she was thrilled to be headed home, she felt a deep sorrow at leaving her father's body behind in a strange land with no one left to mourn him. A part of her wished she'd never pressed him to take her with him in the first place. For if he'd never come home, she would have merely thought he had abandoned her. While that truth would have been painful, it would have at least offered hope that he might someday return.

"You're trembling," Anneliese said softly. "If you are cold, I can give you my shawl."

The shawl in question had previously belonged to Dorthia, as did the dress the girl now wore. Liselotte had given them to Anneliese when her husband retrieved Dorthia's suitcase from the hotel. She'd justified her action, saying it was only fair since Anneliese had so graciously offered Dorthia one of her own. Not wishing to anger either Liselotte or Mr. Robberts, Dorthia shook her head. "I am not cold."

"No? Then why are you crying? I'd think you'd be happy you are leaving our country."

"I'm very happy to be going home. That doesn't stop me from being sad that I'm leaving my father's body behind. It's bad enough that he's dead. Now he will have no one to visit his grave to tell him they cared." In her sorrow, she didn't stop to realize she had no clue where the Germans had buried him.

"I will miss my father as well," Anneliese answered with a sob of her own.

***

Once the ship was in the open ocean, everyone began making their way below deck.

"We should go," Liselotte said, ushering Dorthia and the girls away from the deck.

Mr. Robberts caught Liselotte by the arm. "Not yet!"

Liselotte's face paled.

Even though Dorthia had never seen the man strike anyone

but her, it appeared Liselotte and the girls were equally frightened of him. Dorthia couldn't help but wonder why Liselotte had agreed to marry him.

Mr. Robberts steered Liselotte to the rail, and they stood peering out into the distance. "I didn't mean to scare you. It's just that I'm not looking forward to this cruise."

Anneliese pulled Dorthia close and whispered in her ear. "Papa is afraid."

"Why?"

"Shhh," Anneliese said in hushed tones. "The water makes him sick. Momma said that is why he hasn't returned to America until now. He was afraid of getting back on the ship."

Dorthia nodded her understanding. "You mean he gets seasick?"

"Yes."

"That's not something to be afraid of. Father and I met a man who used needles so the sea would not make him sick. Perhaps I should tell him."

Anneliese's eyes rounded. "You'll do no such thing."

"But if he's scared…"

Anneliese spoke in a determined whisper. "He will not be able to come to the cabin now that the boat is moving. He told Momma he thought the journey over was going to kill him and said he could only go downstairs to relieve himself—even then, he had to carry a bucket."

"I saw there were only four cots and thought I would be sleeping on the floor. Does that mean I'll have a bed of my own?" Dorthia almost felt guilty asking.

"You will, and neither of us will have to share it with anyone." The girl's eyes were bright with the telling. "That's why Momma wanted you to come along. She knows she'll be spending time with Father on the main deck, and she didn't want to leave me and Leni alone."

"We are the same age."

"Yes, but you've traveled on a ship before and know the language better."

"We need to put our things away in case the seas get heavy," Liselotte said, drawing their attention.

Mr. Robberts looked to the sky. "I wish I could tell you it

wasn't to be, but the skies say otherwise. At least it will be a warm rain, and you and the girls will be safe below. Dorthia will help you find your way back." He looked at her for confirmation.

Dorthia bobbed her head, making sure to hide her relief at hearing Mr. Robberts wouldn't be sharing the cabin with them.

# Chapter Six

As the ship crossed the ocean, the days blended together. Afraid calm seas would allow Mr. Robberts to control his stomach long enough to visit the cabin, Dorthia lay awake long after turning in each night, praying for rough seas. Her prayers must have been working, as it had been four days, and the man had yet to return to the room.

While Mr. Robberts stayed out of the room, Liselotte and the girls seemed content to remain in the room when they were not eating or using the facilities. Though Dorthia was grateful to have a safe place with a cot to sleep on, she found the monotony of the confined space maddening. She'd much prefer to roam the ship than stay in the small room watching Liselotte sew and listening to the girls read aloud from books they'd brought with them. It wasn't that she was against reading; she would have gladly joined in to combat the boredom if she were able to decipher the writing. As it was, she merely closed her eyes and listened to their guttural-sounding words, trying unsuccessfully to make sense of what either of them was saying. As she listened, she recalled the times she and her father would take turns reading. The *Red Badge of Courage*, which they'd read on more than one occasion, was one of their favorites to read, as was *Alice's Adventures in Wonderland*. She loved sitting by the fire listening to her father as he read. A good mimic, he would change his tone whenever a new character appeared on the page. While she could still hear him reading in the voices he'd masterfully portrayed, she now had trouble recalling what his real voice sounded like. It hadn't been that long. How could she have already forgotten? A sense of panic rose over her as she searched her mind, trying to hear his words, only to hear him speaking as the befuddled white rabbit or in the sleepy voice of the caterpillar. While she'd enjoyed the voices each time her father had brought the characters to life and constantly begged him to read more, that wasn't what she wanted to hear now. The absence of his voice weighed heavy on her heart. Not only had she left his body behind, but it seemed the memories of him were leaving her as well. It wasn't until a sob escaped and Anneliese and Leni stopped their reading, staring in her direction, that she realized she was crying.

Liselotte set aside her sewing and looked at the ceiling as if debating. Finally, she stood. "Come along, girls. We'll go check on Stephen."

Leni popped off the cot, smiling her approval.

"I don't—" Anneleise began.

"On your feet, child," Liselotte scolded.

Anneleise closed the book, placing it on her pillow without another word.

Liselotte looked at Dorthia. "Some fresh air would do you good."

"I'd prefer to stay here." It was a lie. She wanted more than anything to go topside and look out over the water. While it was a large ship, the fear of making a wrong turn and bumping into Mr. Robberts stopped her.

"Then go for a walk below," Liselotte insisted. "It'll do you no good to stay in this room with your thoughts."

Anneleise jumped on the opportunity. "I should go with her to keep her company."

"Have you thought that perhaps Dorthia wishes to be alone?" Liselotte said, rejecting her request.

"She doesn't mind, do you, Dorthia?" Annelise pleaded.

Dorthia realized she was not the only one who didn't wish to visit Mr. Robberts. "I don't mind."

"Me too?" Leni asked.

"You'll come with me," Liselotte said firmly. The woman moved to the mirror and let out her hair. She ran through the length of it with a brush before pinning the locks back to her head and donning her hat. Next, she pinched her cheeks between her first finger and thumb. She sighed. "I guess we all could use a bit of sun."

"Then let's go," Leni said, opening the cabin door and stepping into the hallway.

Liselotte paused and placed a hand aside Anneliese's cheek. "Don't get into trouble."

"I won't," the girl promised.

Once again, Dorthia felt the pang of not having anyone to worry about her getting into trouble—not that she planned to do so, but it would be nice to have someone to care whether or not she did. She waited for Liselotte to leave, then unbraided her hair and picked up the woman's brush.

"That's Momma's brush."

"I'm not stealing it," Dorthia said, using it to calm her unruly mess.

"I thought we were going for a walk," Anneliese said, watching her.

"Oh, we are," Dorthia handed her the brush. "Unbraid your hair."

"Why?"

"Because it makes you look like a child."

"That's because I am a child."

"Yes, but you look like a poor child."

"I don't understand."

"Mothers of poor children keep their hair in braids to keep it from getting dirty. The children in first class have their hair hanging loose or pinned to their heads because they know they will be able to wash it when it gets dirty."

Anneliese frowned but did as she was told. "Why does it matter?"

"Because if we are going to go to the first-class section, we need to look like we belong."

Anneliese gulped as she ran the brush through her hair. "We're going to the first-class section? Won't they know we don't belong there?"

"I do belong there," Dorthia snapped, pulling the door open.

Anneliese tossed the brush onto her mother's cot and followed Dorthia into the hallway. "You miss your father. That's why you were crying before."

"I tried to hear him." Dorthia felt her lip quiver and lengthened her stride to keep from shedding more tears. "Earlier, when you were reading. I was thinking of all the times my father read to me and how he could change his voice to make the story seem real. I could hear him talking in those voices, but when I tried to hear his voice, his real voice, I couldn't."

Anneliese nodded her understanding. "I can't hear my father either."

Dorthia slowed her steps. "You can't?"

"No." The word came out in a whisper.

"What about Leni?"

Anneliese shrugged. "I don't know. I haven't asked."

"She likes Mr. Robberts."

"She doesn't know Mr. Robberts!" Anneliese snapped, then softened her tone. "Momma's going to make sure she doesn't."

Dorthia stopped in her tracks. "How?"

"By taking us to America. Momma's sister lives there. She wanted us to go with her when she left, but Father, my real father, was sick. Momma knew he wouldn't be able to survive crossing the ocean, so we stayed behind. Then, after he was gone, there was no money for such a journey."

"Is that why she married Mr. Robberts?" Dorthia asked as they began walking once more.

"Yes, Mr. Robberts worked with my father. He would come to our apartment and bring food and pretend to check on Father, but I saw how he looked at my mother."

"Did she look at him back?"

"Not until after Father died. And only then because there was no money for food. He was nice at first. Even though my momma was sad about losing my father, I could tell she liked the attention he gave her."

Dorthia recalled the sadness in Liselotte's face. "She doesn't seem to like him now."

"That's because she found out he was broken. That's what she calls it because of what he does."

"Maybe she should have stayed in Germany and refused to come with him."

"She is his wife. In Germany, wives must do what they are told. Besides, we wanted to come to America. It's okay because once we get to America, we are going to live with Momma's sister. Her husband is a good man. He will make sure we are okay."

"It's good to have someone to watch over you," Dorthia agreed. "I wish I had someone."

"I'll watch over you."

Dorthia whirled on her heels to see who'd said it and saw Tomas standing behind them grinning like a Cheshire cat. She wasn't sure if she should be pleased to see him or angry at him for listening in on their conversation. "Tomas, how dare you spy on us!"

"I wasn't spying. I just didn't want to interrupt," Tomas told them. He grinned once more. "I will, you know."

Dorthia crossed her arms. "You will what?"

"Watch over you."

Dorthia narrowed her eyes at the boy. "Meaning you'll keep following us so you can hear what we say?"

Anneliese snickered.

"Sheesh. I go to the trouble of trying to get to talk to you, and this is how you treat me. I may as well go back to first class."

"What do you mean you've been trying to talk to me? We've been at sea for four days."

Tomas slid a glance to Anneliese. "Yes, but until now, every time I've seen you, you've been with someone."

Dorthia giggled. "In case you haven't noticed, I still am."

"Yeah, but she's not as scary as the woman and man." Tomas chuckled. "Though the man doesn't look all that scary these days. I've never seen a man puke that much."

This caught Dorthia by surprise. "You've seen Mr.

Robberts?"

"He's hard to miss. Even people who don't go looking for him can hear him blowing chunks. Perhaps you should go see for yourself. I'm sure you'd find it satisfying to see the man so ill."

For a moment, Dorthia thought the boy knew her secret. She glanced at Anneliese to gauge the girl's response but saw nothing. "Why would I want to see his misery?"

"Because he slapped you." The boy offered a hapless shrug. "I heard him through the door."

"Oh, no, I don't care to see his misery," Dorthia said, letting out her breath.

"Really? Because I've taken great pleasure in it." He looked at Anneliese and shrugged once more. "Sorry, I know he's your dad and all, but the man is a real goop."

"I don't know this word, goop," Anneliese told him.

Dorthia didn't want to admit it, but she wasn't familiar with the word either.

Tomas shrugged. "Means he's a jerk."

Anneliese bobbed her head. "Ja, he is."

Tomas raised an eyebrow. "You mean you're not mad? Someone called my pop that, and I'd punch them in the nose."

"I'm not mad. You're right, Mr. Robberts is a goop." Anneliese said, then giggled.

"Yeah, I guess all fathers can be," Tomas replied. "Then again, I still think I'd punch a fellow who called my pop one. That's only because I never knew my dad enough to know if it was true, and I wouldn't be happy for someone spreading lies."

"Your father is dead?" Dorthia asked.

"Yep. Lost both my mom and pop," Tomas said without explanation. "That's why my uncle took me in. Speaking of which, he's probably looking for me, so I'd better get back to first class."

"We'll walk with you," Dorthia said, grasping the moment. "That's where we were going."

"But you're not…"

Dorthia looped her arm through his. "You'll take us with you, won't you, Tomas?" Dorthia batted her eyes at the boy.

Tomas considered this for a moment. "Sure, but once we get

there, you're both on your own on account of I have work to do."

Dorthia smiled a wide smile. "That's okay, I know my way around."

Tomas nodded as they started down the passageway. "You should be staying in first class. Your dad had money. Didn't he leave you any?"

"The man who killed him stole it all," Dorthia said, remembering.

"But he had money," Tomas insisted.

"That was stolen," Dorthia repeated.

Tomas glanced over his shoulder as he started up the stairs. "My uncle has money, but he doesn't carry it all with him. If someone stole it, they would only get what he carried with him."

Dorthia stumbled on the steps as his words sank in.

"Exactly," Tomas said. "Where'd your pop keep the rest of his money?"

"I don't know," Dorthia said softly. She was still contemplating this when they topped the stairs. Unlike the lower deck they'd just come from, the walls of the upper deck were lined with smooth, polished wood. Bright lights lit up the outer passageway, giving a hint of what lay beyond the door.

A boy who looked to be a few years older than Tomas stood beside the door, vetting those who entered. Tall with dark hair and even darker eyes, the boy seemed to take great pleasure in looking them over.

Anneliese gasped and took a step back.

Dorthia shot her a warning to be silent, then smiled at the boy.

"Where are you two off to?" he said, ignoring Tomas, who was still waiting to see if they would be allowed to enter.

Dorthia stepped closer and laughed an easy laugh. "Why, to meet our uncle, of course."

The boy looked them up and down once more as if judging their worthiness to pass through the threshold.

Not giving him a chance to make up his mind, Dorthia smiled and pulled herself taller. "I've been showing my cousin around the ship," she said, edging her way close to the opening.

The boy raised an eyebrow. "Cousin?"

"On my mother's side," Dorthia said with a nod to Tomas. "We really should be going, Tomas. Uncle will be wondering what's keeping us."

"Uncle? They're related to you?" The boy looked to Tomas for clarification.

"On my father's side." Tomas grinned and reached a hand to Dorthia. "Come along, Dorthia. We shouldn't leave Uncle Albert waiting."

"I can't believe that worked," Dorthia said once they were out of earshot.

"I was so scared." Anneliese's words still held a note of fear.

"Don't worry, cousin," Dorthia assured her. "Now that he knows us, we shall be able to come up any time we want."

Tomas bobbed his head in agreement. "If anyone gives you any grief, tell them to come find me. Listen, I've got to go; Uncle Albert will be looking for me."

"Tell our dear uncle we said hello." Dorthia laughed.

Tomas answered with an exaggerated bow before hurrying off.

"I don't think I like the way he was looking at us," Anneliese said after he'd gone.

"Tomas?"

"No, the other boy. He looked at us as if we were unclean."

"Look, there's food." Dorthia hurried to the pastry table, plucked up two plates, and handed one to Anneliese. "That's not what his look said."

Anneliese frowned but followed her lead, filling her plate with tasty morsels. "It wasn't?"

"He's a boy. He was looking at you like you were a girl," Dorthia said, slipping into a chair at one of the nearby tables.

Anneliese lowered her plate and looked at her bounty. "But I am a girl."

"A naive one at that. Boys and men want the same thing," Dorthia said pointedly.

Anneliese lowered her eyes. "It is my fault Mother brought you into our home."

"I know," Dorthia told her.

"I want to go back to the room," Anneliese said, rising.

Dorthia took several of the pastries from her plate and folded them into her napkin. "Okay."

The boy was still guarding the door when they left. "Where are you two off to now?" he asked upon seeing them.

Dorthia placed a hand on her stomach. "I know it's not lady-like to say, but we just had our fill from the pastry table, so we are going to walk it off."

The boy laughed a hearty laugh. "I wasn't born yesterday."

Dorthia frowned. "Of course you weren't. You're at least thirteen years old."

"I mean, I know you were just batting your eyes earlier so I would allow you to enter." He took Dorthia by the arm. "It'll cost you more than that if you don't want to get your friend Tomas in trouble."

Knowing she didn't have any money, Dorthia tried to pull her arm away.

The boy firmed his grip. "Now, it don't have to be like that."

"You said it will cost, and I don't have any money."

The boy smiled. "You've got something better than money."

Dorthia exchanged a glance with Anneliese, then without warning, the boy placed his lips on hers. She started to pull away, then decided this was perhaps the nicest kiss she'd ever had.

The boy grinned a knowing grin. "I was right."

She wasn't sure what she expected, but having the boy laugh at her wasn't it. "Right about what?"

"You've done this before."

Feeling the shame in his words, her hand connected to his cheek with a loud pop.

He placed his palm alongside his face. "What'd you do that for?"

"You said I was unclean," Dorthia said heatedly.

Anneliese nodded her agreement.

"I said no such thing. I only meant you're a good kisser. Why, I know guys who'd pay a whole penny to kiss you."

Dorthia blinked her surprise. "You do?"

"Sure I do." His voice was confident. "Some would pay a whole nickel for more. I can introduce you."

Anneliese took hold of her arm. Pulling her close, she

whispered in her ear, "You know what that boy is speaking of, ja?"

"Of course I do."

"We must go. Mother wouldn't approve."

Anneliese was right; her mother wouldn't approve. She, on the other hand, no longer had anyone who would object to her doing something she shouldn't do. Dorthia looked Anneliese in the eye. "You're right. You should go back to the room before your mother wonders where you are."

"You're not coming with me?" Anneliese gasped.

"I am not ashamed to take the boy's money."

"But Mother will be upset if she learns."

"Then don't tell her." Dorthia lowered her voice to a whisper. "The boy will pay me. I need the money. Unlike you, I do not have an aunt to run to once we get to America."

Anneliese knitted her brow. "You'll not be going with us?"

Dorthia had given this a lot of thought over the past few days, wondering what she would say if Liselotte asked her to join them. While she envied the relationship between mother and girls, the sense of caring had never extended in her direction. Nor did she wish to constantly worry about unwanted attention, especially not when others were willing to pay for the same. Dorthia shook her head.

Anneliese let go of her arm. "I'll tell Mother that Mr. Pennington invited you to share the evening meal with him and Tomas. That way, she won't worry if you don't come back to the room right away."

"Thank you." Dorthia watched until Anneliese was out of sight. Taking a deep breath, she turned to face the boy once more.

# Chapter Seven

Though the travelers were weary from the trip over from Germany, most released a collective sigh at seeing Lady Liberty. Seen well before reaching the harbor, the green lady was a welcoming sight for the frequent traveler and a sign of hope for those seeing her for the first time. Invigorated by the knowledge they'd soon be on dry land for the first time in eleven days, the main deck was now a hub of activity. After a trip wrought with heavy seas, the waters were now calm as the ship moved out of the open ocean and made its way down the channel to the pier.

Realizing that departure from the ship was imminent, Dorthia raced down the stairs, hoping to make it to the room before Liselotte packed her sewing kit. She'd earned two dollars and thirty-three cents over the last seven days and wanted to sew the coins into the lining of her skirt to prevent them from being taken. Breathless by the time she reached the room, she paused long enough to slow her breathing before opening the cabin door. Not seeing anyone inside the cabin, she twisted the knob to turn on the light and gasped as she saw Mr. Robberts lying on her bed. She reached for the knob once more.

"Leave the light on." His voice was weak.

"I…I didn't mean to disturb you," she said, staying near the door. "I didn't know you'd returned to the room."

"Only because the waters are calm. When I return to dry land, I expect to sleep for a week." He smiled a weak smile. For someone who'd spent the last eleven days on deck breathing in the ocean air, the man's face was strikingly pale. Then again, it could be due to the dark circles surrounding his sunken eyes.

Not knowing what to say, she said nothing.

"Why are you not on deck with the others? Don't you want to see the ship pull in?"

She realized this was the out she'd been looking for. Without turning her back to the man, she reached for the doorknob.

"Anneliese told Liselotte you plan to leave us once the ship docks. Is that true?"

"It is."

"Where do you intend to go?"

"To find my family." It was a lie, as she didn't have a clue where to begin.

"You are but a child. I will go with you to Boston."

"No!" She forced a smile and told another lie. "Mr. Pennington has promised to help me."

"Liselotte said you've been spending a great deal of time with that boy, Tomas." His voice was cold.

Dorthia swallowed. While she'd been spending a lot of time with boys, Tomas wasn't one of them. Afraid Mr. Robberts would hear the lie in her words, she merely nodded.

"I trust he's been behaving himself."

"Oh, yes. Tomas has been the perfect gentleman." This time, her words spoke the truth, as unlike the other boys who'd paid handsomely for her attention, Tomas hadn't so much as stolen a kiss.

"What did you want?"

"Excuse me?"

"You came to the cabin. You must have wanted something?"

"I have a small tear in my hem and had hoped to use Liselotte's sewing kit." Since it was only a partial lie, she hoped it sounded convincing.

"Go ahead," Mr. Robberts said, waving her to the bed on the opposite side of the room. "My wife won't mind."

Dorthia moved further into the small room, then froze, judging the distance to the door, when Mr. Robberts slowly pulled himself up to sitting.

He used the frame to stand, then, dipping his hand into his pocket, he pulled his clenched fist free and held it toward her. "This is for you."

Dorthia hesitated before finally lifting her hand. One by one, dimes fell into her palm. Eleven in all, each one clinking against the one before it. She did the math in her head: this dollar and ten cents, plus the money she'd earned since being on the ship, gave her a total of three dollars and thirty-three cents. Dorthia blinked her surprise. Though he'd promised to pay her for traveling with them, she never fully expected him to follow through on the promise. She closed her fingers around the coins and shoved them into her pocket with the rest of her money before he could change his mind.

Mr. Robberts' brows knitted together. "You already had money in your pocket."

She nodded.

"You've been stealing from the passengers?"

"No."

"Then where did you get it?"

"I did not steal it," she repeated.

"What have you been doing with your time, Dorthia?"

Dorthia refused to answer.

Mr. Robberts looked her up and down.

Uncomfortable with the way he stared at her, she took a step back.

"You watch that pocket when you're in crowds," Mr. Robberts said.

Dorthia started to remind him that she knew how to protect herself from pickpockets since she herself was a thief but decided against it. "Yes, sir."

"Are you sure you won't change your mind and continue the journey with us, Dorthia? It would be better if it were your decision."

It was her decision, and she'd already made it. Dorthia

ducked when he attempted to touch her face.

"Very well," he said and left the room without another word.

Dorthia watched the door for several moments, half expecting him to return. When he didn't, she went to Liselotte's bed and retrieved her sewing kit. She pulled a needle free along with a wooden spool of thread. Looking at the door once more, she removed the scissors as well and took everything to her cot. She emptied the loose dimes from her pocket, followed by the change she'd carefully wrapped in a linen napkin she'd taken from the upper deck. Placing them on the pillow, she removed her skirt and climbed onto the cot, maneuvering so she could see the door. She cut squares from the napkin, rolled several coins into each, then went to work sewing them into the hem of her skirt. She'd watched the girls enough to sew a stitch, not that she was worried about keeping her stitches even. The stitches didn't need to be pretty, just sturdy enough to hold until they were yanked out once more. While she sewed, she placed the scissors under her leg, leaving the handle within easy reach.

She was just starting the final one when the outer door opened. Her hand flew to the scissors, relaxing once more when Anneliese entered the room alone.

"What are you doing?" the girl asked as she closed the door.

"Fixing my skirt," Dorthia said, jabbing the needle in and out through the fabric once more.

"You should go slower. The stitches won't be pretty."

"The stitches are just fine. Come take a look."

Anneliese approached and lifted the edge of the skirt. Her brow wrinkled. "What is it?"

Dorthia reached under the pillow and pulled one of the dimes she'd saved free. She pressed it into Anneliese's hand. "It's yours."

"Mine?" Anneliese inspected the coin before testing it with her teeth. She frowned. "What do I have to do for it?"

Dorthia shook her head. "Nothing. It's yours."

Anneliese knitted her brow. "What's the catch?"

"No catch, I promise. You told your mother I was spending time with Tomas and his uncle. If she'd found out the truth, she would have…well, I don't really know what she would have done, but she believed you, so the coin is yours."

"You don't need it?"

"I have more." Dorthia finished her stitch, used her teeth to disconnect the thread, then patted the cot. "Sit. I will sew the coin into your skirt."

"But it's only one coin," Anneliese argued. "It will be safe in my pocket."

"One coin that will feed you for a week," Dorthia told her. She lifted the edge of Anneliese's skirt, rolled the fabric around the coin, and began to stitch it into place. "You are to tell no one about this."

Anneliese frowned. "Not even Mother?"

Dorthia shook her head. "No one. From now on, you'll wash your own dress so that you alone know the secret it holds. If you ever get in trouble, that dime will keep you from starving to death."

"What kind of trouble? Mother said there is plenty of food in America."

"There is food, but you still have to pay for it." Dorthia paused her sewing to look Anneliese in the eye. "I always had food until I didn't. Wasn't there a time when you were hungry?"

Anneliese nodded. "The same as you after my papa died."

Dorthia finished sewing, then knotted the end of the thread. "It isn't much, but it will have to do for now."

Anneliese ran her fingers along the stitching. "Perhaps one day I will be able to add more."

"Yes, and when you do, their weight will give you comfort. The stitches do not need to be pretty, but you will need to make sure they hold well enough that you don't leave your money lying in the dirt for someone else to find."

Anneliese stood and twirled in place. "I can't even feel it."

"That's because…"

A knock at the door drew their attention.

Anneliese hurried to the door and opened it to see Tomas standing there. His normally pristine white uniform was scuffed at the knees and he had the beginning of a black eye.

Tomas jerked his finger toward Anneliese. When he spoke, his words came out in heavy breaths. "I just overheard her papa telling my uncle that you stole money from him."

Dorthia's eyes grew wide. "That's an outright lie. I did not steal money from him.”

“He said you did.”

“I did not steal from him.” Dorthia glanced at Anneliese. “Did Mr. Robberts do that to your eye?”

Tomas touched his cheek. “Of course not.”

“Then what happened?” Dorthia asked.

“It doesn’t matter. I just need to know if you took his money.”

“I did not steal from him,” Dorthia said firmly.

“It’s the truth,” Anneliese said, coming to Dorthia’s defense. “My father offered to pay her ten cents a day to be our governess while on the ship.”

“He told my uncle you stole that and more from him; how much money do you have, and where did you get it?”

There was something in the way he said it that bothered her. “I only have the money he gave me and no more.” While Dorthia would be willing to give back the money Mr. Robberts had just given her, she wasn’t about to relinquish the money she’d earned fair and square.

“Show me!”

Once again, she felt him to be accusing her of something. “I can’t. I’ve hidden it.”

“It better be hidden good. Mr. Robberts told my uncle to summon the police once the ship docks. He said it would be your choice to go to prison for stealing or stay with the family until you work off your debt. They will arrest you if you are lying.”

Prison? All those days living on the street and going hungry just to avoid going to prison, and now that she’d returned to the States, she would be locked away through no fault of her own. It wasn’t fair. Dorthia firmed her jaw. “I will not go to prison for something I didn’t do.”

Tomas studied her as if judging the truth of her words. “I could get you off the ship with the first-class passengers. It wouldn’t be hard—most of them have seen you and wouldn’t think anything of your leaving with them. You’ll still have to show your papers to the customs officers. You do have your papers, don’t you?”

Dorthia sighed. “No, Mr. Robberts has them. He said he was

keeping them safe, but he'd probably planned this all along."

"He wouldn't have kept them with him," Anneliese said, shaking his head. "They would be in his bag. I'll get them."

"No," Dorthia said. "I'll get them. That way, he won't see the lie on your face when he asks if you helped me."

Anneliese nodded her agreement and stepped aside.

"You must go," Dorthia said softly. "That way, when he asks, you can truthfully tell him the last time you saw me, I was in the room."

Anneliese hugged her briefly before starting for the door.

"Wait. Tomas, you step into the hallway too."

The boy knitted his brow. "Why? I'm not scared of her pop."

Dorthia smiled. "No, but this way, Anneliese will be able to tell her papa I was in the room alone."

Tomas opened the door and checked the hall before stepping outside. "Don't be long."

"I won't. Now it's your turn," she said to Anneliese. "Don't worry, you'll be telling the truth when you tell your papa you know nothing."

"I wish we were sisters," Anneliese said and hugged her once more.

"Me too." It was a lie, as if they were sisters, she would have no choice but to go with them. "Now go." Dorthia waited for her to close the door, then hurried to Liselotte's bed and unfastened Mr. Robberts' bag. Since he had spent the vast majority of the trip on the main deck, the contents of the bag were well organized. Two sets of clothes remained folded and untouched since being placed inside the bag and a stack of paperwork off to the side. Dorthia pulled the paperwork from the bag, leafing through the stack until she saw the document she was searching for. She felt a pang in her heart at seeing her father's signature and hugged the paper to her chest as if doing so would somehow bring him closer. It did not. She set aside the rest of the papers and opened her own bag to put her travel papers inside. Though she'd left the States with seven dresses and three pairs of shoes, she was returning with one change of clothes and a single pair of shoes that now pinched her toes. Had her father been alive, she had no doubt she would have arrived home with enough clothing to fill a trunk. She chided herself for being nostalgic and closed her bag once more. She started to leave, then realized she hadn't returned Mr. Robberts' paperwork to his suitcase. She picked up the stack of papers carefully returning them to the bag. As she did, she caught sight of a brown leather pouch sticking out from beneath his clothes. She pulled the pouch free, worked to unwind the string that secured the flap to the button, and gasped at seeing the envelope filled with paper money. She sank to the cot, debating her next move. That money would go a long way in not only seeing she never had to go hungry but also ensuring she could find a place to sleep. Her heart raced as she lifted the bills from the envelope. As she lowered the money to her pocket, she realized that stealing from Mr. Robberts would also be stealing from Liselotte and the girls. While she wasn't overly fond of Liselotte, she'd come to care for Anneliese very much. She'd come to terms with stealing from others, especially since she could easily procure the money without having to stop and consider the consequences of her actions. Walking up to someone unaware and quickly pilfering money from their pocket left her able to move away without making eye contact. She preferred it that way—it was easy to stave off guilt when most of her victims were faceless.

That was not the case today. If she took Mr. Robberts' money, it could have dire consequences for more than just him. A part of her figured he owed it to her for everything he'd put her through. Plus, he'd ruined her good name by telling Tomas' uncle she was a thief. It might be true, but he didn't have to tell anyone about it. What must Mr. Pennington think of her and why did she even care?

She was a thief and worse…

Dorthia peered at the money, knowing that even though Anneliese would have no part in her actions, if she followed through, Mr. Robberts would take out his anger on the girl, who would then hate her until her dying day.

She couldn't do it, not like this, even if a large part of her felt it would be justified. Dorthia returned all the money to the leather envelope but made a point of placing the pouch at the top of the stack of clothes so that Mr. Robberts would know she had not stooped to his level. Fastening the suitcase once more, she snatched up her bag, leaving the room before she had a change of heart.

***

Dorthia clutched her satchel as she stood waiting to depart the ship. A sadness washed over her as her gaze trailed over the nearby buildings, and she recalled a not-so-distant past when she'd stood looking at the New York skyline with her father half listening as he regaled her with boring tidbits surrounding the structures. "Oh, Father, I miss you so," she whispered into the air. "What I wouldn't give to have you standing here now."

As it was, she had no plan past making it off the ship without being arrested and hauled off to prison. It crossed her mind that perhaps she should have agreed to go on with Mr. Robberts and his family, as at least the threats were known. She swiveled her head, searching the crowd as if expecting him to be there smiling his victory, and relaxed slightly at not seeing him. The line moved forward. One step closer to land and the freedom it offered. *Then what*, a nagging voice inside her brain asked. She didn't respond, as she hadn't a clue.

"Dorthia!"

She jumped at the sound of her name, then relaxed once more when Tomas pushed his way through the throng of passengers waiting to depart. "You're in line. I trust you made it through customs?"

Dorthia bobbed her head. "Other than my bag and the clothes I have on, I didn't have anything to declare."

"You're lucky. You have your papers and do not appear to be in ill health. I can remember once when they quarantined the whole ship and made us dock in the harbor within sight of land because they didn't want the sickness to leave the ship."

"I think I would be tempted to jump over and swim to shore," Dorthia told him.

"Don't think some didn't try."

"What happened to them?"

"Some were captured and brought back to the ship."

"And the others?" she asked, knowing the answer.

"The channel can be unforgiving. So can people who are afraid. Where will you go?" Tomas asked, changing the subject.

"I don't know." The look he gave made her wish she'd lied.

Tomas firmed his chin. "Then I shall go with you."

"Why would you do that?"

"To protect you, of course."

Dorthia laughed and once more regretted her actions when Tomas narrowed his eyes.

"You do not think I'm capable of protecting you?"

"Of course you are. You've done a fine job of watching over me on the ship."

"Then why did you laugh?"

"Because I don't need protecting."

"Sure you do. You're a girl. Girls need protecting."

"I can take care of myself." Dorthia moved forward. She could see the gangway that connected the ship to the shore. It wouldn't be long now.

"You have no family and no money. How are you going to take care of yourself?"

"I'll find a way."

Tomas narrowed his eyes. "By giving yourself to boys?"

So that was what had been bothering him. The accusation in his voice stung, and Dorthia felt the heat in her cheeks when the woman standing behind them gasped. "Who told you that?" Dorthia hissed.

"Then it's true. You've been selling yourself to him and others for a few measly coins?"

Several of the passengers were now turned, waiting for her to answer.

"What I have or haven't done on the ship is none of your business."

"How could you?" Tomas spat.

Those standing near mumbled their agreement.

She fought back tears, refusing to let any of them see how much his words cut her. "Obviously, you have never been hungry. For if you had, you would know the answer to that question. I pray you never have to do something that will make others look at you the way you are looking at me now." Dorthia gazed at them all in turn. "That goes for all of you who are standing here judging me now."

Past caring what anyone thought of her or following rules

of society that she could no longer adhere to, Dorthia pushed her way forward and departed the ship without a backward glance. As she made her way to shore, tears soaked her cheeks. By the time she left the pier, her tears had morphed into heaving sobs, which lasted long after her tears stopped flowing.

# Chapter Eight

Having been to New York on multiple occasions with her father, the streets felt welcoming. Then again, it could merely be because, for the most part, she could decipher what was being said around her. Sure, there were still pockets of individuals speaking in the language of their country, but even those people seemed to know enough English to make themselves understood.

Dorthia walked without direction until she was standing in front of the Grand Central Terminal. She stared at the building for several moments, wondering how she'd gotten there, then realized she'd been following the path she and her father had taken after riding the train down from Boston on several occasions. Upon arriving at the terminal, her father always regaled her with details about the building. She used to love stepping off the train, crossing the rails, and then heading to the dining concourse on the lower level of the building, where the smells of food flooded her senses. While her father preferred stopping in the Oyster Bar to get sausages and onions, she'd always strolled straight to the pretzel cart, walking away with two, one of which she tucked away to eat after they were in for the night. When leaving the city, it was the same. She would eat one while waiting in the station for their train and save the other for their journey back to Boston.

Entering the building, she headed down the ramp to the lower level. Oh, how she'd always loved this part of their journey. Dressed in their finest, she'd slip into the shoe shop where her father would patiently wait to see what would catch her eye. Something always did, and he'd buy it for her without question—anything for his best girl.

She'd once asked him why he never remarried. He'd laughed and said he didn't have enough money to spoil two girls. In truth, she knew he missed her mother too much to remarry. Before they left Boston, she'd heard him talking in the wee hours of the night and snuck downstairs to find him sobbing over her mother's photo. She'd listened without interrupting as her father had told the woman in the frame it was time to make new memories and that they'd be moving to a new home once they returned to Boston. That had shocked Dorthia as the two-story apartment was the only home she'd ever known. She'd wanted to ask him about it but remained silent, as she hadn't wanted him to think she was spying on him. She didn't have to wait long to learn of his decision, as he'd told her at supper that first night on the ship to Germany. She'd told him she didn't wish to move. He told her it was too late; their things were being packed and would be waiting for them in their new home when they returned. She'd been so angry at him that she hadn't spoken to him for two days. When she'd finally relented, he told her he'd chosen the new home because the memories in the old one were eating him alive. Since she'd never known her mother, she hadn't understood missing someone so much. That had all changed since her father died.

Still caught up in her nostalgia, she paused at the shoe store she had visited with her father during their last visit to New York. She'd dragged him inside and left with three new pairs of shoes. Caught up in the memory, Dorthia slipped inside and began to browse the children's section. Spying a pair of shiny black loafers, she plucked them from the stand, aiming to try them on for size.

A silver-haired man wearing a black waistcoat waltzed to

where she stood and snatched them from her. "You'll do well to leave your grubby little hands off the merchandise," he sneered.

Grubby little hands? How dare he! She pointed a finger, intending to tell him what she thought of him when she saw the dark ring of filth that led from the base of her thumb and trailed along her first finger. She pulled back her hand, but not before she caught sight of her image in the mirror. While she didn't quite look like a street urchin, she was a far cry from looking as if she could afford to be shopping in a high-class establishment such as was nestled within the halls of Grand Central Terminal. Stores which were filled with wares from designers around the world. She hurried from the shop without a word. As she walked toward the women's lounge, her toes dug into the ends of her shoes, each step a painful reminder of things she could no longer afford.

She ducked into the women's lounge, tears brimming in her eyes as she moved past the sitting area and stopped in front of the line of sinks to scrub the filth from her hands. When she finished, she used her fingers to tame her hair. A woman wearing heavy eye makeup and a black lace dress that stopped just below her knees entered the lounge and stepped up to the mirror beside her. The woman's hair was pulled away from her face with ivory combs, while the length was curled into tight ringlets that danced about her chin as she moved.

Dorthia stared in amazement as the lady pinched at her cheeks with her fingers and thumb until they were rosy. Then, she watched as she removed a gold tube of lipstick from her clutch. The woman lifted the cylinder, exposing a brilliant shade of red that she used to paint her lips. The transformation was stunning. The woman returned the tube to her bag, leaving it unclasped as she reached for a hand towel. She plucked two instead, heaving an exaggerated sigh as one floated to the floor.

As the woman bent to retrieve the wayward linen, Dorthia reached into her bag and retrieved the cylinder, shoving it into her pocket just as the woman righted.

The lady caught Dorthia watching and frowned.

Anger coursed through Dorthia's veins. How dare the woman look at her as if she were nothing more than a street urchin. *But that is exactly what you are*, a little voice in her head reminded her. Ignoring the inner voice, Dorthia firmed her chin and went back to taming her hair with her fingers.

The lady removed one of the hair combs. "Here, use this," she said, offering Dorthia the comb.

Dorthia's anger dissipated as she took the comb and worked it through her hair several times. As her hair smoothed, a sting of guilt washed over her. She lowered her eyes and held out the comb. "Thank you."

The woman started to take it, then shook her head. "You keep it. This one too," she said, removing the other.

Dorthia shook her head. "No, they are too beautiful."

The woman smiled. "I want you to have them. Would you like me to put them in for you?"

Though she could have put them in place on her own, Dorthia nodded, then watched in the mirror as the woman moved behind her and made quick work of pulling her hair into a long braid. Dorthia held her breath as the woman dipped her fingers into her bag. She let it out once more when the woman withdrew a red ribbon, which she used to secure the end of the braid.

The woman placed a comb on both sides of Dorthia's head and nodded her approval. "They are perfect for you."

Dorthia reached a hand into her pocket, aiming to return the lipstick.

"Keep it," the woman said, waving her off. "Just be careful wearing it. A shade like that can get a girl in a lot of trouble."

Dorthia's jaw dropped. "You knew I took it and still gave me the combs? Why?"

The woman looked in the mirror and sighed a deep sigh. "Because you remind me of someone I once knew."

Dorthia wrinkled her brow. "How can lipstick get me in trouble?"

"With the boys."

"Boys don't wear lipstick."

"No, but they like girls who do." The woman winked.

"Boys like me just fine even without lipstick. My father took me to Germany on business. We were only supposed to stay a month. Only Father died, and a man... I didn't like him so much, but the boys that came after I didn't mind." She wasn't sure why she said it other than once she started, she couldn't stop. Then again, perhaps it was the need to share her secret with someone who might understand her plight.

"Why did you come to Grand Central? Are you planning on taking the train?"

"I used to come here with my father." Dorthia shrugged. "I don't know where I am to go. I only just arrived back in the States today."

"Don't hang around this building long. The police walk the floors to keep the beggars out. I know it doesn't feel like it, but you've been given a gift."

Dorthia took exception to this. "What gift? No one's given me anything."

"Oh, but they have. You are a beautiful girl and carry yourself well. You can ask for more than the average girl on the street. Don't lay with just anyone. And not even a kiss unless they pay you first." The lady brushed Dorthia's face with her thumb. As she did, Dorthia saw the glint of the ring that sparkled on her finger. "Do you have another dress in that bag?"

Dorthia nodded.

"Clean yourself up and put on a clean dress. Unlike others, you won't go hungry." The woman started to leave, then hesitated. "Save your money, and when you find a way out of this life, take it."

"How will I know?" Dorthia asked.

The woman sighed. "When an opportunity arises, take it. Listen, Hun, I'd like to tell you another way, but girls like us have to work with what we've got. I wish it wasn't so, but it is the way of it. I'd like to help you out, but I've turned away so many, and it just isn't fair."

Dorthia waited for her to leave, then pulled out the tube. Uncapping it, she stared at it, wondering how anything that could make a woman look that beautiful could get her into trouble. Not wishing to risk it, she recapped the tube and shoved it back into her pocket.

She moved about the terminal until she reached the great hall and had yet another memory of her father filling her with the history of the building. Built to handle two hundred trains an hour, the building encompassed forty-eight acres. One of the first all-electric buildings, the large arched windows were designed to funnel in light beams on sunny days.

Dorthia moved through the bustling crowd, searching each face as if expecting her father to appear and tell her he was still alive and it had all been a horrible nightmare. When he failed to materialize, she continued on her way, walking in the light beams until she reached the large four-sided clock in the center of the room. The day was already half over and she didn't have a plan. Moving to the waiting room, she found the bench she'd last shared with her father and sat clutching her bag in her lap as she pondered her next move.

Heading to Boston would be the logical choice, but that would cost money, and even if she were to go, her father had never told her the address of their new home, not that it mattered, as there would be no one there to greet her when she arrived. Dorthia sighed. The thought of returning to Boston without her father held no joy and would be no different than living in Germany—everything would feel cold and unwelcoming. She clutched her bag closer. She did not know what the future held, but she knew she would not be returning to Boston, where she would always be searching for something she'd never find.

Pushing to her feet, she walked against the crowd and took the ramp to the dining concourse lower level and headed straight to the pretzel stand. Dressed in all white, including a wedge cap, the man behind the cart was the same gentleman she'd purchased from every time she and her father visited New York City. He smiled at her, and for a moment, she wondered if he recognized her.

"What'll it be, kid?"

Kid? In the past, he'd always greeted her by calling her young lady; then again, at the time, she'd actually looked like one. She thought about the lipstick tube in her pocket and wondered if she should have painted some on after all. Maybe later. The last thing she wanted was to get lipstick on her pretzel. She looked at the plate-sized twisted dough, knowing she should only order one, but she was tired of looking at things she couldn't afford. "Two pretzels, please."

The man looked her over. "That'll cost you a nickel. You

got any money?"

Dorthia withdrew the dime from her pocket. She narrowed her eyes and firmed her chin. "Of course I do."

"Now, don't go getting sore; I have kids come through here all the time, wanting me to feed them out of the goodness of my heart. While I wish I could, I have a family to feed." He pushed back his hat and reached for the pretzels.

"Could you please put them in separate bags? I want to save one for later."

The man hesitated. "That'll cost you another penny for the second bag."

"It never costs any extra when I'm with my father." Dorthia made a point to look at a gentleman sitting alone on a bench with a paper folded over his lap. "Father works hard for his money too; perhaps I should go get him and see what he has to say about the extra penny."

The pretzel vendor followed her gaze. Aware he was being stared at, the man on the bench scowled.

"There you go, getting sore again. Can't you tell when a guy is fooling?" he said, handing Dorthia the bag with the pretzel. "Of course you can have two bags. Give me a second to bag the other one. I'll even add a little extra salt at the bottom for good measure."

Dorthia stooped to place the first pretzel inside her bag and then hoisted it over her shoulder. She took the second pretzel and held out her hand for her change.

"There you go. One shiny nickel." The man held the coin just out of reach. "Are you sure you don't want two more pretzels? I'll put them in two separate bags."

"I will ask my father if you want since it was he who told me I should only buy two. However, he's in a very sour mood and might not take too kindly to my interrupting him now that he's reading his newspaper." Dorthia nodded to the same man, who now had the paper stretched in front of his face.

"No need to bother your old man. I was only joshing with you," The pretzel vendor handed her the coin, glancing nervously at the man as Dorthia shoved it into her pocket.

Knowing the pretzel vendor was watching, Dorthia walked toward the man on the bench, who looked up over his paper when she approached. She smiled and nodded at the empty space beside him. "Please, sir, may I share your bench?"

He offered the briefest of shrugs. "I suppose you can sit on the other end."

"Thank you." Dorthia sat and tucked her bag under the bench. She saw him watching her and held out her pretzel. "Would you like a taste?"

"No, I would not." He motioned toward the vendor. "When you were standing over yonder, I got the distinct impression you two were talking about me."

"Yes, I'm sorry for that." Dorthia made it a point to look directly at the vendor, who was still watching them.

"Well? What were you saying?" he asked when she didn't offer more.

"The man didn't think the money I gave him was mine." Dorthia lowered her eyes. "He even tried to make me pay extra for a second bag. I told him you were my father and that you'd given me the money."

The man folded his newspaper and placed it across his lap. "That money was yours?"

"Yes, sir."

"You didn't steal it?"

"Oh, no, sir. I worked real hard for it," Dorthia said without saying how.

The man stood.

"Sir, you forgot your bag," Dorthia said when he started to walk away.

"I'll be back. I'm just going to have a little chat with the man."

"Oh, but it really is okay," Dorthia insisted.

"No, you just sit there and keep an eye on my bag. I know how to handle guys like that."

Dorthia struggled with her conscience as she stared at the bag, which looked to be very well made. A bag like that would bring a pretty penny at the market, perhaps even more, if there were something inside worth selling. The man pointed his finger at the guy behind the cart. She thought about her own father, knowing he, too, would have insisted on having a chat with the man. She sighed as she remained rooted in place—

stealing from the man would be akin to stealing from her father.

A wide smile played on the man's lips when he returned as his eyes drifted to his bag. "I guess you are an honest one at that."

"I told you it was my coin," Dorthia replied. "What did you say to him?"

"I told him in no uncertain terms he should not attempt to take advantage of young ladies such as yourself." The man scooped up the paper and lifted his bag. "He believes you are my daughter. If he gives you any more grief, tell him I just went to get a shoeshine, and I'll be back to settle things with him. That should set him on his heels."

As Dorthia sat finishing her pretzel, she contemplated her next move. Though she thought she had enough money for a hotel, she doubted anyone would rent a room to a child. Even if they did, the money she had wouldn't last forever. She'd told herself everything would be all right if she could just get back to America. Now that she was here, other than being able to understand the language, nothing had changed. As a weariness crept over her, Dorthia closed her eyes to keep from crying.

# Chapter Nine

"Wake up!"

Dorthia opened her eyes to see a policeman standing over her with his hands resting on his hips and a deep scowl on his face.

"This is a train station, not a home for wayward children. Come along now, on your feet," he bellowed, kicking at her shoe. "We don't allow your kind in here."

"My kind?" Dorthia shrugged off the veil of sleep. "And just what kind would that be?"

"Vagrants," he said, reaching for her arm.

"Why of all the nerve." She pulled her arm away and firmed her chin. "I'll have you know I'm here with my father."

"Sure you are. And just where might this father of yours be?"

"He went to get a shoeshine," Dorthia said, using the story she'd concocted before falling asleep.

"If I had a nickel for every time one of you kids tried to pull the wool over my eyes, I'd be as wealthy as a king. Now, on your feet before I thump you over the head and drag you out."

"I do have a father." Dorthia pointed toward the vendor cart.

"If you don't believe me, just ask the pretzel man."

The police officer pushed back his hat and looked in the direction she pointed. "What does the pretzel man know?"

"He knows I have a father because he spoke to him not more than a few moments ago." Dorthia saw the pretzel vendor watching and pointed once more, hoping to raise the man's ire. It worked. The man closed the hatch on his box and stormed in their direction.

"Listen, I don't know what this kid is telling you, but I've already told her father it was a big misunderstanding."

The policeman rocked back on his heels. "What was a misunderstanding?"

The pretzel man jabbed his thumb in Dorthia's direction. "The kid thought I was trying to pull one over on her, but I was only joshing. I told her old man the same thing."

The policeman cocked an eyebrow. "You spoke with the girl's father?"

"I told you I did," the pretzel man said, bobbing his head. "Bout twenty minutes ago."

"And he was here in this room."

"It's not like I've been outside. Listen, I have a customer at my cart. Can I go now?"

"You can go." The officer waved him off, then turned his attention to Dorthia. "You need to find your father and stay with him. People see a kid such as yourself unattended, and they'll think I'm not doing my job."

"Yes, sir," Dorthia said, gathering her bag, and hurrying up the ramp. She rushed past the four-sided clock and continued on until she pushed through the doors and stood rooted in place outside the upper-level entrance as others exited behind her. Though she knew it was getting late, she hadn't expected it to be on the verge of darkness. A memory flashed in her mind as she recalled her and her father's last visit to New York City and how he'd warned her not to go out in the streets alone at night. Even when they ventured out together, he had tucked his arm through hers to ensure she didn't wander off. When she'd asked him why he was so protective, he'd told her about the gangs that roamed the city at night. Later that evening, as they'd dined outside the hotel, she heard a noise and jumped. Her father had patted her hand with his and told her she never had to feel unsafe when they were together. She had taken him at his word until that one fateful day in Germany.

"Oh, Father, what am I to do?" Dorthia whispered to the air. "It's late. I'll never be able to find a safe place to sleep before nightfall." Her plea was answered by a jolt when someone exited the building and ran into her.

"Move out of the way," the man grumbled as he skirted around her.

"Dang kids," another man sneered. "The city's overrun with the little varmints. They've been sending them out of the city via the trains in droves, and yet we still have a mess of them. Makes a man wonder if we'll ever be able to walk down the street without worrying about one of those kids reaching their grubby little hands in our pockets."

"Take it easy, Manfred," a third, younger gentleman said. "It's not good for a man of your age to get your ticker out of sorts. Besides, it's not only the kids who pick the pockets. Johnathon had his pockets rifled just last week, and there wasn't a kid in sight."

Dorthia slunk out of the way as more people filed out of the building seeking to hail a cab. Men in suits, women in fine dresses, and families poured past, all seemingly excited to have reached their destination. A man exited the terminal holding the hand of a little girl whose eyes were bright with wonder.

The girl looked at Dorthia and frowned. "Father, that girl has stains on her dress," she said without lowering her voice.

"Don't pay her any mind, Evelyn." The man lifted a hand to the motorcars as he glanced in Dorthia's direction. "She's a street rat."

"What's a street rat?" the girl asked.

"A feral child who hasn't any manners," the man replied.

"How dare you judge me!" Dorthia blurted. "You know nothing about me or what I've been through. What would happen to that girl if you were to die today?"

"Come along, Evelyn—the girl is obviously mad. She should be in an asylum instead of being allowed to threaten the tourists." A motorcar pulled up to the curb. The man hoisted his suitcase and gripped the girl by the arm. As they walked, the girl looked over her shoulder and stuck out her tongue.

Dorthia answered in turn. The gesture felt good until she saw an elderly woman in a wide-brim hat frowning her disapproval.

"Such a vulgar child. Whatever must your mother think?" the woman said, clutching her pearls.

A white-haired man carrying a tan suitcase and leaning heavily on a cane ambled up beside the woman. "Come, my dear. We mustn't let the waif spoil our evening."

"No, of course not," the woman replied, turning away.

It dawned on Dorthia that she liked it better in Germany. At least then she couldn't understand what was being said about her. While dirty looks were difficult to swallow, hurtful words were even more painful. All thoughts of going into the city left her. She was tired of being treated like she didn't matter. Tired of her heart aching every time she saw a child with their parents and tired of being looked at as if she were …what was the word the woman had used? Vulgar, yes, that was it. Even repeating the word inside her mind made her cringe. None of the boys on the ship had looked at her that way. She smiled. On the contrary, they'd all seemed pleased to see her any time she was near. Then again, she'd always worn one of her good dresses whenever she went to the upper deck, not the stained traveling dress she was currently wearing. Dorthia waited for the surge to stop and then stepped back inside the building, her breath coming easier as the doors closed behind her.

She walked past the travelers without making eye contact and made her way back to the women's lounge. She checked to make sure she was alone, then set her bag on one of the rocking chairs. Digging through her bag, she removed a dress that showed little wear. Stripping off her traveling dress, she set that one aside and pulled the other over her head. She walked to the mirror to study her image and sighed as she pressed her hands along the fabric to smooth the wrinkles. Deciding she didn't wish to look like a child, she removed the ribbon, undid the braid, and used the combs to change the style of her hair. Okay, she might not look like she was made of money, but she should be able to walk amongst those in the station without drawing too much attention to herself.

Dorthia's gaze fell to her feet where her toes pressed painfully against the ends of her scuffed shoes. She grimaced as she wiggled her toes and realized each digit was sore from pushing into the leather. She recalled some of the homeless children she and her father had seen living on the streets. Most of them were without shoes in the summertime; perhaps she could go without them as well. Recalling how the woman in the wide-brim hat had gaped at her, she decided against it. Instantly, her mind went to the shoes she'd seen in the window at the shoe store. Fine shoes like that wouldn't hurt her feet—provided the man would sell them to her. Of course, he would once she showed him that she had enough to pay for them. Dorthia glanced at her discarded dress, mentally counting the money hidden within the hem. *Don't be silly,* she silently chided. *You'll need that money to eat. When I do, I'll steal more.*

Making up her mind, she hurried to the rocker and used her fingernails to rip out the hem, placing each of the coins into the deep pocket of the dress she had on. Fearing she would change her mind, Dorthia shoved the discarded dress into the bag and hurried from the room with the bag draped over her shoulder. She ran down the wide hall, through the main concourse, and down the ramp until, at last, she was standing in front of the shoe store. Gathering her courage, she lifted her chin and waltzed into the room and straight to the shoe display, which had previously piqued her interest. The salesman, who was busy helping another customer, looked her over but made no move to ask her to leave. Dorthia removed the shoe from the stand, turning it from side to side. Satisfied with the quality, she sat on an empty chair across from the woman. Tucking her feet under the chair, she folded her hands in her lap, waiting her turn.

The man went into the back and brought out several boxes, setting them on an empty chair beside the woman.

"You go help the girl. I can try these on myself," the woman said when the salesman stooped to remove the shoe she'd been trying on.

The salesman glanced at Dorthia. "Are you quite sure?"

"I've been putting my shoes on for over fifty years. Go, I know where to find you should I find myself in need of assistance," the woman said, then winked at Dorthia.

Dorthia returned the wink, then pushed from her chair. She walked to the counter and pointed at the Red Goose shoes she'd been admiring. "I would like those shoes, please."

"They are two dollars and ninety-five cents," the salesman said.

Dorthia gulped. Two dollars and ninety-five cents would buy a lot of sausages.

"You're looking a bit peaked," the salesman said dryly. "Perhaps you should ask your mother to come inside so she can make a better choice. Say, a pair of Buster Browns instead. They are a respectable brand that will save your folks about seventy cents."

Dorthia stared at the Red Goose shoes, debating. Seventy cents was a lot of money. What if she couldn't find a boy who wished to pay a nickel to kiss her? She hid her disappointment and nodded her head. "Okay, I'll take the Buster Browns instead."

The salesman pulled out the Ritz Stick and placed it against her foot. Satisfied with the measurement, he pulled two boxes from the drawer beneath the counter, opening them to display both black and brown leather shoes. Though the toes were covered, the top of the shoes were open and held in place with a thick strap that prevented them from coming off. "They come in both black and brown. Which of them are to your liking?"

Dorthia wrinkled her nose. While there was nothing wrong with the shoes, they were not the shoes that had caught her eye. Still, seventy cents was worth the sacrifice. She pointed to the black pair. "Those will do."

The salesman set the other box aside, pulled out one of the black shoes and handed it to Dorthia to try on. She pulled her foot free of the shoe she was wearing, squinting as her toes rubbed against the leather. Sucking in her breath, she pushed her left foot into the first shoe and sighed her relief when the toes failed to touch the end.

"Better?" the salesman asked.

"Much," Dorthia said, reaching for the right shoe.

"Marvelous. Now stand up and let me see. Marvelous," he said once more after using his thumb to judge the fit. "Those shoes should hold you a few months."

"A few months?" Dorthia exclaimed.

The salesman wrinkled his brow. "Yes. Those shoes will not serve you well in the winter. You'll need boots, unless you're planning on being inside or taking the train to where it is warm."

*Boots, of course.* She hadn't even thought of that. She lifted her foot, removed the shoe, and then repeated the process with the other foot. "I would like a pair of boots, please," she said, handing the man the shoes.

"Are you sure? The weather is still quite warm. Perhaps you should ask your mother."

"I do not wish to further burden my parents. If you would get me those boots, please, and make them a half a size bigger," Dorthia said, hoping the extra would allow her to make it through winter before growing out of them.

The man swallowed, and his Adam's apple bobbed. "Bigger?"

"Yes, please. A half a size."

The salesman looked to the ceiling. "Would you like me to wrap them?"

"No, sir. I wish to wear them now."

"As you wish. They will be three dollars and twenty cents." He eyed the shoes she'd come in with. "Shall I dispose of those for you?"

Dorthia recalled the day her father had purchased them for her. The saleswoman at the Boston store told them they'd come all the way from Paris, France. While they'd fit splendidly at the time, she'd rather go barefoot than cram her feet back inside. "Yes, please."

"You'll give her a forty-cent credit on her old shoes," the woman sitting across from her said the moment the salesman scooped them up.

The man's eyes grew round. "Why on earth would I do that?"

"Because we both know you'll shine those shoes up and sell them. Even at a discount, those shoes will bring you enough to make you a profit."

"Fine," the salesman huffed. "Forty cents credit it is."

"And a new pair of stockings," the woman said. "Unless you would like me to take my business elsewhere."

The man plucked a pair of stockings off the shelf. "Anything else?"

"Just the stockings and the boots," she said, flashing a satisfied grin.

The salesman placed the stockings on the counter.

Dorthia gaped at the woman. "Thank you."

The woman smiled. "Think nothing of it. We women have to stick together after all, now, don't we?"

Dorthia started to tell the lady that she wasn't a woman yet but decided against it, worrying she would regret butting in. "Yes, ma'am."

"Here you go, one pair of boots, a good half size too large," the salesman said, entering the room. "And I want it noted that I am selling you these against my better judgment. You'll remember that if your parents wish to make a fuss about my selling them to you. Understood?"

"Don't worry," Dorthia said, shoving her foot into the first boot. "I assure you you'll not hear a word from either my mother or father."

"Very well, then, with the discount, that will be two dollars and eighty-five cents." He held out his hand, watching as Dorthia counted out the money, then smiled a forced smile. "I'll bid you farewell, little missy. May you wear them in good health."

"Thank you." As she turned from the counter, Dorthia offered the woman a genuine smile.

Leaving the shop, she walked up the ramp toward the main concourse. As she did, she replayed the last few moments in her head. Not once did the man question whether she belonged there, and yet she was the same person he'd yelled at earlier that day. No, she wasn't the same; she'd combed her hair, washed her hands, and put on a clean dress. Could dressing the part really make such a difference? Deciding to test her theory, she continued walking to the upper-level exit. Once outside, she stood rooted in the same spot where she'd stood only an hour before. As people exited the building, they skirted around her. While a few grumbled, none spoke about her the way others had when she wore the dirty dress and worn shoes.

Feeling more confident, Dorthia wandered about the

building in search of a place to spend the night where she wouldn't call too much attention to herself. While she didn't think the policeman would recognize her, she didn't wish to take any chances at being thrown out into the streets or worse. The sun had long set; now, instead of being filled with sunlight streaming through the massive windows, the enormous room was washed in the glow of the many chandeliers that hung throughout the building. The glow from the light reminded her of the lateness of the hour and how weary she still was from her trip across the ocean. Seeing no benches, she returned to the waiting room. Unlike earlier in the day, the room was quiet, with no more than thirty or so people spread out amongst the benches. Dorthia chose an empty bench in the middle of the room. She looked longingly at the bench, which would allow her to stretch out. Afraid it would draw attention to the fact she was alone, she sat and closed her eyes. She jerked awake, noted the silence in the room, then closed her eyes once more. Sometime later, through the fog of half-sleep, an infant's cries pierced the air.

Opening her eyes, Dorthia searched the room. A woman with a small boy balanced on her left hip walked down the aisle pushing a baby carriage in determined strides. An older boy who looked well into his sixth year followed close behind, half pulling and half dragging an oversized suitcase. Dorthia scooted out of the way when the woman paused at the bench where she was sitting.

The woman smiled her gratitude as she set the smaller boy on the bench and helped the older boy hoist the suitcase onto the end. She then scooped up the screaming infant and handed the baby to the older boy, before turning and rifling through the bottom of the carriage. She pulled out two small, worn quilts, giving one to each of the two boys before retrieving the infant. She stood bouncing the baby as the older boy folded his quilt and sat it on the bench between himself and his brother. The younger boy inched up on the bench using the folded quilt as a pillow. The older boy covered him with the smaller quilt before lying down and sharing the quilt pillow with his brother. Once the boys were settled, the woman sat, undid the buttons on her dress and offered the baby her breast.

The infant's squalls morphed into eager gulps as the room grew quiet once more.

The smallest of the boys raised his head. "I'm hungry too, Momma."

The woman furrowed her brow. "I know," she said softly. "Go to sleep; we'll find food tomorrow."

"You said that yesterday."

"Go to sleep, John," the woman said more firmly.

Dorthia's heart clenched at the mention of the boy's name. She wasn't sure if it was because the boy shared the name of her father or if she knew all too well how difficult it was to go to sleep on an empty stomach, but ignoring her own hunger pains, she reached under the seat and pulled up her bag. Reaching inside, she removed the jumbo pretzel and offered it to the woman.

Tears formed in the woman's eyes as she reached for the pretzel without argument. "John, Joseph," she said, getting the boys' attention.

Both boys woke up and instantly sat staring at their mother with wide eyes.

The woman tore off a large section and handed it to the older boy, who immediately passed it on to his sibling, then looked to his mother for his share. "Eat it slow," she cautioned, "I don't know when there will be more."

Joseph nodded his understanding as he nibbled off bite after bite.

The woman handed Dorthia the remaining dough.

"I've had plenty," Dorthia said, waving her off. "And money for more."

The woman studied her as if trying to judge her sincerity. "Are you sure?"

"Yes, ma'am."

"You can call me Mrs. Harper." A sadness touched the woman's eyes. "I have nothing to give you in return."

Dorthia smiled. "Oh, but you do."

"I do?" Her voice was hesitant.

"The policeman doesn't like that I'm here without my father. I wish to sleep but fear him coming and taking me away. If I could just rest my eyes for a little without worry…"

Mrs. Harper smiled for the first time since entering the room. "By all means, child, sleep."

"You'll wake me before you leave for your train?"

"Don't worry, our train doesn't leave until tomorrow afternoon. We have no place to go until then." Mrs. Harper motioned to the bench. "Rest your head, child; I'll let no trouble come your way."

Dorthia stretched across the bench and, using her hands for a pillow, closed her eyes.

# Chapter Ten

Whispered voices pulled her from her sleep. Dorthia opened her eyes and sat, her gaze searching the room. She relaxed at seeing a man and woman chatting several rows away. The woman next to her slept with her head tilted forward, the baby nestled in her arms. Afraid she would drop the child, Dorthia moved to lift the baby from her arms.

Instantly awake, Mrs. Harper's eyes sprang open as she clutched the infant to her chest. Her eyes were puffy with dark circles, and she glared at Dorthia as if she were the reason for all her troubles. "What are you doing?"

Dorthia gulped. "You were sleeping and I was afraid you'd drop the baby. If you don't mind, I'll hold her while you sleep."

The woman relaxed. "You've held a baby before?"

"Yes, my cousin. When Father and I went to visit relatives in Chicago."

Mrs. Harper looked over at the boys, who were both sound asleep. "Okay, but just for a few moments."

Dorthia nodded and reached for the baby once more.

The woman stifled a yawn. "If she wakes, place her thumb in her mouth, and she'll likely settle again." Within seconds of turning the child over, Mrs. Harper's breathing changed to soft snores.

Terrified of dropping her, Dorthia cradled the baby's head in the crook of her arm. She'd lied when telling Mrs. Harper she had held a baby before. While she had held her cousin, he was a year old. Unlike this infant, who was no longer than the length of her arm, he had been big enough to hold up his head and toddle away on his own. She studied the baby and wondered if she'd been that small when coming into the world. Doubtful, as her father had told her that her mother had died bringing her into the world, and she couldn't imagine something this small killing a person. She glanced at the woman sleeping beside her and further wondered why it was possible for her to give birth to three children when her mother couldn't survive birthing one. It dawned on her that if her mother had survived, she would not be in the predicament she currently found herself in. Children stayed with their mothers, and she would not have had a reason to go to Germany with her father.

The baby squirmed. Dorthia rocked her as she'd seen Mrs. Harper do and smiled triumphantly when the baby settled once more. For as long as she could recall, she'd told herself she didn't want any children as she didn't want to end up dead like her mother, but sitting here holding the baby, she thought she would make a very good mother. The more she considered it, the more she thought it to be true. Perhaps she'd even be a better mother than the woman sitting next to her who could not even afford to feed the boys she had now. As the thought came to her, Dorthia held the baby closer. Babies grow up; even her cousin ate real food, and he was still a baby. She looked at the infant's face and how her tiny eyelashes touched her cheeks, and marveled at the way she suckled in her sleep. It dawned on her that she could leave right now while the baby's mother was sleeping. She had money left and knew how to get more.

*And how would you keep her safe?* her inner voice asked. *You can't even sleep without fear of being tossed into the street.*

*I'll tell them I'm the child's mother. They won't make me go if I have a baby. A baby...I never wanted one before because I was afraid I would die. This way, I can have one without having to worry.* Making up her mind, Dorthia inched her way down the bench. As if the infant knew of her plan, she opened her eyes and began to wail.

Dorthia fed the baby's thumb into her mouth. Too late, the woman woke and instantly reached for the child.

Her child, not Dorthia's.

As the crying continued, Dorthia was almost glad her plan had been foiled. Almost, because now she would never have a baby of her own.

"Hush, Rachel," the woman cooed, placing the child on her breast. "You'll wake your brothers, and they, too, will want to be fed. They'll need to be patient just a little longer, and everything will be as it should."

"Does she understand your words?" Dorthia asked.

Mrs. Harper shook her head. "Not yet, but she likes it when I speak to her. Sometimes it helps to tell someone else your troubles."

"You can tell me," Dorthia said, watching the baby suckle.

"You have been kind enough. I shouldn't burden you with my troubles."

"You'd rather burden the baby?"

The woman smiled a sad smile. "You are smart for a young girl."

The comment caught Dorthia by surprise since everyone always thought she was older than she was. "I'm not so young."

Mrs. Harper raised an eyebrow. "You're younger than you look. Am I wrong?"

"No." Dorthia sighed. "How could you tell?"

"I'm a mother. Mothers know things."

"How?" Dorthia repeated.

"I don't know the why of it. I just know that ever since I became a mother, I've known when my children need something. That's why we are making this trip to Charleston."

"Your husband isn't going with you?"

Mrs. Harper closed her eyes for the briefest of moments. "My husband is dead."

"How did he die?"

"He fell from a great height."

"A building?" It was a guess, but her father had told of such things happening.

The woman's brow furrowed. She tugged the blanket over the infant's ears as if afraid the baby would hear. "Yes, he was working on the Woolworth building. They told me he lost his balance and gave me ten dollars, of which I had to use some to bury him. The money ran out too quickly, and I did not know how I was going to feed my boys. I tried to find a job, but they don't like to hire women. The ones who do will not hire a woman with a suckling child."

"Will Charleston hire you?"

"No, but my husband's parents live there and will help. It was his mother who sent enough money for the tickets. There was more, but the landlord demanded I pay him for the rent. He threatened to send me to jail and my children to the asylum if I didn't pay. I kept out enough to cover the tickets for the train and gave him the rest. I was so scared; I didn't want them to take my children." Mrs. Harper turned toward her, and as she spoke, her lips trembled. "I've already lost so much. I'd rather die than be without my children."

Dorthia's breath caught in her throat. For a moment, she thought the woman knew of her foiled plan. "My mother died when I was born. When I was little, I used to think she'd rather be dead than have a baby."

Mrs. Harper sucked in her breath and placed her hand across her mouth. Gathering her composure, she lowered her hand and used it to pat Rachel's bottom as she shook her head in earnest. "You mustn't think that. I know your mother would have given anything to have lived to watch you grow up."

"That's what my father used to say."

Mrs. Harper's hand stilled. "Used to?"

"He's dead."

Joseph woke and sat upright next to his mother, who repositioned the baby to free up her right hand, which she placed on his knee. Dorthia longed to trade places with the boy, if only for a moment.

"If you don't mind me asking, how did your father die?"

"He was murdered by a pickpocket while we were in Germany." Dorthia wasn't sure why she opted for the truth, other than a small piece of her thought that perhaps a woman who loved her children as much as Mrs. Harper appeared to love hers might find it in her heart to love another.

"Germany?"

Dorthia nodded. "Yes, ma'am."

"The authorities caught the man? Is that how you made it home?"

"They caught him for stealing a necklace in the square, but they do not know he murdered my father," Dorthia replied. "I lived on the streets until Mrs. Robberts found me and took me home to live with her."

"Oh, that's good she took you in."

Dorthia laughed.

"You don't agree?"

"Mr. Robberts liked me too…" Dorthia wanted to say more, but the words wouldn't come.

"Oh, you poor child," Mrs. Harper cried out. Shifting the baby once more, she took hold of Dorthia's hand.

Dorthia blew out a jagged breath. "They brought me with them when they came to America. We arrived just yesterday. They wanted me to go with them, but I didn't wish to follow them."

"No, of course, you wouldn't, not after that."

"After what?" Joseph asked.

"Never you mind," his mother told him. She turned to Dorthia once more. "Where will you go?"

"I don't know," Dorthia said and purposely allowed a sob to escape. "I was thinking I could go with you."

"NO!" Joseph said, pushing from the bench. "Tell her she's not coming with us!"

"What's wrong, Momma?" John asked as he sat and wiped the sleep from his eyes with his fists.

"Tell her," Joseph said before his mother had a chance to answer.

The baby squirmed, and Mrs. Harper bounced her in her arms. "Joseph, keep your voice down before you wake your sister."

"That's right," the boy fumed. "Rachel is my sister. I don't need another one. You said I am the man of the family now that Father is gone. We don't need another mouth to feed. Listen to me, Momma. You know it's true."

Dorthia opened her mouth to tell them she wouldn't be a burden.

"Of course we can't take her with us." Mrs. Harper looked at Dorthia as if willing her to understand. "My husband's parents are being more than generous in offering to take us in. I wouldn't dream of taking advantage of their generosity by saddling them with another mouth to feed. I'm sorry."

"That's okay," Dorthia said, ignoring the sting of rejection. "I am nearly a woman. I have ways of making money and don't need anyone to tell me what I can and can't do."

"Joseph, sit," Mrs. Harper said, patting the bench beside her. She waited for him to comply, then handed him Rachel. "Hold the baby for me; I want to talk to Dorthia for a moment."

"She's not coming with us," Joseph said firmly.

"That's enough of your sass, young man," she said, motioning Dorthia further down the bench. Once they'd moved to the other end, Mrs. Harper sat next to her. "This way you have of making money. I take it was something you learned from Mr. Robberts?"

Dorthia firmed her chin. "What do you care?"

"Just because I can't take you with me doesn't mean I don't care," the woman said softly. "That part about your being a woman, you are not there yet, are you?"

Dorthia frowned, not understanding the question.

"Have you had blood come from between your legs?"

"Once when…"

"No, I mean other than that?"

"No."

"You will. When you do, it will mean you are becoming a woman. I'm telling you this so you won't be frightened. Once that happens, you need to be careful and not let any men or boys lie with you until after you are married."

"Why not?"

"Because that is the way babies are made."

"What if I want a baby?"

"You don't." Mrs. Harper softened her tone. "Not right now."

"I might."

Mrs. Harper relaxed against the bench and spoke without

looking at Dorthia. "If you have a baby without being married, they will take it away, and you will never see the child again. You may have more over time, but there will not be a day that goes by that your heart doesn't ache for that child."

Dorthia studied Mrs. Harper's tear-stained face. "Someone took your baby?"

"They did. I was but a child myself. My parents had too many children and couldn't care for us all. I left home thinking I could do better for myself. I couldn't and ended up doing the things a girl does to survive." She turned then, looking at Dorthia. "You know the things I speak of."

Dorthia nodded.

"Giving birth nearly killed me. I was too young and my body too small. But I loved that baby and would have done anything to keep her had they let me."

Dorthia considered her words. "Do you think that's what happened to my mother? That her body was too small?"

"Perhaps. It could have been a number of things, but I know had she lived, she would have loved you. You'll understand when you have a baby of your own someday."

Dorthia glanced at Rachel. She didn't really want a baby; she wanted that baby. "Why wouldn't they let you keep the other baby?"

"Because I was an unwed mother. Mothers need to be married to properly provide for their children."

Dorthia glanced at Rachel and then lowered her gaze. "I'm sorry."

"For?"

"While you were sleeping, I thought to take Rachel and leave. I didn't know they wouldn't let me keep her." Dorthia wasn't quite sure who the 'they' were, but she thought it might be the same policemen who didn't want her sleeping in the terminal.

"I know."

Dorthia couldn't believe her ears. "You do?"

Mrs. Harper nodded. "I saw it in your eyes when I took her from you."

"You're not mad?"

"No harm was done. Besides, I know what it is like to want

someone to love you."

"Is that why I want a baby? So she will love me?"

"Yes. It's also why you lie with boys."

Dorthia started to tell her she did it for the money, but she wasn't all that sure that Mrs. Harper was wrong. "Your husband died. Is that why they wanted to take your children away?"

"Partly, yes. We women can't care for children on our own, as we aren't allowed to work jobs that pay enough to provide for our family."

"Will Charleston allow you to keep your children?"

"I'll be okay living with Mr. Harper's parents until I remarry. My husband's mother has written to tell me one of Mr. Harper's brothers has expressed interest in taking me as a wife. He sounds like a good man, as he agreed to provide for his brother's children."

"Is the brother nice?"

"I wouldn't know. I have yet to meet him."

"You've never met him and yet you're willing to get on a train to go marry him?"

Mrs. Harper nodded. "There is nothing left for us here. I have to think taking the train will give us a fresh new start."

"I used to like riding the train with my father. I'm not sure I would enjoy it so much these days," Dorthia said softly.

"Perhaps one day you'll ride one to a place that will make you happy."

"Does Charleston make you happy?"

"My hope is it will." Mrs. Harper glanced at her children. "Mr. Harper spoke highly of his family. I'd like to think his brother will be good to me and the children."

"I'm hungry and need to go to the washroom," John said, approaching.

Mrs. Harper motioned to her other son. "Joseph, take your brother to the water closet."

Eager to comply, Joseph slid across the bench and handed off the baby.

"Straight there and back," Mrs. Harper said firmly.

"Yes, Momma," Joseph promised.

"When are we going to eat?" John asked when Joseph took his hand.

"Soon," Joseph said, leading him away.

Dorthia waited for the boys to round the corner then rose from the bench. "I need to use the washroom too," she said, following them out into the main concourse and staying close behind as they went into the men's washroom. She hurried to the women's dressing room, did her thing, and stood outside the men's washroom, praying she hadn't missed them. She didn't have to wait but a moment.

Joseph scowled upon seeing her. "What are you doing here?"

Dorthia returned his scowl. "I was going to take you to get something to eat, but if you're going to be rude, I won't bother."

John pulled away from his brother. "I'm hungry."

"Momma told us to come straight back," Joseph reminded him.

"John is hungry, and I know you are too. I have enough money to get us all a sausage."

John's face brightened. "A whole sausage?"

"Yes," Dorthia promised.

"I'll share mine with Momma," Joseph said. "She'll need to eat if she's going to make enough milk to feed the baby."

"I'll buy your mother one of her own," Dorthia told him.

"I won't change my mind about you coming with us," Joseph told her.

"I don't want to come with you anyway," Dorthia lied. She started walking, leaving it to them if they wanted to follow, then smiled when both Joseph and John moved up beside her. She led them through the main concourse, then down the ramp to the dining concourse, stopping in front of the Oyster Bar. "If anyone asks, you are my brothers, and our mother sent us to get the morning meal."

Joseph furrowed his brow. "Why would they care?"

"Because people don't like kids wandering around on their own." Dorthia's stomach rumbled as she opened the door and went inside. Until that moment, she hadn't realized just how hungry she was.

"It smells so good in here," John said, sniffing the air.

A burly man with deep-set eyes moved from behind a counter and blocked their way. "What do you kids want?"

Dorthia smiled a broad smile. "We would like four sausages if you please."

The man sized them up. "Four, you say? Do you have any money?"

"Of course I do. I wouldn't expect you are going to give them away for free," Dorthia said, matching his tone. She pulled her hand from her pocket to show several coins. "I would like them wrapped, please, so we can share our meal with our mother."

The man plucked several coins from her hand. "For another nickel, I'll give you some milk to wash them down."

John turned to her with hopeful eyes. "Can we have milk too, sister?"

"Of course, we can." Dorthia smiled and handed the man the coin.

The man motioned to the wall beside the entrance. "Stand over there out of the way, and I'll bring them out shortly."

"Why are you doing this for us?" Joseph asked once they reached the far wall. "It's not like I've been nice to you."

Dorthia considered her words. "I think you're just scared because your father died, and your momma told you that you are the man of the family. The man of the family is supposed to provide money for food and you have no idea how. I don't think you're mad at me. I think you're mad at your father for dying and leaving you to look after them."

Tears pooled in Joseph's eyes. He angrily batted them away. "How do you know?"

"Because I, too, know what it feels like to hate someone you love," Dorthia said softly.

# Chapter Eleven

Dorthia saw the relief in Mrs. Harper's eyes the moment they rounded the corner.

"Where have you boys been?" Her voice held a note of panic.

Joseph opened his mouth to explain. "Dorthia took us…"

Mrs. Harper cut him off. "Dorthia is not your mother. I am. I told you to come straight back."

"But, Momma," John started.

"Don't you 'but Momma' me." She narrowed her eyes at Dorthia. "Do you not know how worried I was? You admitted to wanting to steal one of my children."

"I wasn't trying to steal the boys," Dorthia mumbled.

"How was I to know that?" Mrs. Harper glanced at the clock. "You've been gone twenty-five minutes."

Dorthia lowered her eyes. "I'm sorry. I thought…"

"No, you didn't think," Mrs. Harper scolded. "If you did, you would've known how worried I would be when my children didn't come back. You need to go. I'll not have you corrupting my boys."

"No, Momma!" Joseph said, stepping in front of Dorthia.

"She stays."

Mrs. Harper arched a brow. "You'll talk to your mother like that?"

"Dorthia wasn't trying to steal us. She took me and John to get food." Joseph held up the bag so she could see.

Mrs. Harper's face paled. "Sausages?"

John pulled his hands from behind his back to show the glass jar he'd been hiding. "And milk too!"

Mrs. Harper lowered to the bench and placed her hands over her face, sobbing. John thrust the milk into Dorthia's hands and crawled onto the bench beside his mother. Climbing onto his knees, he wrapped his arms around his mother's neck. "Don't cry, Momma. Dorthia got you a sausage too."

In her hurry to help, Dorthia hadn't stopped to consider the fact Mrs. Harper would be mad at her taking the boys with her to get the sausages. She hadn't wanted to get them in trouble; she'd merely wanted to share her good fortune with them. Instead, she'd made a mess of things. She turned to leave, knowing they'd be more apt to sort things out without her there.

"Momma, Dorthia's leaving," Joseph said as she walked away.

A moment later, a hand took hold of her arm.

"Oh, Dorthia, what must you think of me?" Mrs. Harper said, pulling her close. "I'm sorry. I've just lost so much."

"I'm sorry too." Dorthia sobbed. As she stood there in Mrs. Harper's embrace, she felt the smallest glimmer of hope for the future, which lasted the briefest of seconds.

Mrs. Harper pulled away and lifted Dorthia's chin with her finger and used her other hand to wipe away her tears. "Please stay with us until we have to leave."

***

With their hunger momentarily satiated, the boys grew bored sitting and waiting for their train. Dorthia helped Joseph hoist the heavy suitcase onto the carriage and regaled them all with what she could remember about the architectural details of the building as they wandered around the terminal. Dorthia pointed to one of the large chandeliers. "There are fifteen of those, all over eleven feet tall, and each one is covered in gold."

John stared up at the chandeliers, mouth agape.

"I'm going to climb up there and cut one down. Then we'd be rich and Dorthia could come live with us," John mused.

Before Dorthia had a chance to answer, Joseph smacked John on the back of his head. "It's not real gold ya dope. And you can't just climb up there and cut them down. They're too big."

"That's right," Dorthia agreed. "My father told me they weigh twelve hundred pounds each."

John studied her with round eyes. "That's a lot, huh?"

Dorthia nodded. "Yes, John, that's a lot."

"Just think of the mess it would make," Mrs. Harper mused. "All that glass falling onto the marble. I wouldn't wish to be the one who had to clean that up."

"I'd like to watch it fall," John said, looking up once more. "Do you think Papa was that high when he fell?"

Mrs. Harper pulled the baby closer and turned away.

From the way her shoulders shook, Dorthia could tell the woman was crying.

Joseph smacked John on the back of the head once more. "Ya dope. Why'd you have to go and say that for? Now you made Momma sad."

"I didn't mean anything by it," John said. "I was just wondering because it is so high and the man that came to the door said Papa fell from a great height."

Mrs. Harper turned to face them once more. "That's enough, boys. I'll not have you squabbling about your father's death. Dorthia, do you have any more fascinating things to share with us?"

Dorthia quickly pointed to the clock which was the focal point of the room. "The clock has four sides. My father said that it is so people don't miss their train."

"That's nothing," John said, wrinkling his nose. "We saw that when Momma was buying our tickets. We already knew it had four sides."

Dorthia grinned. "Yes, but did you know there is a secret staircase hidden within the information booth?"

Joseph scratched his head. "Are you sure?"

Dorthia bobbed her head. "I'm sure. It is a spiral staircase that takes you to the information booth on the lower level."

"Boy, Dorthia, you sure are smart," John beamed.

"It was my father who was smart. I'm just repeating what he told me."

"How many times did you come here with your father?" Mrs. Harper asked.

"Four, that I can recall."

"Then John's right," Mrs. Harper said. "You are smart to remember all of this."

Dorthia sighed. "I think Father would be happy that I did."

"I'm sure he would," Mrs. Harper agreed.

Dorthia pointed at the stairs. "Want to know a secret?"

"Another one?" John asked.

"Yes." Dorthia turned and pointed in the opposite direction. "My father said they were supposed to build a matching pair on the opposite side of the room, but then decided it would be silly to do so because they wouldn't take you anywhere."

"Stairs to nowhere." Joseph laughed a hearty laugh. "What were they thinking!"

Dorthia nodded her agreement. "Those are the only stairs. The rest of the building is made with ramps."

John wrinkled his brow. "You're wrong."

"No, I remember my father's words. He said those are the only stairs."

John grinned and pointed toward the information desk. "You're forgetting the secret stairs."

Dorthia smiled. "You're right, John. Now who's the smart one?"

"Me!" John said, poking his thumb at his chest.

"What else can you tell us?" Joseph asked.

"Nothing. That's all I can remember." Dorthia sighed. It was the truth, because while she had no trouble recalling what he'd told her, the rest of him seemed to be slipping from her memory. Dorthia swallowed her panic. "I can't remember his voice or face and it's only been a few months. What if one day I lose his words as well?"

John tugged on his mother's skirt. "Will I forget what Papa looks like?"

Mrs. Harper clutched the locket around her neck. "No, John. But if you start to forget, come to me, and I will show you your father's photograph. Then we will remember together."

As Dorthia stared at the locket, she recalled a similar one her father had given her for her fifth birthday. Inside the gold case was a photo of both her mother and father. She'd looked at it countless times  since she'd received it, and yet she still couldn't summon the images inside. She'd left it at home in their apartment. It had been her father who'd told her not to bring it, saying it was too ostentatious for a child to wear something so ornate. Though she'd left that at home, with her father's pocket watch, her father had left his ring and their papers in the hotel. Though Mr. Robberts had retrieved her suitcase, he'd not brought home any of her or her father's belongings, telling her the hotel had already disposed of her father's suitcase. It hadn't dawned on her at the time to question why the hotel would save a bunch of dresses and get rid of the things that would have brought her greater joy.

John sneezed.

Instantly, a memory flooded her senses. She'd gotten something in her eye on the train during their first trip to New York City. Immediately after departing the train, her father had taken her to the Grand Central Emergency Hospital here in the building. "There is a hospital!"

Mrs. Harper shook her head. "There is no need for a hospital; it was only a sneeze."

"No, I'm saying that is what else I know. There is a hospital here in the terminal. I know because my father took me there."

"You were sick?" John asked.

"No, I had something in my eye. But there were several who were sick sitting in the waiting room. They were sneezing and coughing something fierce. Father was afraid I would get sick, so he made them put me in a private room." She smiled. "The waiting room was room A. They took the splinter out of my eye in room B, and then they let me sit in room C until my eye stopped hurting."

John beamed. "You remember your father!"

Dorthia sighed. "I can remember things we did together, but not what his face looked like."

Mrs. Harper glanced at the clock as she shifted the baby to her other arm. "Boys, we should be making our way to the terminal. It is nearly time for us to catch our train."

"The train terminal is just down that ramp." Dorthia managed a smile as she pointed the way.

"Aren't you going to walk with us?" John asked.

Dorthia shook her head. "No, it's too far, and then I'd have to walk all the way back up again." It was a lie. The truth was she knew it would be too painful to watch them get onto the train without her.

"Come with us," Joseph blurted. "Momma, tell her she can come."

Dorthia couldn't believe her ears. She searched Mrs. Harper's face, waiting for her response. Her breath caught in her throat when the woman nodded her agreement.

"If she has enough money to buy a ticket," Mrs. Harper said, shifting the baby once more.

Dorthia's heart sank as she reached into her pocket, thumbing her fingers along the three remaining coins. She wasn't sure how much a ticket to Charleston cost but knew any time she and her father traveled, he'd paid for the tickets with paper money. No matter if she chose the cheapest ticket they had, she didn't have enough, even if she used the secret dime she'd left in the hem of her skirt. She removed her hand, showing them the coins.

"I'm afraid it isn't enough," Mrs. Harper said softly.

"I know," Dorthia replied.

Mrs. Harper lifted her hand to Dorthia's cheek. "I'm sorry."

"It's okay," Dorthia said, not meaning it. Nothing about them going without her was okay except that they had indeed offered to take her with them. "It makes me feel better knowing you offered."

"It's not fair!" John burst into tears, burying his face in his mother's skirt.

Mrs. Harper removed her hand, using it to comfort her son. "Nothing about life is fair." She peeked at the clock once more, then held out her arm to Dorthia.

Dorthia walked into her embrace, staying there for several moments. As she backed away, John moved to put his arms around her.

"Please come with us," he sobbed.

Dorthia knelt to look him in the eye. "I can't. But I promise to remember you always."

"It's not the same," he sobbed.

"I know." Dorthia agreed. "You help take care of your baby sister."

"I will." John sniffed, then returned to his mother's side.

Dorthia waited for Mrs. Harper to turn away then reached out her hand to Joseph. The boy frowned but took her hand, his eyes growing wide when he felt the two coins she'd placed into his palm. She held a finger to her mouth to silence him.

"Why?" he whispered as he pocketed the coins.

"It's a long way to Charleston. Those sausages won't hold you forever. Save them for as long as you can. Don't tell anyone you have them. John will whine his way into your mother's heart, and she'll want to feed him too early. You'll know when the time is right, and when you do, use them to buy you all something to eat. Make sure your mother eats too. She'll need to keep up her strength to feed the baby."

Joseph nodded his understanding. "What will you do?"

Though she didn't have a clue, she didn't wish to add to his burden by admitting it. "I have plenty of change to get me by for a bit, just not enough to get me passage on the train ride."

"Joseph," Mrs. Harper said, interrupting. "Help me lower the suitcase off the carriage so I can change your sister."

"I'll help him," Dorthia said, welcoming the distraction.

Once the carriage was cleared and the baby changed, Mrs. Harper motioned Dorthia close and lowered her voice to keep from being overheard. "I know you don't want to hear this, but you'd do better in an asylum than getting with child or thrown into prison."

"I'm not going to an asylum," Dorthia said firmly.

"That's what I said at first, but I quickly found it was not fun being on my own. After they took the baby, I didn't care what happened to me, so I agreed to go to the asylum."

Dorthia couldn't believe her ears. "You were in an asylum?"

Mrs. Harper nodded. "I didn't love it, but the streets can be frightening if you don't have a gang to protect you and even scarier if you do, because then you have to do what the leaders tell you to do."

"What do they tell you to do?"

"Mostly the things I was already doing, but it's different when you don't have a choice."

"You're telling me I won't have to answer to anyone in the asylum?"

"No, I'm saying the safest place for an orphan girl your age is in the asylum. Not selling your body and living on the streets. I got lucky. Not all do."

Dorthia nodded her head, but in truth, she'd stopped listening after hearing the words "orphan girl." As much as she wanted to pretend it wasn't so, an orphan was precisely what she was.

"Think about what I've said," Mrs. Harper said firmly.

"I will," Dorthia promised.

"Momma, the train," Joseph said, pointing to the clock.

Mrs. Harper nodded. "Yes, come along, boys."

It took all Dorthia had not to follow after them and beg the conductor to look the other way as she boarded. The only thing that kept her from doing so was the sting of rejection if he refused. She remained rooted in place long after they were out of view—a part of her waiting for Mrs. Harper to return and tell her they would stay in New York City and find a way for them to all stay together. As the moments wore on, she knew that wasn't to be.

Time spent with the Harpers made being alone once more almost unbearable. The once fond memories of walking the halls of Grand Central Terminal with her father were now overshadowed by a newfound loneliness that engulfed her. The air in the building became increasingly heavy, and she knew she had to get outside before she suffocated. Dorthia made her way toward the exit as if she were trudging through mud, her heart breaking with each step as she mourned a life that could have been.

# Chapter Twelve

Once again, Dorthia found herself wandering without direction with only the weight of the three coins in her pocket and the hidden dime to add a subtle hint of security. As the day wore on, she grew weary and began searching for a suitable place to spend the night. Seeing a sign for a hotel, she hoisted her bag and entered. Walking straight to the front desk she pulled herself taller. "I'd like a room for the night." She held her head high to appear more confident in the asking.

The desk clerk looked down his nose at her and raised an eyebrow. "We do not rent rooms to children."

"I'm not a child. I'm seventeen," she said, willing him to believe her.

"You're no more than ten at most." He lowered the pencil and began scribbling something on the paper in front of him.

Dorthia pulled the pencil from his hand. "I told you I am not a child."

The man eyed the pencil. "Could have fooled me."

Dorthia returned the pencil. "I just don't like being ignored. Now, are you going to rent me a room or not?"

"Not."

Dorthia pulled the coins from her pocket. "I have money to pay."

"Be that as it may, unless you have a father or husband, I couldn't rent this room to you even if you were thirty."

Dorthia frowned. "Of course I don't have a husband. What does my having a husband have to do with anything?"

"Rules are rules. You're not likely to find a reputable hotel that will rent a room to a female of any age who is traveling without a male escort," he said, returning to his task.

"That's utterly ridiculous," Dorthia told him.

"Listen, kid, you may talk like an adult, but I don't make the rules. I just enforce them. You got a beef, take it up with the people who made the rule."

"And who would that be?"

The man shrugged. "How would I know? They don't pay me enough to ask questions. And they certainly don't pay me enough to deal with you or any other of those suffrage women." He snapped his fingers to get the attention of a man standing by the door.

The man hurried to the counter. "Yes, Mr. Davidson?"

"Boz, the lady here needs help to the door."

"Certainly, sir," he said, reaching for Dorthia's bag.

Dorthia batted his hand away. "I can carry my own bag."

"She's one of those suffrage gals." Davidson chuckled. "Holding up signs, demanding to be treated as equal to men. Can you imagine them allowing women to vote?"

"I'm not interested in voting. I just want a place to sleep for the night," Dorthia said.

"That's what they all say. The next thing you know, you'll be asking to buy the hotel just so you can rent the rooms to women."

"I just might. What are you laughing at?" Dorthia asked when the man chuckled once more.

"Because, little Miss High and Mighty, even if you were seventeen, which we both know you are not, women can't own property unless they are married."

"Actually, that's not true," Dorthia replied.

"It is too. Women cannot own property unless they are married on account of they need someone to manage it for them."

"That isn't the part that is untrue. I never said I wasn't married. I only said what does having a husband have to do with renting a room?"

Davidson dismissed her with a wave of the hand. "Get this brat out of here before I turn her over my knee."

"Well, I never!" Dorthia said.

"Yeah, well maybe that's your problem," Davidson snorted.

"Listen, kid," Boz said, following her outside.

Dorthia narrowed her eyes. "I'm not a kid."

"You want to act older than you are?" Boz sneered. "I have a way for you to earn a little dough."

"What do I have to do?" Dorthia asked.

Boz reached a hand out and stroked her hair. "Be nice to men, starting with me."

Dorthia recalled Mrs. Harper's warning about keeping her legs closed. "Do I got to do more than kiss?"

"Kiddo, kisses I can get for free. I don't know anyone but boys who'll pay you for a kiss. You want some real dough? You come see your uncle Boz." He twisted her hair around his finger. "Don't tell anyone I told you that or I'll cut that pretty little tongue right out of your mouth."

Dorthia's heart raced. For a moment, she thought about kicking him in the shin, but knew that would only anger the man who still held her at a disadvantage. She nodded her understanding, breathing a sigh of relief when he finally let her go. Grabbing her bag, she ran down the street to the echo of his laughter. After a while, she glanced over her shoulder, didn't see anyone following, and slowed her steps. That man wouldn't have dared talk to her like that if her father were still alive. Then again, she wouldn't have had to beg for a room if he were. As her pace slowed, anger fueled her steps. It occurred to her that she wasn't angry at the man for laughing at her; she was furious with her father. This was all his fault. If he hadn't coddled her the way he had, she wouldn't have been able to sway his decision about taking her to Germany.

Dorthia had been walking for some time when she noticed a four-story building with a group of boys milling around. Upon reading the sign that read NEWSBOYS LODGING HOUSE, her heart skipped a beat. This was the place Mrs. Harper had told her about that rented rooms to children. As she neared, one of the boys stepped in front of her, blocking her way.

A tall kid with hooded eyes and a drawn face, he was dressed in rags. The boy sneered at her. "Whatcha want?"

"I'm looking for a room for the night." She attempted to step around him.

He blocked her way once more. "They don't give rooms to no girls."

"I'm not looking for them to give me anything," Dorthia said, showing him her coins. "I have money to pay." She regretted saying it the moment the words left her mouth, as several of the other boys moved closer, peering at the coins.

One of the boys made a move to reach for the coins. To her surprise, the boy she'd been speaking to slapped his hand away.

"Leave her be," he said, then turned to Dorthia once more. "This house don't allow no girls. Especially dimwitted ones."

Dorthia closed her fingers around the coins, shoved her hand into her pocket, and narrowed her eyes at the boy. "Who are you calling dimwitted?"

"You, ya dope! Coming around this place flashing your money around."

"I wasn't flashing my money. I was showing you I can pay for my room."

"Not here you can't on account of they don't allow girls." He shoved the boys aside. "Now go on and git before one of these dopes takes those coins from ya."

Dorthia turned and willed herself not to run. She was tired of being afraid, tired of being told girls had no place. She dipped her hand into her pocket and felt the coins—a cool reminder that some boys thought her worthy of more. Her stomach growled, reminding her of her hunger. Since she couldn't use her money on a room, she decided to get something to eat. Her father used to say he could think better on a full stomach. Perhaps after eating, she'd be able to find someplace to spend the night. She'd lived on the streets before, proving she didn't need a bed, just a safe place to rest her head for the night. She'd survived the streets of Germany; surely she could learn to navigate living on the streets of New York.

***

Having discovered a doorway that was recessed enough to provide a bit of shelter, Dorthia spent her evenings sleeping in the entryway and days walking aimlessly around the city. By high noon each day, she made her way to the market. She wasn't sure why she was drawn to that part of the city; perhaps it was because there were so many shoppers that it was always easy to find an easy mark. Then again, it could be because no one seemed to pay her any mind as she wandered in and around the carts, checking out the vendors. If she caught anyone looking at her, she'd quickly sidle up to an adult and pretend to be with them. She doubted the ruse would last long, as her good dress was covered with grime and quickly becoming worn. She needed a new dress, but thus far, she hadn't dared to steal enough to purchase a new one. Her needs were small, and since no one would allow her to pay for a room, she was content pilfering a few coins a day to keep from starving.

In her former life, she'd merely need to point to whatever she wished for, and it would be hers, but that life no longer existed. She was no longer drawn to the things that once would have captured her attention. Now, instead of pretty silk and fabric that could be turned into a lovely dress, she focused on food and, more importantly, food that would keep her feeling full the longest. While she loved pretzels, she'd quickly discovered that eating one would not keep her satisfied as long as eating a sausage or meat pie. She'd never had to make those decisions when her father was alive, as there was always money for more.

Dorthia forced herself to stop thinking about things she couldn't change. Her father had taught her to read at the age of four. By the age of six, she could write her letters and do simple arithmetic, but though he made sure she was ahead of most children her age, he'd never taught her to live life without him. No, that was a lesson she was learning on her own.

# Chapter Thirteen

Cool wind whipped through the city streets as flakes of white tumbled aimlessly from the sky. A shiver traveled down the length of her as she recalled the winter days spent living on the streets of Berlin after her father died. At least she'd had a coat then and a bramble of branches that funneled the steam beneath to keep her from freezing. Up until now, the doorway had proved sufficient, but in the coming months, she would surely freeze to death if she didn't find a more suitable place to shelter and clothing that would protect her from the elements.

Dorthia rose from the stoop with a tinge of fear. In the months since arriving in New York City, she'd only stolen enough to get her through the day. Over the last week, she'd upped her game, knowing she needed to procure enough to purchase new clothing to help keep her warm. As she made her way to the market, she chided herself for being so conservative with her pilfering and not having already stolen enough to purchase what she needed. It was cold, and she had no coat, so she now looked exactly like what she was—a street urchin. Meaning she looked like someone to be wary of and with that came the heightened risk of getting caught. Then again, if she were caught, she wouldn't have to worry about freezing, as surely they would have fireplaces within the prison walls. As she rubbed her arms against the chill, she almost welcomed an end to the loneliness that greeted her with each waking day.

Dorthia made her way to the market, then moved in and out of the early morning crowd, dipping her hand into pockets and relieving strangers of their change. She found her next mark, a woman in an expensive-looking coat and wide-brimmed hat, and boldly stepped up beside the woman unnoticed. She waited until the woman stopped to inspect some vegetables, then made her move, snaking her hand into the lady's coat. Just as she clutched the woman's coin purse, she saw a boy near the cart watching her. He started in her direction as Dorthia withdrew her hand. At first, she thought he was going to rat her out, but instead, he walked to the opposite side and engaged the woman in conversation long enough for her to open the coin purse and remove a couple of bills. Unlike the boy in Germany who'd taught her the skill, she was mindful of her victim's needs and always left something behind. Dorthia quickly pocketed the bills and then returned the coin purse, hoping she'd left the woman enough money to pay for her purchase. She moved away from the lady, but not before mouthing her thanks to the boy for his help.

A lady in a fur coat stopped in front of her. As Dorthia stood there watching the woman light a cigarette, she noticed a gold chain dangling from her wrist. That the woman was wearing gloves was encouraging, as it should prove easy to remove the chain without her noticing its absence. Dorthia bided her time, following after her mark. She got her chance moments later when the woman stopped at a table to check out bolts of fabric. Not wishing to ruin the fabric, the woman held the cigarette low as she used the opposite hand to search the table. Dorthia sidled up beside the woman and stealthily unlatched the chain and hurried away without being caught. As she slid the chain into her pocket, she recalled the first time she'd taken something other than coins. While she'd been successful in taking the bracelet, she'd nearly gotten caught when she stopped but a few steps later to throw up.

Baylor, who had initially shown her the move, had been

with her at the time. Even with the limited communication, she knew he'd been disappointed in her. She knew without him saying he thought her no good at being a thief. That was because she lacked the German words that would have explained to him that she was no better than the man who'd killed her father over a stupid gold watch. The second time had been easier, and now Dorthia could procure a bracelet with only a simple flashback memory of the first time she'd become a real thief.

As Dorthia's pocket grew heavier, her mood brightened. While she didn't dare count her money in public, the weight of the coins, the bills, and the addition of the newly procured bracelet felt like enough to purchase what she needed to help keep her warm. Still, she didn't think it would hurt to get just a few more coins to be sure, so she continued to walk through the market, looking for an easy mark. She'd found the woman and lifted her arm, intending to reach into her coat pocket.

"Stop thief!" a man's voice boomed.

Dorthia yanked her hand back, watching as nearly a dozen children bolted in different directions. She thought to join them in their retreat, but common sense kept her rooted in place. While she'd been thinking about relieving the woman of her coin purse, her hand was nowhere near the woman's pocket when the man yelled. She further doubted that every child who ran was guilty of thievery at that precise moment.

The woman whose pocket she'd been about to dip scowled at her. "Why didn't you run off with the rest of them?"

Dorthia stood her ground. "Why should I?"

"Because you're one of them."

Dorthia feigned innocence. "One of who?"

"A thieving little varmint," the woman replied.

Dorthia pulled herself taller. "Why, I'm nothing of the sort. You take that back."

"Oh, yeah," the woman said, looking her up and down. "If you aren't an urchin, then where, pray tell, is your coat?"

"It's on the line waiting to dry," Dorthia said, reciting the lie she'd rehearsed enough that her face wouldn't betray her. "My mother had to wash it after my baby sister put her grubby little hands all over it."

The woman considered this for a moment. "If your mother

is so worried about your appearance, then why does she allow you out of the house looking the way you do?"

"My mother can't help the way I look." At least that part wasn't a lie. Dorthia offered a heavy sigh. "Our tenement is without a boiler. My poor mother nearly froze her fingers just cleaning the stains from my coat."

The woman wavered, offering Dorthia the same soulful sigh. "It's a shame the conditions we are made to live in."

"Yes, ma'am," Dorthia agreed.

"And what brings you to the market this day?"

Dorthia looked to make sure no one was watching, then pulled the chain from her pocket. "My baby sister needs food. My mother asked me to try to sell this at the market to get enough money to provide a proper meal."

The woman arched an eyebrow. "It's real?"

Dorthia bobbed her head. "Yes, ma'am. Given to her by my father. Mother would keep it but for my baby sister needing to eat. Mother's milk is gone," Dorthia added when the woman didn't look convinced.

"Oh, your poor mother must be beside herself. I'll tell you what I'll do. I'll give you a whole dollar for the bracelet."

"No, I couldn't," Dorthia said, shaking her head. "Mother was in tears when she handed it to me. She said I mustn't take less than two dollars for it."

The woman brought the bracelet to her mouth, tested it with her teeth, and nodded her consent. "Two dollars it is."

Dorthia smiled and held out her hand.

# Chapter Fourteen

Dorthia pulled her coat closed and lowered her head against the bitter winter's chill as she stomped through the snow-filled street. Her mood was as sour as the scowl on her face, as she'd only managed to dip a few coins during the brief outing.

"Yo, Dorthia, whatcha doing out on a day like this?"

Dorthia lifted her head and saw Vito, one of the many newsies who earned his way hawking newspapers. She offered him a smile. "I need a new dress."

"You got money to buy one?"

She cast a glance at the tenement. "Nope."

Vito nodded his understanding, then reached into his pocket, pulled out a pair of gloves, and offered them to her.

"You know I can't wear them," she said, shaking her head. It wasn't that she didn't want them, but she needed to feel her way around the pocket or risk getting caught.

"Sure you can. Just take them off before you go to work," he said, shoving them into her hand.

Dorthia slipped them on and marveled at the fit. "Where'd you get them?"

Vito offered a grin that showed a missing front tooth. "You ain't the only one with skills."

"What do you want for them?"

His grin widened as he flicked his tongue over his lips. "Same thing as the last time."

She inspected the gloves once more. "Okay. You come find me when you're done."

Vito hoisted his papers when a man exited a tenement across the street and headed in their direction. "GERMAN ULTIMATUM SENT TO PORTUGAL!" he shouted when the man neared.

The man reached into his pocket, flipped Vito a coin, and reached for the paper. Tucking it under his arm, the fellow proceeded without a word.

Dorthia sighed.

"What's the matter, kid?"

"You just stand there and people throw money at you."

"What's the big deal? You're paid for what you're selling."

"Yeah, but I won't be able to do that for long on account of I don't want a baby." Actually, she didn't mind the baby part; it was the dying while giving birth, or having her baby taken away from her, that she wanted no part of. She hadn't had to worry about that yet, but Mrs. Harper's warning was always on her mind. It was also the reason she'd taken to hoarding her money, as she promised herself she would stop as soon as she became a woman.

"You worry too much. I've been with a lot of dames, and none of them have had babies. How old are you anyhow?"

The question caught her off guard.

"Don't you know?"

"I was seven."

"Naw, you don't look seven. You look at least eleven. When was ya born?"

"March 16, 1907."

Vito turned the paper to see the date. "Let's see, it's March 3, 1916 now, so that makes you…"

"Nine, on my birthday," Dorthia said before he could do the math.

Vito's eyes rounded. "You mean you're only eight? You're

nothing but a baby."

Dorthia narrowed her eyes. "You take that back!"

"Now don't ya go getting sore. I didn't mean nothin' by it. I just meant you shouldn't be doing the things you do at your age."

"You didn't seem to mind before you knew how old I am."

"That's on account of you look older. I didn't know you were a…"

"Don't you say it!" she said, cutting him off.

"Aww, don't go getting all sore; you being so young might not be so bad after all. Why just this morning, I overheard Mr. Wilks saying how he needed to find a new girl."

"Mr. Wilks?"

Vito nodded toward the end of the street. "A couple blocks down at the flower shop. I heard him say his other girl was too old to sell them."

Dorthia scratched her head. "You can't sell flowers when you're old?"

"I guess not, on account of that's what he said."

Dorthia glanced at the building, her gaze traveling to the rooftop. "I'd best be getting my dress, then."

"You get a job and you can buy your own dresses."

Dorthia nodded to the ill-fitting coat Vito was wearing. "You're telling me you bought that coat?"

Vito chuckled. "Course not, on account of I gotta pay for my room at the lodge and eat."

"Yeah, you're lucky you're a boy. They don't rent rooms to girls."

"They do at the lodge on Rivington Street."

Dorthia knew the lodge he was referring to, as she'd stayed there a couple of times when the weather had been exceptionally bad. While she'd welcomed the warmth, she'd drawn the line at the classes, which were ridiculous in her mind. She'd left after discovering they were merely in place to teach girls of the street to behave like ladies. She knew how to behave like a lady; her father had seen to that. Knowing how to act right had gotten her nowhere. She spat on the sidewalk and wiped her mouth with the back of her coat sleeve. "No thanks."

Vito shrugged. "Suit yourself. I kinda like having a roof

over my head. You've got dough. I've seen it. Whatcha saving all the money for anyway?"

"I'm going to buy myself a ticket to Charleston." The revelation surprised her as much as it did him. While she'd thought about the possibility each night as she closed her eyes, she'd never spoken the dream out loud.

"Charleston?"

"Yep, it's far away."

"What's in Charleston?"

"My mother."

Vito blinked his surprise. "You've got a mother?"

"Of course I do. Doesn't everyone?"

"I suppose some kids do. I just didn't think you were one of them on account of you ain't never said nothing."

"Well, I do have one, and as soon as I get enough money, I'm going to find her." As the words spilled from her mouth, Dorthia ached for them to be true.

"How come you're not in Charleston with your mother?"

Before she could answer, a man yelled for a paper and Vito darted across the street. Not wishing to speak about the woman she barely knew anymore, Dorthia took this opportunity to leave.

***

Dorthia revisited the conversation with Vito as she went inside the tenement building and climbed the stairs to the rooftop. While Mrs. Harper had offered to allow her to go with her, it had been two years since their brief meeting. Would the woman remember her? Even if she did, would she still be willing to share her home? And what about Joseph? The boy hadn't wanted her to go with them in the first place. He'd only relented after she had shared her money with them. What if they now had enough to eat? Would the boy still be so eager to agree to share his family with her?

Dorthia thought of little John and how accepting he'd been. That was then. The boy was two years older now. Two years… that meant Rachel was no longer a baby. She'd be walking— no, running all over the place now. Dorthia smiled, picturing the little girl running to greet her. The image was short-lived. She was a street urchin with nothing to offer. While she could still

117

earn a bit of money selling her favors, even that prospect would end as soon as she became a woman. Then she'd be nothing more than another mouth to feed. Why would Rachel or any of them rush to greet her when all she'd be was an added burden?

Dorthia reached the last stair and opened the door to the rooftop, thankful to find linens blowing in the frigid breeze. Among them were several dresses that looked like they'd fit. She crossed the rooftop in determined strides, hoping to select a dress and make her way back to the street before anyone knew the garment was gone. As she reached for the dress, she was consumed with the guilt that always plagued her when taking from someone close to her own age. It wasn't as if this was a wealthy area, such as the one where she and her father used to live. No, this was a tenement house. A place where the girl would be sad to find it gone, as the family might not have the means to replace it.

Dorthia pushed the thought from her head, reminding herself that the clothes were hanging to dry. Lots of clothes, so the people who lived in the building were much better off than she. Plus, if the dresses were left to dry, that meant the girl probably had another one to get her by. More than that, she obviously had a roof over her head to keep her warm and dry. Surely if the girl knew of her plight, she would be willing to share her good fortune.

*That doesn't give you the right to take what does not belong to you.*

Dorthia froze as the words came to her in her father's voice, a voice she'd long since forgotten. "But I'm cold, Father, and tired of worrying about how I will survive."

When no answer came, she walked to the edge of the rooftop. Taking a breath, she looked over the side, her breath billowing out like steam as she peered at the sidewalk below.

*Papa died falling from a great height.*

This time, it was John's voice she heard. As she stood there staring over the side, she wondered what death was like. Would it stop the cold that gripped her like a chilly vise? Would it stop the loneliness that plagued her days? Would it stop the constant fear of the unknown or diminish the guilt of disappointing a father who was no longer here? Would she meet her mother who gave up her life so that she herself could live? Or be reunited with her father who'd sacrificed his own happiness so she would not be sad growing up without a mother?

Her father had once told her that one day, when he was old and grey and she had a family of her own, he would leave her to be with her mother once more. He'd lied to her; he had not been old or grey, and she had no family to share her sorrow. It wasn't fair that he got to be happy and see her mother again, while she was now living in fear.

Dorthia pushed up on her tiptoes, craning her neck, debating as a strong wind whipped across the roof, pushing into her as if it wished to help her with her decision.

*What if Father was wrong?*

This time, it was her own voice cutting through the jumble of thoughts in her head. Her mother died in Boston, and her father was killed in Germany; what if they had never found each other in death? It was that thought alone that made her lower to the ground and turn away from the edge of the roof.

As she plucked a dress from the line and hid it inside her coat so her body could help warm the fabric, she felt none of the guilt she'd previously felt. She also knew she was not going to Charleston. While dreaming of joining the family had been a pleasant way to spend her evenings over the past two years, she now knew the dream to be just what it was. A way to stave off the guilt of everything she'd done. Saving money for the purported trip had been a way to justify stealing from others who were fortunate to have more than she. As such, she was able to live with her conscience and not give thought to the girl whose dress she would steal. While she hadn't fully given up on seeing her parents in death, she wasn't ready to take a chance on things she couldn't be certain of. What she was sure of was that she would be staying in New York City and running the streets with all the other thieves, for she, too, was one of them.

# Chapter Fifteen

Dorthia arrived at the flower shop to find several girls standing inside. Dressed in rags, the girls glared at her as she entered.

A freckle-faced girl with dark circles beneath her eyes stepped in front of her. "What are you doing here?"

"I was told Mr. Wilks was hiring."

"He's not hiring you," the girl sneered.

"Why not?"

"He only hires street kids."

"What's your point?"

"You're not one of us."

"I am too," Dorthia said with conviction of her new epiphany.

"Ain't neither. Look at the way you dress." The girl took hold of Dorthia's hand and laughed. "Why, your fingernails aren't even dirty."

Dorthia pulled her hand back. "Just because I live on the streets doesn't mean I have to be a slob. My father told me when looking for a job, you'd better have a good appearance."

"See, you have a father," the girl said. "That right there tells me you're not one of us."

Dorthia firmed her chin. "Had a father—he's dead. Now if you'll excuse me."

One of the other girls spoke up. "I've seen her around. She likes talking to the boys."

The third girl chimed in, "Talking ain't all she does with the boys."

Dorthia narrowed her eyes at the girl who'd just spoken. "What I do or don't do is none of your business. Now if you'll excuse me…"

"You'll wait your turn," the freckle-faced girl said. "We were here first."

Dorthia's heart sank. Vito had told her to hurry, but she'd wanted to make a good impression, so she'd taken the time to run to the Rivington Street Bathhouse and take a shower. She'd even paid extra for an extra towel to dry her hair, so it didn't freeze when she went outside.

The curtain opened, and a man stepped out. Slim, balding, he walked hunched over as he carried a large basket full of cut flowers. He eyed them each in turn as he skirted the counter.

The freckle-faced girl spoke up. "Mr. Wilks, I was here first."

One of the other girls gasped. "That's a lie. Shelley and I came with you."

"Yes, but I walked through the door before you, so that makes me first," the freckle-faced girl replied.

"I don't care who was here first," Mr. Wilks said. "I care who will do the best job."

The freckle-faced girl jutted her hand in the air. "That's me."

"No, me," the other two girls said at the same time.

Mr. Wilks glanced at Dorthia. "What about you?"

"I don't know, since I have no idea what the job entails." Dorthia shrugged. "I suppose I would be able to do anything if I set my mind to it."

Mr. Wilks regarded her with a raised eyebrow but offered no additional comment as he set the basket of flowers on the counter and nodded to the freckled-faced girl. "Pretend I am a customer who would like to purchase a dozen flowers. Tell me what you'd do."

The freckled-faced girl merely stared at him.

Undeterred, he turned to the next girl and repeated the question. Once again, the question was met with silence as he repeated the question to the third girl.

She motioned to the basket. "Pick out your flowers."

Mr. Wilks gathered as many of the flowers as he could and stared at her expectantly.

The girl held out her hand and smiled triumphantly when Mr. Wilks handed her a penny. The smile faded when the man returned the flowers to the basket and held out his hand to retrieve the coin.

Mr. Wilks turned to Dorthia. "Are you ready to sell me some flowers?"

All three girls gasped when Dorthia shook her head. "No, sir."

"Why not?" There was no malice in the tone.

"Because you haven't told me how much to charge."

Wilks smiled his approval. "They are a penny apiece or a dime a dozen."

Dorthia committed the price to memory. "A dozen is twelve, yes?"

His smile grew. "That's correct."

"I'm ready."

"Good day, Miss. I'd like to purchase a dozen flowers."

Dorthia counted out twelve flowers and handed them to the man. She smiled. "That will be ten cents, please."

Mr. Wilks handed her a dime.

Dorthia recalled something from when she lived with her father and took a chance. "It's cold outside. Shall I wrap them in paper to keep them warm?"

Mr. Wilks beamed his approval as he handed her the bouquet. The smile was short-lived when Dorthia went through the motion of wrapping them and returned them to him. "I thought you were going to wrap them for me."

"Oh, I would if you were a real customer. But since you are pretending to buy them, I was only pretending to wrap them."

"Splendid," he said, returning the flowers to the basket. "How did you know to wrap them?"

"Because my father used to bring me flowers when we lived

in Boston."

"Where is your father now?"

"Dead."

"And your mother?"

"Also dead."

"Where do you live?"

Dorthia knew the girls were listening, as good sleeping places were hard to come by. "Will not telling you keep me from getting the job?"

"No, I don't suppose it would."

"Then I'd prefer not to say."

The freckle-faced girl pointed a finger at her. "See, I told you she's hiding something!"

Before Dorthia could object to the accusation, Mr. Wilks motioned to the door. "That will be all. You may leave."

The girls sighed a collective sigh and started for the door.

"Not you," Mr. Wilks said when Dorthia moved to follow. He waited for the others to leave before speaking once more. "I will pay you ten cents a day to start. If you do a good job, I will raise it to fifteen cents. Is that agreeable?"

It was less than what she'd been collecting when dipping pockets. Then again, if she weren't saving money to go to Charleston, she doubted she would need much. She nodded her agreement.

Mr. Wilks clasped his hands together. "Splendid! Now, go collect your things and hurry back so we can get started."

Dorthia frowned. "My things?"

"Yes, your belongings."

"I don't have any belongings." It was true; her money was hidden in an old sock deep in her coat pocket, and she'd discarded her old clothes at the bathhouse.

Though she'd braced herself for disappointment, Mr. Wilks seemed unbothered by the news.

"Very well then, we'll start now," he said, handing her the basket of flowers. "A penny apiece unless they want a dozen. Then they pay a dime. Got it?"

"Yes, sir."

"Good." Motioning for her to follow, he walked to the door and pointed out the window. "You'll stand on that corner as you can collect the traffic from the trolley. Get on out there with you. You do a good job today, and we'll talk about the rest of the benefits later."

Dorthia started to ask him what benefits were, but decided against it as she didn't want him to think she wasn't smart enough to do the job he'd just hired her for. As if afraid Mr. Wilks would see her thoughts, she gathered up the basket and hurried to the corner before he could change his mind. She stood there for several moments, watching as people walked past her without so much as a second glance. Then, recalling how Vito drew attention to his papers, decided to give it a try.

"Flowers, for sale, a dime for a dozen!" she shouted to a man who was passing her by. While he made no move to stop, the fellow behind him stopped and pulled out a dime. Handing it to her, he waited for her to count out twelve flowers before continuing on his way.

Dorthia started to put the coin into her pocket, then stopped. Her money was in that pocket, and she didn't want to get this dime confused with the money she already had. Switching the basket to the other hand, she put the flower money in the one that wasn't being used.

A lady stopped before her as she spoke; her breath came out in steamy puffs. "Can I pick my own flowers?"

"Yes, Ma'am, as long as you pay me my dime," Dorthia said and held out her hand.

The woman reached into her change purse and used her index finger to fish out a dime. As she did, Dorthia couldn't help noticing the beautiful gold bracelet draped across the woman's wrist, so loose and shiny. Dorthia knew she'd easily be able to remove it without the woman noticing. It was by pure will that she didn't act on the impulse, as somehow the bracelet managed to slip from the woman's wrist on its own. This caused a whole new inner struggle as Dorthia debated telling the woman of her loss. She hadn't stolen the bracelet; the woman had lost it. She herself had once lost a button off her favorite coat and had been terribly upset when she found it was missing. Surely the woman would miss something that appeared to be worth so much. Then again, if it were, it should bring a healthy amount at the pawn shop and give her enough to purchase a new outfit when it came time. In the end, Dorthia decided the woman was well off enough that she wouldn't miss it and allowed her to walk away without calling her attention to the bracelet lying at the bottom of the basket.

Dorthia drew her coat closer to her face to block the chill as she continued selling flowers. Now and then, she would move the stems aside to see if the bracelet was still there, but she never once thought to remove it from the basket. It was still there at the end of the day when she slowly made her way back to the flower shop. She opened the door and hesitated at seeing Mr. Wilks standing behind the counter. She'd been so intent on getting out of the cold that she hadn't thought to put the bracelet in her pocket.

He waved her inside. "Come along, girl. Close the door before you let all the heat out."

Dorthia turned to close the door, thinking she would have time to hide the bracelet before Mr. Wilks saw it. Too late, as he appeared behind her and lifted the basket from her arm.

He smiled his approval. "You sold them all."

"Yes, sir."

A frown creased his brow as he pulled the chain free. "What's this?"

"A woman dropped it into the basket as she gathered flowers."

He studied the bracelet. "Dropped it, you say? Are you sure you aren't the one who removed it?"

"No, sir."

"You didn't think to return it?"

"Oh, I thought about it, alright. But since I was thinking of removing it before it fell, I didn't see the harm in keeping it."

His tone softened. "I'm not your father, so I'll not try to act like one. You can do anything you want outside those doors, but I'll not have you steal from inside these walls. Is that clear?"

Dorthia bobbed her head. "Yes, sir."

"Keep that in the basket for a couple of days. If the lady misses it, she may come back to see if you have it. If she doesn't come back, it is yours to keep."

Dorthia couldn't believe her ears. Not only was he not angry with her, he was going to allow her to keep it. "You mean you're not mad I didn't give it back?"

He shrugged. "If you can live with your choices, then so can I. Take off your coat, and I'll ask Mrs. Wilks to bring you down a bowl of soup to warm your belly. She likes to cook, so as long as you stay, she'll see that you are fed." Mr. Wilks studied her for a long moment, then motioned for her to follow. They walked to the back of the store, where he opened a door to reveal a small room with a metal-framed bed and a wooden bookshelf with several dozen books. "The mattress doesn't have much stuffing, but you're welcome to use it if you'd like."

"You mean I can stay here tonight?"

"You can stay as long as you work for me."

Dorthia recalled Mr. Robberts' visits to her room and swallowed as understanding dawned on her. It all made sense now. She wondered what time she could expect him in her room, then decided it best to find out the truth now rather than be surprised in the wee hours of the night. "Mr. Wilks. If you're going to be visiting my room, I'd much rather you do it now. I'm awfully tired and would like to get some sleep tonight."

Once again, a frown furrowed his brow. "I'll not be having my way with you. Nor will I allow anyone to bother you while you are under my roof."

"You won't?"

He left without answering and returned a few moments later to hammer a hook into the door frame. After tugging on it several times, he measured the distance and set to screwing something into the wooden door. When he'd finished, he latched the hook into the eyelet screw and asked Dorthia to open the door.

She could not.

He unlatched the door and stepped outside the room. "You are welcome to lock that door anytime you wish so that you feel safe when you're inside. It's your room now. You can keep your belongings here, and no one will bother them. The only rule is you can't tell anyone. Word gets out, and I'll have every beggar child in the city looking for a place to rest their head."

***

Dorthia wiped the tears from her eyes with her thumb. "Mr. Wilks was true to his word. That mattress was as hard as the frame it lay on, but it didn't stop me from having my first good night's sleep in years. For the first time since my father was killed, I felt safe."

"You were a family?"

Dorthia shook her head. "No, the arrangement was purely business. Mr. Wilks was a man of few words, only speaking to me when necessary. Mrs. Wilks would leave my food outside my door and pick up the empty dishes after I finished."

"But she was nice to you."

"Nice as strangers can be, I guess. I never spoke to the woman other than a thank you here or there."

"It seems strange they would offer so much but give so little."

"I was just happy to have a roof over my head."

"How long were you there?"

"Three glorious years." Dorthia yawned.

Emily lowered her pen. "If you're tired, I could come back tomorrow."

Dorthia considered this a moment. "I'm fine for a bit longer. I know your head is full of questions. Go ahead and ask them."

Not one to waste an opportunity, Emily opened her notebook. "You said you worked as a flower girl for three years. By my calculations, that would make it the year 1919. Is that correct?"

Dorthia nodded. "I was twelve years old when they left."

Emily halted her scribbling. "They who? The Wilkses?"

"Yes. Caught me by surprise too. Woke up one day to see them wielding suitcases and saying how they were moving to Ohio to live with their son."

"They didn't give you any warning?"

"I told you they were all business. I knew no more about them than they knew about me. I had no clue they even had a son. There were signs that something was amiss, but nothing that worried me at the time."

"What kind of signs?"

"In the week before they left, they didn't get any flower deliveries. Mr. Wilks would drive down to the dock every Monday morning and bid on what flowers came in. But he'd not gone there that week. While I noticed the absence of fresh flowers, it didn't occur to me to question it."

"So they sold the store?"

Dorthia shrugged. "Beats me. All I knew was I was without a home for the first time in three years."

"You were older. That must have been scary."

"I was street savvy by then. Not a lot fazed me."

"What did you do?"

"I collected my things and left."

"Please, my readers…"

"Want the nitty-gritty," Dorthia said, cutting her off.

"It's what sells." Emily's tone was unapologetic.

"Even when I was working, if an opportunity presented itself, I'd dip a pocket. I'd also manage the occasional ring or bracelet, but never a watch. I was a thief, but as long as I stayed away from watches, I wasn't like the man who killed my father." Dorthia stopped staring at Emily, willing her to understand. "I might have resigned myself to my fate, but it didn't mean I was proud of the person I'd become. I'd always looked older than my age, and when I began to develop, I developed well."

"Meaning the boys started to notice you."

Dorthia nodded.

"How long were you on the streets that time?"

"About a year."

"And that's when you went out on the train?"

"No, that's when I went into the asylum." Emily started to ask another question. Dorthia waved her off. "My body was changing, and Mrs. Harper's words weighed heavily on my mind. I knew I was playing with the devil, but trading favors was still less risky than dipping pockets. When I was little, as long as I was properly dressed, no one seemed to notice when I'd slip up beside them. But as I developed, everyone seemed to know I was there. I can't tell you how many times I nearly got caught. I guess I decided I'd rather die than go to prison, so I did what a girl had to do to get by. You know, I am tired. Do you mind coming back tomorrow?"

"Not at all," Emily said, closing her notebook. "Do you need anything before I go?"

"No, my nurse will be in shortly."

# Chapter Sixteen

Dorthia had no sooner finished breakfast than Emily appeared in the doorway of her room.

Emily hesitated. "I don't want to interrupt."

"I'm finished." Dorthia waved her in. "I know your head is full of questions. Go ahead and ask them."

Not one to waste an opportunity, Emily opened her notebook. "You said you worked as a flower girl for three years."

"That's right."

"You went back to…"

"I did what I had to do to survive," Dorthia said, cutting her off. She softened her tone. "That all changed when I met Dr. Todd."

"Dr. Todd."

Dorthia smiled. "He had a way about him that would make kids trust him. I'd resigned myself to my fate and was headed down the wrong road when he found me." As she spoke, the memories came flooding back.

***

Dorthia heard voices in the outer room. Thinking she had

overslept, she hurried to dress. Even before opening the door, she knew something was amiss. Her intuition proved to be correct as when she lifted the hook from the clasp and opened her bedroom door, she saw both Mr. and Mrs. Wilks standing near the counter, holding suitcases. Her breath quickened. Not in all the time she'd been working for them had they gone anywhere that required them to take luggage. Mr. Wilks hadn't mentioned a holiday; then again, it wasn't like he shared much with her on any given day. Her mind considered the ramifications. If they were going on vacation, would they allow her to continue to sleep in the building? She swallowed her panic, waiting for an explanation as the couple lowered their cases.

"We're leaving." Mr. Wilks' words were without emotion. "And we'll not be coming back."

Dorthia searched her mind for a response, but words failed her.

"Did you hear me, girl?"

Dorthia nodded.

"Go collect your things."

For the briefest of moments, Dorthia thought they intended to take her with them.

"You'll not be able to stay here once we are gone," he said, removing that glimmer of hope.

Dorthia hurried to her room to collect her things without comment. As she gathered the few belongings she'd managed to squirrel away in her time living here, she fought to stave off the tears.

As she exited her room, Mr. Wilks offered her a pillowcase. "For your belongings," he said, handing it to her. "You did nothing wrong. We are just too old to do this anymore. Understand?"

Dorthia nodded, though in truth, she understood nothing except that for the second time in her life, she'd been lulled into a false sense of security. Even though their relationship lacked any semblance of the love her father had showered on her, after years of having no one, she'd settled into a comfortable coexistence with the couple.

Worry lines tugged at Mr. Wilks' jowls as he pulled several

coins from his pocket and pressed them into her hand. "I'm sorry it is not more." Without waiting for a response, he pointed toward the door.

Not wishing to add to his distress, Dorthia turned and began a slow trek to the door. By the time she exited the building, the tears she'd been holding back trickled down her cheeks. Following the path she'd taken each morning for the past three years, she walked to the corner and stood watching the streetcar ambling toward her as she fought to collect her thoughts.

The streetcar stopped.

Mindless of a destination, Dorthia stepped onboard and dropped a coin into the box, her only thought to get away.

***

Bricks warm against her back, Dorthia leaned against the building with her left leg bent against the wall in a stork-like fashion, with the hem of her dress draped just above her knee. Showing off a body that had matured well beyond her years, she'd loosened her top to reveal just enough cleavage to garner attention. Though she'd been tempted to paint her lips red, Mrs. Harper's warning had frightened her against doing so. While not abstaining altogether, she restricted her offerings to heavy petting. Sure, it limited her earnings, but in the two weeks she'd been back on the streets, she'd managed to make enough to stay fed and, on occasion, had used some to spend the night in the News Girls lodging house. Feeling guilty about spending her money so frivolously, she mostly slept curled up in the alley just outside the building.

A group of boys exited the theater. One of them saw her and offered a loud whistle as he set out in her direction.

Another boy grabbed hold of his shirt. "Don't waste your time on that one. She's a tease."

The whistler looked her up and down. "She doesn't look like a tease. She looks like she means business."

The boy released him. "You want to waste your dime on grabbing, groping, and kissing, go on ahead, but don't expect any more than that."

Once released, the boy hurried to where Dorthia stood. He placed his hand on the wall, crossed his feet at the ankles, and looked her up and down. "Is it true what my friend said?"

Pretending not to have heard their conversation, Dorthia shrugged. "Depends on what he said."

The boy touched her shoulder. "That you're a tease."

"Oh, that. Your friend is mad because I wouldn't give him what he wanted."

"What did he want?"

"He wanted to lie with me."

"Why'd he want to do that?"

"On account of I kissed him."

"Why'd you do that?"

"Because he paid me."

"Maybe he thought you owed it to him to lay with him since he paid you."

"No," Dorthia said, shaking her head. "I made it perfectly clear when he paid me that he was only getting a kiss."

The boy moved in closer. "Would you give me a kiss?"

Dorthia looked him over. "Sure, if you pay me."

The boy eyed her bare leg. "What if I want to touch your leg?"

"Then you'll have to pay me."

"And if I pay you even more, will you lay with me?"

"I will not," Dorthia said firmly.

"Why not?"

"I don't want a baby until I have a husband to provide for me."

"I ain't asking you to marry me!"

"Good, because I am not ready to be married. I'm not ready to have a baby either, which is why I won't lie with you."

"Who said that's how babies are made?"

"Mrs. Harper."

"Naw, I think Mrs. Harper was just funnin' you. I've laid with lots of girls and ain't none of them had no babies."

Before she could answer, a shrill whistle pierced the air.

The boy glanced in the direction of the whistle and released her. "Dang do-gooders got to spoil everything," he mumbled then hurried off in the opposite direction.

Dorthia watched as the man labeled a do-gooder approached. She wasn't sure what a do-gooder was and, for a moment, wondered if she, too, should run. The man must have read her mind as he slowed and raised his voice to be heard.

Well-dressed and clean-shaven, he kept his voice low so she had to strain to hear. "Please, wait. I'm not going to hurt you. I just want to talk to you for a moment."

Dorthia remained rooted in place as she had a flash of a memory of her father speaking to a horse that had gotten spooked when a motorcar rumbled past.

"Please, I'd like to help you." There was something about the man's voice that seemed like he genuinely cared.

She hesitated. "Help me how?"

"I can help you get off the streets."

"Who said I live on the streets?"

The do-gooder inched his way closer. "It's okay. I'm not going to hurt you."

"What's it to you where I live?"

"Wouldn't you like a bed to sleep in?" he asked, taking another step closer.

"Where I sleep is none of your business." Dorthia narrowed her eyes. "I can take care of myself; I've been doing it for six years."

"Six years is a long time. Aren't you tired of being out here all by yourself?"

Actually, she was. While the Wilkses never treated her like family, it was nice knowing she wasn't alone.

The man must have sensed her indecision as he took a step closer. "What are you? Thirteen or fourteen? You could be with kids your own age. I know most of them. They would welcome you into their family."

Dorthia's heart clenched. "You want me to join your family?"

"In a way, yes. There is a nice asylum just a few blocks from here. You'll get fed and will have your own bed to sleep in."

Asylum! All this talk about having her own bed, and being a part of a family, and he was looking to take her to the one place she'd been working to stay out of. Dorthia spat in the dirt. "That's what you can do with your asylum." She bolted, speeding off in the opposite direction without giving him a chance to say another word.

She ran until she had no more breath to run. As she slowed,

she replayed the man's words in her head. He made it sound like asylums were a good thing. She recalled Mrs. Harper's words, and how she had planned on taking her boys to one until she received the letter from Charleston. Surely she wouldn't have even considered it if they were all that bad. Dorthia pivoted and ran back to where she'd last seen the do-gooder.

He was gone.

As she stood there searching for the man, she told herself she didn't care, that what he had said was probably lies aimed to trick her into going with him. Still, a bigger part of her was tired of living on the streets and always looking for something she couldn't seem to find.

# Chapter Seventeen



*1920*

Having made her way back to the market, Dorthia ambled along, studying the horde of shoppers as she searched for her next mark. A woman at the silk vendor wagon held out her hand to receive several bills, which she promptly shoved into the pocket of her sweater.

*Perfect.*

Dorthia started in her direction, only to veer off at the last moment when a little blonde-haired girl peeked around the woman's skirt, staring directly at her.

Not so perfect after all.

Dorthia smiled at the girl, then began searching for another mark. She keyed on a gentleman who'd just pulled his wallet out to purchase a meat pie. Looking dapper, with a smoothly shaved face and a dark, tailored suit, the man stuffed his wallet into the side pocket of his suit coat and bid the vendor farewell with a tip of the hat.

Dorthia figured the man must be unfamiliar with city living, as anyone who'd spent more than a moment there would know that to be a pickpocket's dream scenario. Smiling at her good fortune, Dorthia began stalking the man, waiting for just the right moment to relieve him of his wallet. The man seemed to be in no hurry as he wandered down the street, pausing now and again to look over a vendor cart while taking a taste of his pie.

Dorthia closed the gap, then paused, quickly looking in the other direction when the man glanced over his shoulder. The man began walking once more. Dorthia counted to ten, then began following.

As the man reached the next street, he stepped off the curb, taking several quick steps to avoid being struck by an approaching buggy. Instead of continuing to the next set of vendors, he altered his course, taking a less populated street.

Though she knew better than to attempt a dip without a crowd to disappear into, Dorthia was determined not to let her prize get away, so she followed. Halfway down the street, he ducked into an alleyway.

Dorthia slowed her pace, debating whether or not to follow. As she reached the entrance to the alley, her breath caught as she came face to face with the man. He grinned a wide grin as if he'd been expecting her. "You need to find another line of work. I knew you were there the whole time."

She feigned innocence. "I don't know what you're talking about."

He reached into his pocket and pulled his wallet free and stuffed it into the pocket of his pants. "You're not a very good liar either."

She took a step back.

"Now, don't go running away. You haven't heard my proposition yet."

Dorthia halted her retreat. "What proposition?"

"A job."

Dorthia was intrigued. "What kind of job?"

"One that'll put a roof over your head and pay you a dollar a day."

Dorthia blinked her surprise. "A whole dollar? What do I have to do?"

"If you come with me, I'll show you."

"Come with you where?"

"To the job." Though the man was smiling, his eyes were

dark. "Wouldn't you like to earn enough money so that you don't have to worry about getting sent to prison for stealing?"

"Yes."

"Then come with me. I'll show you the job, and if you don't like it, you can leave."

"Can't you just tell me what the job is so I will know if I like it or not?"

"What's your name, sweetheart?"

"Dorthia."

"Dorthia, such a pretty name. No, Dorthia, I can't tell you, because if I tell you and you don't like the job, then you might run off and tell others. If you do that, then everyone would want to earn that dollar, and I only have so many dollars to go around. That's why it's so important to keep this job a secret. Does that make sense?"

Actually, it did. "Mr. Wilks told me not to tell anyone where I slept for the same reason."

The man's brows knitted together. "Mr. Wilks?"

"Yes, I used to sell flowers for him. He moved, so I don't work for him anymore."

The man's face relaxed. "Then I guess he won't mind if you work for me. Will he?"

"No, sir. I don't suppose he will."

"What about your parents?"

"Dead. Both of them."

"Good."

Dorthia frowned. "What's so good about it?"

"I just meant we don't have to worry about anyone coming to look for you."

"No, sir," Dorthia told him. "You don't have to worry about that at all."

The man smiled as he extended his hand. "Come along, Dorthia, and I'll show you to your new home."

She hesitated, debating if she should go. She thought about the do-gooder, regretting she had not gone with him when she had the chance. The bottom line was she was tired of living on the streets and willing to take the chance at the happiness he offered.

Instead of retracing their steps, he took her through the alley, keeping her hand tucked securely in his own. Dorthia couldn't believe her luck; not only would she be earning a lot of money, but the man—she realized she had not asked his name—had told her she would be part of a family. They'd walked two blocks when she saw him. It had been a year since she'd last seen him, a year since he'd tried to convince her to go into an asylum. Though she'd only spoken to him for a few moments, his face was ingrained in her mind. Perhaps it was because not a day had passed without regretting her decision not to go with him to the asylum. But had she gone, she would not be headed to the new family she was heading to now. Still, he had seemed concerned about her wellbeing, so a part of her wanted to let him know she was going to be okay.

Dorthia yelled to get his attention. "Hey, do-gooder! I've got a new job and I'm going to have a family!"

The do-gooder stuck his head out the window of his motorcar. This time, there was nothing soothing about his voice. "THAT MAN IS NOT YOUR FRIEND!" he yelled.

The man beside her tightened his grip on her arm as he turned and began dragging her in the opposite direction.

Dorthia struggled against his grip. "Ouch! You're hurting me."

"Pipe down, ya brat!" he said, yanking her forward.

Dorthia didn't know why the man was so angry, but suddenly, going with him didn't seem like a good idea. She struggled against his grip, but the man was too strong. Not having any other choice, she dipped her head and sank her teeth into his arm.

"Yeow!" The man released his hold on her and raised his fist.

Dorthia ducked to miss the blow, then darted across the street.

A horn blared as the do-gooder pulled up beside her. Reaching his hand across the seat, he opened the door of his motorcar. "Get in!"

Dorthia climbed in and pulled the door shut, breathing a sigh of relief as the automobile sputtered forward.

"Did he hurt you?" the man asked after a moment.

"Not so much." Dorthia rubbed at the red marks on her arm,

wondering what she'd done to make the man so angry. "He seemed so nice. I don't understand what I did to make him want to hurt me."

"The only thing you did wrong was agree to go with him." The do-gooder's words were spoken without accusation.

"But he was so nice," Dorthia repeated. "He was taking me to a family, and then I saw you. I just wanted to let you know I'd found a family. Why did that make him so mad?"

"Did he ask you if you had any family?"

"Yes. I told him I did not. So why was he mad?"

"He was mad because he got caught."

"Caught?"

"The man's name is Randall. He wasn't taking you to a family; he intended to take you to Orange Street to lock you up."

Dorthia frowned. "Lock me up? You're saying he's a policeman?"

The do-gooder shook his head. "No, I'm saying he's a very bad man who runs a house of ill repute."

*Ill repute?* She'd heard that term before. "What is a house of ill repute?"

The man hesitated as if choosing his words. "It's a place where men go to lie with women and girls."

"Oh, I don't lie with men and boys," Dorthia said, shrugging him off.

"You won't have a choice," the do-gooder said firmly. "Please, let me help you."

"How is it you know so much about that man and what he does?"

"I'm a doctor. I've treated the girls who've been lucky enough to get away," the man said softly.

"You just want to take me to the asylum," she said, recalling their last conversation.

"Have you ever been in an asylum?"

"Of course not. I'm way too smart to get caught."

"What about Randall?"

"I didn't know about him. Now that I do, I'll know not to go with him. I only went with him because he offered me a job."

"Guys like Randall have a way of getting what they want.

What kind of job?" he asked before she could say anything.

"He didn't say."

"He didn't tell you what it was, and you were still willing to go with him?"

"Of course. He said he'd pay me a dollar a day."

"You would have never seen any of the money. What if I offer you a job?"

"What kind of job?"

He laughed. "Now you're asking."

"I'm a fast learner."

"I can see that. I'll see that you get a job in the infirmary at the asylum."

"You're a do-gooder. How do I know it is not you trying to trick me?"

The man slowed and angled the motorcar to the curb and raised his hands. "As God is my witness, I'm not trying to trick you. And you wouldn't be locked up. You'd be free to leave if you decide you don't like it there. I'd see to it myself."

Having been sleeping in door jambs of apartment buildings for the past two weeks, Dorthia wanted more than anything to believe him. "How do I know I can trust you?"

"You'll have to take my word on it."

"You're saying I'll be a doctor?"

The doctor laughed an easy laugh. "No, not a nurse either, but you'll be my assistant on days when I am at the asylum. And I'll find another job for you on days I'm not there."

"Why?"

"Because it's what I do."

"No, I mean, why me? There are a lot of kids living on the streets. Why not help one of them?"

"Would you prefer me to help someone else?"

"No!" The word came out so quickly that it was as if someone else had said it.

"Okay, then."

"Will you take me there now?"

"In a bit, yes. But first, let's get you cleaned up."

# Chapter Eighteen

Dorthia held up the mirror, turning her head from side to side, studying her reflection. While she'd agreed to get cleaned up, she had thought that meant going to the bathhouse for a quick shower, not being taken to the doctor's house, which also served as his office, so his nurse, Mrs. Charlotte, could cut her hair.

Dressed in a black dress, wearing a white apron with her silver-streaked hair pulled into a tight bun, the woman obviously knew nothing about cutting hair, as most of Dorthia's was now lying in a pile on the floor.

Dorthia raised a hand to what was left of her beautiful brunette hair, which wasn't a lot since it now fell just above her ears. "It's so short."

Mrs. Charlotte clicked her tongue. "You're lucky I didn't shave it off."

Dr. Todd smiled a kind smile. "It's the easiest way to get rid of the bugs."

A shiver traveled the length of Dorthia's arms. While she didn't want bugs, she loathed the fact that she now looked like a boy. She stared at her discarded locks, wishing for a way to reattach them. "But I look like a boy."

"Better to look like a boy than be covered in bugs." Mrs. Charlotte took the mirror, placing it on the chair before leading her to the sink and handing her a towel. "Cover your eyes."

Dorthia did as told, gasping as Mrs. Charlotte poured foul-smelling liquid over her head and began rubbing it into her scalp.

Though the liquid was cool, it burned her scalp. Dorthia sneezed. "It's hot and smells disgusting."

"It's kerosene, and you'll live," Mrs. Charlotte said, combing through what little hair was left. "Lucky for you, those critters will not."

Dorthia sighed, suddenly glad her father was not there to witness her shame. "I have bugs, I look like a boy, and I smell disgusting." The words came out in a sob.

"Not to worry, Dorthia," Dr. Todd told her. "The bugs will be gone after this, and your hair will grow back."

Dorthia noted how the doctor's calm, confident tones reminded her of her father.

Mrs. Charlotte pointed to the sink. "Bend over so I can rinse your head."

Dorthia ducked her head over the opening while the woman carefully poured a bucket of tepid water over her scalp. When finished, Mrs. Charlotte took the towel she was holding and gave her a fresh one. "Dry off as much as you can while I get the grease."

Dorthia gulped. "Grease?!"

"For your hair. If there is anything left alive, they will not be able to hang on." Mrs. Charlotte walked to the cupboard and pulled out a small, lidded dish, which she then opened and passed under Dorthia's nose.

"It smells like lavender and rosemary," Dorthia replied. Though she wasn't overly fond of rosemary, it was much better than the pungent odor of the kerosene.

Mrs. Charlotte nodded her approval. "You know your herbs."

"Only the ones Mr. Wilks carried in his flower shop."

The woman frowned. "You know Mr. Wilks?"

"Yes, ma'am. I worked for him for three years. He let me

live in the room under the stairs." Dorthia clasped her hand over her mouth, then slowly pulled it away. "I wasn't supposed to tell anyone I slept there, but I guess it's okay now since they moved, and I don't work for him anymore."

"Mr. Wilks." Mrs. Charlette glanced at Dr. Todd. "If I recall right, he's the man who lost his little girls to the fever years ago, right?"

A frown tugged at the corner of Dr. Todd's mouth as he nodded his agreement. "That is correct. By the time they called for me, there was nothing I could do. I don't think his wife has said more than a handful of words to anyone since."

"Poor woman," Mrs. Charlotte agreed. "Something like that has to weigh on a mother."

While Dorthia wanted to be sad that Mrs. Wilks lost her daughters, a part of her felt relieved at hearing the news. In the years she'd lived there, the woman hadn't acknowledged her with more than a grunt or nod of the head. Perhaps the woman didn't hate her after all. "I just thought she didn't like me," she said, airing her thoughts.

Mrs. Charlotte shook her head. "I doubt that was the case, child. Losing someone you love weighs on a person; I imagine losing two at the same time would be almost too much to bear."

While Dorthia felt a sense of loss at never having a mother, she had never actually mourned the woman. She'd lost her father, and that was as much as she thought she could bear. "Mrs. Harper lost a baby. She seemed really sad when she spoke of it."

Mrs. Charlotte nodded her agreement. "I'm sure she was," the woman said without asking who Dorthia was speaking of. Instead, she took hold of Dorthia's chin with her left hand as she dipped her right hand into the bowl and gathered a hunk of grease, and began slathering it over her head. She repeated this several times before releasing her grasp and using both hands to massage the grease into her scalp.

Dorthia closed her eyes, enjoying the pressure of the woman's touch.

"Don't you go falling asleep on me until you get in the bath," the woman said, removing her hands.

Dorthia opened her eyes. "I get to take a bath?"

Mrs. Charlotte chuckled. "You don't think those bugs stopped at your hair, do you?"

Dorthia peered at her arms, looking for the bugs. She saw nothing. "If I have bugs, then why can't I see them?"

"They're there. See those little bumps?"

Dorthia peered closer and nodded.

"Those are bugs under your skin."

"You're not going to cut them out like you did my hair?"

"No, child. We don't do surgeries to remove the bugs. I'll run you a bath and add a bit of lye. Between that and the lye soap, it'll cure what ails you. Come on, we'll leave the doctor to his paperwork, and I'll see to it."

Dorthia followed as the woman led her down a long hall and into a large room with a toilet, a free-standing sink, and a footed tub.

Mrs. Charlotte leaned over the tub, pressed the rubber stopper into the drain, and turned on the spigot. She added some powder, which instantly turned to suds, then turned her attention to Dorthia. "Strip down while I get your water ready. Put your clothes on a pile in that basket so I can take them out to the barrel."

"Barrel? You're going to wash them for me?"

"Heavens no, child," Mrs. Charlotte said, shaking her head. "I'm going to burn them. Same with the rest of your things."

Dorthia gulped. While her clothes weren't fancy, they still fit. "There must be some kind of mistake. Dr. Todd didn't say anything about burning my clothes."

"Did you agree to go to the asylum?"

Dorthia nodded.

"Then you won't need your clothes. They'll give you new ones and wash them for you every week."

Okay, that sounded promising. "What will I wear until then?"

"Don't you fret yourself about that. Just go on and get in that bath while the water's still warm, and I'll bring you something to wear. Don't go getting your hair wet. You need to leave that grease in and give it time to do its job. Understand?"

"Yes, ma'am."

"Good. Now out of those clothes and into the bath." Mrs.

Charlotte turned the spigot to turn off the water. When she spoke, her tone softened. "I'm sure it's been a while since you've enjoyed a good bath. There's no hurry to get you to the asylum, so take your time."

Dorthia waited for her to leave the room before undressing and stepping into the sudsy water. It was hot, but that didn't stop her from climbing inside the bath and sinking in to where only her head was above water. It was glorious.

A bath. A real bath with hot water and soapy bubbles. While she'd had a shower at the bathhouse from time to time, there was always a line, and never time to dawdle. As she lay there soaking, she couldn't recall the last time she'd felt so clean. "Before Father died." She sighed. "No, in Germany. That was the last time I had a bath."

She closed her eyes and felt her troubles begin to slip away.

When she opened her eyes once more, the water had cooled. She lounged in the bath a little longer then used the soap bar to scrub the filth from her body. When she'd finished, she splayed her hands in front of her face, studying the wrinkles. She was just about to call out to ask Mrs. Charlotte to bring her some clothes when she saw a dress hanging on a hook on the back of the door. A small stack of clothing sat on the bench next to the door, along with the shoes she'd worn in, which looked to have been freshly polished. While her shoes were there, the clothes she'd removed were gone, along with the basket she'd put them in. All without her seeing.

*I must have fallen asleep.*

Dorthia climbed out of the tub and hurried to dress. The dress wasn't new, but it was free of stains and smelled clean when she slipped it over her head. She pulled on the undergarments and shoes before opening the door to the outer room.

Dr. Todd looked up from his desk. "Feel better?"

She frowned. "I wasn't sick."

"I meant after taking a bath."

Dorthia bobbed her head. "Oh, yes, sir. I most certainly do."

He smiled.

"Thank you for the dress."

"It's only temporary. You'll be getting a uniform when you

get to the asylum."

"A uniform?"

"Yes, the headmistress prefers all the children in her care to be dressed alike. It keeps the children from feeling inadequate if their clothes are not as nice as someone else's," he said by way of explanation.

"You said I can leave if I don't like it there. What if I want to leave and the only clothes I have are the ones they give me?"

"You make a good point. I will ask to have the dress you are wearing returned. I'll have it cleaned and pressed and keep it here for you. If you decide not to stay, I will return it to you."

She studied him, debating his trustworthiness.

His smile widened. "Have I lied to you yet?"

Dorthia shrugged. "I don't think so."

"And I won't. My father always said a man is only as good as his word."

Dorthia sucked in her breath. "My father used to say the same thing."

Dr. Todd jumped on the opportunity. "Dorthia, where is your father now?"

The question caught her off guard. "I don't know."

"When was the last time you saw him?"

"When the man killed him," she said softly.

"You saw your father killed?"

She nodded.

"Then why did you say you don't know where he is?"

"Because I don't. I was scared, so I ran away. When I went back, he was gone." Tears welled in her eyes before trickling down her cheeks. "I didn't see where they took his body and don't know if he found my momma in heaven."

"Your mother's dead too?" Dr. Todd's voice was full of concern.

Dorthia brushed the tears with her hands. "Father said she died so I could live."

Dr. Todd pulled a handkerchief from his pocket and handed it to her. "She died giving birth to you?"

Dorthia felt the heat of the accusation. "Yes. I killed her."

"You did not kill her."

Dorthia narrowed her eyes. "Are you calling my father a

liar?"

Dr. Todd sat back in his chair. "No, of course not. I wouldn't presume to make such a judgment on a man I've never met. I'm merely saying you mustn't blame yourself for your mother's death."

Oh, how she wanted to believe him. "Why not?"

"Because women die during childbirth for a number of reasons, none of which are the fault of the child. And just because it happened to your mother doesn't mean it will happen to you," he said as if reading her mind. "That's not to say you should do things that will have you finding out anytime soon."

"Like the things Randall wanted me to do?" she said, leaving out the fact that she'd already done some of those things.

"Precisely."

"How do you know I didn't kill her?"

"I'm a doctor. It's my job to know."

"Dr. Todd? Do you know if my father found my mother in Heaven?"

"Was your father a good man?"

"Yes, sir," Dorthia sniffed. "Father was a very good man."

"I'm a God-fearing man, and as such, I would think they have found each other."

She swiped at the tears. "I wish I could be sure."

"Dorthia, why don't you think they found each other?"

"Because Father died so far away."

"Far away? Where?"

"Berlin."

Dr. Todd raised an eyebrow. "You were in Germany when you saw your father killed?"

"Yes."

"Did your father die in the war?"

She shook her head. "No, the war hadn't started yet."

"How old were you?"

"Seven."

"What were you doing in Berlin?"

"My father went to Germany to discuss a bridge. They were building it, and they wanted my father to look over the plans and location to make sure it would hold up. He was an engineer, so he knew things like that."

"You had relatives who sent for you after he died?"

"I have relatives, but they don't know where I am."

Dr. Todd pulled his pocket watch from his pocket to check the time, and for the smallest of seconds, he reminded her of her father.

Dorthia blinked as another round of tears threatened.

Dr. Todd stood and placed his hat on his head. "Young lady, how about we go get some supper? While we are eating, you can tell me what happened, starting with your trip to Germany and how you got here."

She smiled. "I would like that very much."

# Chapter Nineteen

It was near dusk when they finally reached the entrance to the asylum, an imposing red brick Victorian building that took up most of a city block and was surrounded by a tall black wrought-iron fence. Dorthia paused at the gate, studying the steep roof pitches and asymmetrical façade. Oh, how her father would have loved this building. As she stood there gazing at the building, she could almost hear him touting the merits of the structure as he had done with similar buildings in the years before his death.

"It's a Victorian," Dr. Todd said, following her gaze.

"A Queen Anne to be exact." Dorthia used her index finger to trace the lines of the roof. "See how things don't line up with the front-facing gable?"

Dr. Todd nodded his approval. "I'm impressed."

Dorthia laughed. "Father said I could tell the difference in buildings even before I could count past ten. This was a favorite of his."

"Your father knew of this house?"

"Not this one, just the style." Dorthia shook her head as she recalled a story her father had told her many times over the years. "Father loved Victorians. Especially Queen Annes. He fell in love with the style when he and Mother traveled to San Francisco before I was born. There was a row of them along the bay on Steiner Street that Mother fell in love with. She had almost convinced Father to move there, but then there was an earthquake that destroyed most of the city. That was the year before I was born. Father told me he refused to move to a place where houses could be shaken from their foundations. I think he carried that guilt with him always as he purchased a small Victorian home for us before we left Boston. He'd planned on surprising me with it when we returned from Germany, but he slipped and ended up telling me about it on the way over."

"That's the home you were telling me about over supper?"

"It is."

"And you have no idea of the address?"

"No. As I said, it was supposed to be a surprise." Dorthia frowned. "What do you suppose will happen to the house now?"

"It's been years since you and your father left for Germany. I would expect the house to have been long sold by now."

The thought of someone living in the house saddened her. "And who got the money from it?"

"I wish I had the answers you seek, but I'm afraid I do not."

"I bet my grandmother was sad when Father and I did not come home," Dorthia replied, speaking of her father's mother. The woman lived in Chicago, and although she could only recall meeting her once, her father had said her grandmother had come for an extended stay to help him care for her after her mother died. He'd also told her that her grandmother had offered to take her to her home in Chicago. While Dorthia had been pleased to hear he hadn't wished to send her away, she now wondered what her life would be like if he had agreed. *I wouldn't be here.*

"I'm sure she misses you both very much," Dr. Todd said, interrupting her thoughts.

Dorthia sighed. "I'm ready to go in now."

Dr. Todd hesitated. "The fence doesn't scare you?"

She frowned. "Should it?"

"No. But I believe you are the first who hasn't been bothered by it."

"Father liked fences. Buildings and structures don't scare me; it's the people they are meant to keep out who worry me."

"You'll be safe inside." He palmed his hand toward the gate. "After you, my dear."

The door leading into the building was massive and solidly built. As it swung open, the outside charm of the building was lost in a sea of white from floor to ceiling.

Dorthia gasped. "Why, it looks like a hospital!"

Dr. Todd chuckled. "You say that like it's a bad thing."

"I like that the building is clean. But where is the color Queen Annes are known for? Father would not approve at all."

Dr. Todd furrowed his brow. "You're not going to change your mind about staying here, are you?"

"No, I guess since I'm already here, I should give it a chance."

"Good. Come, and I will introduce you to the headmistress."

Dorthia followed, listening to their shoes connect to the tile floors as they turned and walked down the long hallway. This hallway was much like the entrance, only wider, with multiple doors and the occasional gold-framed painting on the wall. Brilliant red crocks were spaced evenly down the corridor. She knew they were there in case of a fire and further knew her father would be pleased to know they were there. They passed several doors before stopping.

Dr. Todd rapped on the door, entering after a woman's voice called out for him to do so.

"Wait here for a moment." He opened the door and stepped inside.

Dorthia stepped closer so she could hear.

"Dr. Todd, I did not expect to see you today." The voice sounded cheerful.

"I brought a friend to see you."

"Oh?"

"A girl. She's in my care, but I feel she would be more comfortable staying here with you and the children."

"Oh, I see. One of your special cases, I assume." The woman's tone had changed.

"Indeed. Dorthia will be working for me when I am in the

building, and I told her she does not have to stay if she doesn't wish to remain."

"Dr. Todd, I know you mean well, but I have enough to deal with without you bringing in another of your strays."

Strays? Dorthia narrowed her eyes. Why of all the …

"Dorthia is different," Dr. Todd replied. "The girl comes from a family of means. She is left orphaned through no fault of her own, and I am personally going to make it my mission to find her kin."

Dorthia gasped. She sucked in her breath as her hand flew to her mouth.

"Dorthia," her name sounded harsh coming from the woman's tongue, "since you are obviously listening to our conversation, you may as well enter."

Dorthia let out her breath, then moved into the room when Dr. Todd stepped aside and motioned for her to enter. While she wanted to apologize for eavesdropping, she did not. The door was open after all.

A thin, stern-faced woman dressed entirely in black with her hair pulled into a bun, the headmistress looked her up and down. "Are you one to spy on your elders?" she asked without waiting for an introduction.

"I was not spying. The door was open, and I couldn't help but hear." She looked at Dr. Todd with hopeful eyes. "Are you really going to find my family?"

"I can't make any promises that I will find them, but I can promise to try. In return, you have to promise to give this establishment a try. I know it won't be easy since you've been on your own so long, but you will try, won't you?"

Dorthia glanced at the headmistress before answering. "Yes, sir."

Dr. Todd smiled a triumphant smile. "Splendid."

"I will have Clara show her to the washroom where she can be scrubbed."

"I've just had a bath," Dorthia told her. While she enjoyed baths, she felt getting two in the same day was one too many.

"Every child who comes in reports to the washroom," the headmistress said sternly. "This asylum prides itself on cleanliness and cannot have you bringing anything in."

"I didn't bring anything," Dorthia said, standing her ground. "Mrs. Charlotte burned everything I own."

"I am speaking of bugs," the headmistress said dryly.

Dr. Todd placed a hand on her shoulder. "Dorthia doesn't have any bugs. My nurse saw to that under my instruction."

"She cut off my hair too!" Dorthia removed her hat to show what was left of her hair.

"I assure you," Dr. Todd said firmly. "Dorthia is clean and free of bugs."

"Very well, Dr. Todd, we will have it your way." The headmistress sighed. "She will still wear the uniform."

"Of course," Dr. Todd agreed. "If you can have the clothes she is wearing placed in my conservatory, I will pick them up when I come to do my rounds."

The headmistress raised an eyebrow. "You wish to keep them?"

"I do. I promised Dorthia I would keep them for her in case she decides to leave."

The headmistress raised an eyebrow. "Dorthia, please step into the hall so I can have a word with Dr. Todd."

When Dorthia walked into the hall, Dr. Todd pushed the door closed. It failed to latch and opened just enough for her to see into the room.

"Dr. Todd, this surrender is most unusual. You know how we do things here. I'll not have you undermining my authority like this ever again."

"How is treating a child with respect undermining your authority?"

"We have things set up the way we do for a reason."

"Set up? You mean by placing a child into hot water and allowing their skin to be scrubbed raw?"

"A little fear never hurt anyone. Plus, it gives my staff the upper hand. We need children to respect the staff."

"No, you want them to be afraid of them. There is a difference. Dorthia doesn't have bugs, nor does she need to be so afraid of staying here that she prefers to return to the streets, where she'll end up selling her body for the rest of her life just to survive."

"Are you saying the child is promiscuous?"

"I'm saying she's a child but looks fifteen. You of all people know what children are forced to do to stay alive out there. That she's survived on the streets this long without being pulled into a house of ill repute is a miracle." Dr. Todd began pacing the floor. "She watched her father die and has lived on the streets for six years, and yet it hasn't broken her spirit."

"She has a sad story, as does nearly every other child in this asylum. You have brought me numerous children over the years. What makes her so special?"

Dorthia leaned in closer so she wouldn't miss his answer.

"She reminds me of Rebecca."

"The girl you pulled out of the house on Roosevelt Street?"

"That's the one. She was fourteen when we found her and had been imprisoned since she was eleven. If I don't get Dorthia off the streets, she could face the same fate."

"You promised her she can leave if she does not like it here. Do you plan on holding to that promise?"

*Of course he does*, Dorthia thought. Then again, she had trusted Randall as well. Was it possible that Dr. Todd was simply telling her what she wanted to hear just so he could trick her into coming to the asylum? She leaned in, eager to hear his answer.

"I never make a promise I don't intend to keep. Speaking of promises, I told Dorthia she could work for me on days when I visit the asylum."

"Dr. Todd, this is highly irregular. Isn't it enough you got the child off the street?"

"Not this time. In speaking with Dorthia, I can tell she comes from a well-to-do family."

Laughter filled the room. "Dr. Todd, have you never heard a child lie? Why, I have a boy in here at this very moment who contends he is the heir to the throne."

"You are speaking of the boy who eats the chalk?" The doctor's voice held no humor.

"His father was a drunkard who pulled him through the door to this establishment by the lobe of his ear. I assure you, there is no royal blood in that family. It is simply the boy's way to keep from being punished."

"Even so, I believe Dorthia is telling the truth when she tells me her father was an engineer."

"What makes you so sure?"

"How many children do you know that could look at this building and tell you its design?"

"Impressive. However, I am not sure it is solid proof. I am sure I could find someone among the children who would know this to be a Victorian building."

"No, I said it was a Victorian. It was Dorthia who corrected me, telling me it was a Queen Anne."

"Very well," Headmistress said after a moment. "I suppose I can find it in my heart to grant special dispensation for this child if you would be willing to pay for her board."

"You expect me to pay for her board?"

"You asked for special dispensation. If you do not wish to pay her tuition, the girl will be integrated with the other children. It is the way it must be to avoid looking as if I am showing favoritism. Surely you understand my position. If you truly believe the girl comes from a wealthy family, then I am sure they will be pleased to reimburse you once she is returned to them."

"Very well," Dr. Todd said, donning his hat. "You may deduct Dorthia's tuition from my pay."

*I get to stay.* All those years of trying to stay out of any asylum, and now she found herself happy knowing she would be allowed to stay. Why that made her so happy, she did not know; maybe it was the fact that the doctor had promised to help find her family, or perhaps it was that he actually believed in her. Suddenly worried the headmistress would discover her listening and refuse to let her stay, Dorthia moved away from the door.

A moment later, Dr. Todd opened the door. "Dorthia, the headmistress would like a word with you."

"Is it your wish to stay here with us?" the headmistress asked when she entered the room.

Dorthia couldn't believe it. All those years of being afraid of getting caught and being made to go inside an asylum, and here she was being given a choice. She nodded her head.

"Use your words, please, Dorthia."

"Yes, ma'am. I wish to stay as long as I'm happy here," she

added just in case.

The headmistress leaned back in her chair. "Yes, Dr. Todd has made it clear it is your choice whether to stay or go. All the same, I want you to promise me that if you do choose to leave, you will come to see me and explain your decision before leaving. Can you abide by that request?"

Dorthia glanced at Dr. Todd, who smiled his encouragement. She nodded once more.

"Your words, please," the headmistress reminded her.

"Yes, ma'am, I agree to discuss my leaving with you first."

"I will allow no promiscuity in this asylum. There will be no kissing or otherwise engaging in flirtatious activities. Is that understood?"

Dorthia wasn't quite sure what flirtatious activities were, but she doubted anyone inside the asylum would have the means to pay for such things anyway. "Yes, ma'am, I understand."

"Very well, I will ring for Clara to take you to the washroom so that you can receive your uniform," Headmistress said when Dorthia started to object.

Dr. Todd turned to address her. "I'm going to take my leave now. But I'll be back in two days' time to check on you. Follow the rules, and if there is anything you are not sure of, I'm sure Headmistress will be happy to find someone to help you."

"I will ask Clara to have one of the girls show her around and stay with her until she settles in. I believe Mary will be a good fit."

"Mary would be a splendid choice," Dr. Todd said, nodding his agreement. He bowed, then lifted his hat to his head. "I'll bid you ladies adieu and see you in two days."

"The doctor is going out of his way to see that you are well cared for. It is your duty to try to get along in here so you do not let him down."

Dorthia hadn't thought about her leaving as letting the doctor down. But when put to her like that, she knew she would try her best to like it here. The man reminded her of her father, and the last thing she wanted to do was let him down. "Yes, ma'am."

Headmistress lifted a small brass bell from her desk and

clanked it from side to side.

Footsteps sounded in the hall, and a girl stepped into the room. If not for the fact that she herself looked older than she was, Dorthia would have thought them to be around the same age.

"You rang, Headmistress?"

"Clara, I want you to take Dorthia to the sisters so she can be fitted for a new dress and shoes."

Clara's brow furrowed. "You don't want her to have a bath?"

"No, Dr. Todd brought her in. He saw to the task before she arrived. Take her to get changed and tell the sisters she is only to get her uniform. Tell them to set aside her clothes and I will collect them myself later."

"Yes, Headmistress," Clara said, bobbing her head.

"Clara?"

The girl hesitated.

"After she is dressed, find Mary and tell her I want her to help Dorthia settle in."

"Yes, ma'am." Clara directed her attention to Dorthia. "Come with me. You're lucky you've already had your bath," she whispered once they were away from the door.

"You don't like baths?" Dorthia asked.

"Shhh. Keep your voice down in the halls."

"Why?"

"It's the rules. There is to be no talking in the halls, and if you must talk, you should keep your voice to a whisper, as the halls have ears."

Dorthia snickered. "That's impossible. Halls cannot have ears."

Clara stopped. "In this place, there are always ears. I will advise you to watch your tongue and be warned: never say or do anything that you don't want others to hear or see."

Dorthia gulped. "Is it a bad place?"

"Only if you do something bad."

Okay, that made Dorthia feel a little better, as she had no intention of doing anything bad. "How long have you lived here?"

"For as long as I can remember."

"You've never wanted to leave?"

Clara shrugged. "Where would you have me go?"

"I don't know."

"There are some that would wish to leave, but this place is all I have ever known."

"Do you work here?"

"I assist the headmistress."

"How much does she pay you?"

Clara laughed, then caught herself and lowered her voice. "I don't get paid."

"How can it be a job if you don't get paid?"

"I have enough."

"Enough what?" Dorthia pressed.

"I've seen the children that come in here. Most arrive after having lived on the streets for years. I've heard their stories and listened in horror at things they have done or have had done to them. I do not have those stories." She looked Dorthia in the eye. "No one has ever touched me where I do not wish them to touch."

Dorthia turned away from the implied accusation as a chill ran the length of her arms.

"I am free to move around as I please," Clara said, returning to her answer. "I have the headmistress' ear, and no one bothers me. I have clothes, a clean bed to sleep in, and I don't have to worry about going to prison for stealing a loaf of bread. It happens, you know."

Though she herself had been lucky to have never been caught stealing, she knew all too well the horrors of living on the street. "If it's so good in here, why is everyone afraid to come inside?"

"You were living on the streets. Yes?"

"Yes."

"Why were you afraid to come in here?" Clara asked, turning the question back on her.

"I'd heard it was a bad place."

"Compared to what?"

"I don't understand."

"Bad compared to what? If you had a nice home with parents who love you, then yes, this place is bad. But if you are living on the streets and stealing, fighting, or selling your body to survive, then I'd guess this place isn't so bad."

"You know, you're pretty smart for someone who's never been to school."

"Don't be ridiculous. Of course I've been to school."

"But you said you've never left here."

"So that doesn't mean I haven't been to school. We have classrooms and teachers here."

"There are classrooms?" Dorthia gasped. While her father had worked with her and brought in tutors to see that she knew the fundamentals at an early age, and she'd kept up with her reading while living in the room under the stairs, she herself had never set foot in an actual classroom.

"You'd better get used to it. The headmistress doesn't tolerate children who don't take their studies seriously."

Though Dorthia knew Clara meant it as a warning, she was thrilled with the prospect of continuing the education her father had started.

# Chapter Twenty

The washroom turned out to be an open room with multiple rows of deep, round tubs, each filled with what looked like scalding water. There were children in two of the tubs, neither of which appeared to be at all pleased with their current predicament. On the contrary, the women hovering over them appeared to be enjoying themselves very much. Both women looked up when she and Clara entered, the one nearest greeting them with the most wicked grin.

"Go," she said, motioning to one of the tubs.

Clara waved the woman off. "No bath. Just uniform and shoes."

The woman scowled. "Must bath."

"No bath," Clara repeated. "Just clothes. The headmistress wishes for the clothes she is wearing to be washed."

"*Geh deine Kleidung holen!*" The woman smiled and pointed to a counter at the back of the room. "*Dann nimm dich und deine widerlichen Käfer mit!*"

Clara smiled. "Thank you."

"Why are you thanking her when she is being rude?"

"Are you sure? She was smiling."

"Smiling because she knew you couldn't understand her. The woman just referred to you as a wretched child and said I am covered in bugs." Dorthia narrowed her eyes at the woman. "*Ich habe keine Käfer, und du bist nicht sehr nett,*" she said, telling the woman she did not have bugs, further calling her on being rude.

Clara blinked her surprise. "You don't have a German accent. How is it you know it so well?"

Realizing Dorthia had understood her words, the woman's face grew pale as she uttered her apologies. "*Es tut mir leid.*"

Dorthia turned and walked to the back of the room without responding.

"What was all that?" Clara asked as she drew near.

"I didn't want her to know that I only speak a little German," Dorthia whispered. "I told her she wasn't being nice. And she apologized."

"You don't look happy about that."

"I've not even been here an hour and I'm already causing trouble. I'm afraid the headmistress might not be happy with me."

"Don't you worry about that. She'll be happy you stood up for me."

"But she warned me not to cause trouble."

"I'll take care of it."

Dorthia breathed a sigh of relief; the last thing she wanted to do was get kicked out before she even gave the place a try.

A woman just as large as the other two rounded the back wall and stopped at the counter.

"Dorthia needs a uniform," Clara told her.

"Ja." The woman looked Dorthia over, then pulled a dress from the shelf. She placed it on the counter before walking around the divider and holding a ruler to Dorthia's foot. She mumbled something under her breath, then made her retreat once again.

Dorthia looked for a place to change and saw nothing that would allow any privacy, so she loosened her dress and disrobed where she stood.

"What are you doing? There are boys in the room."

Dorthia laughed. "So?"

"It's not proper for a girl to allow a boy to see her without clothes."

"They don't have any clothes on either and they don't seem to mind."

"You are not ashamed for them to see you undressed?"

"It's nothing new. Besides, they are too busy with their baths to notice me." Dorthia smiled when she unfolded the dress and saw that it looked the same as the one Clara had on. While not a designer dress, it was pretty and clean. Dorthia pulled it over her head and marveled at the fit. "It's like it was made for me."

Clara nodded. "You're lucky you got Miss Eleanora; she's the best at sizing."

The woman returned, handing over a pair of shoes along with a pair of black stockings, which Dorthia hastened to put on while Clara followed the woman to the back room.

"Miss Eleanora will speak to the others," Clara said when she returned. "The headmistress will not learn of this."

"Why are you being so nice to me?" Dorthia asked as she slipped into her stockings.

"Is it a sin for someone to be nice?"

"No, but it's an asylum. I thought everyone was supposed to be mean."

"You'll find some who are and some who want people to think they are. Not everyone is always as they seem. Some will try to test you to show you they are the boss. My advice: don't start any fights, but don't let anyone push you around. Someone finds they can push you around, and you won't like it so much in here. Come. I'll take you to Mary."

"Is Mary nice?"

"Mary has a good way about her." Clara's smile waned. "You listen to her; she knows things."

"What kind of things?"

"Too many to say." Clara pressed her finger to her mouth, silencing further questions as she opened the door. Clara led her down the long hallway, turning before reaching the headmistress' office. She stopped halfway down that hallway and opened the door to a spacious, windowless room with multiple groups of children mulling around. The first thing she noticed was the children all appeared clean. The girls wore the same blue gingham dress as she'd been given while the boys wore white shirts, black knickers that stopped at the knee and black stockings. What surprised her most was that every child in the room had on shoes, and near as she could tell, not a one of them were scuffed.

"Wait here. I'll get Mary." Clara paused, surveyed the room, then approaching a small group of children, pulled aside a pretty blonde girl who stood a head shorter than Clara. Dorthia sized her up from a distance. Though she was shorter, Dorthia figured them to be around the same age. She also knew they were speaking about her as the girl kept glancing in her direction. A moment later, Clara returned with the girl at her side. "I've got to go. Mary will see to you from here on out."

"Clara tells me you like boys," Mary said as soon as Clara was gone.

Dorthia looked toward the door. When Clara was warning her about people, she didn't realize she was amongst those who weren't as they seemed.

"Don't be upset with Clara; it's her job to know things. She also said the headmistress allowed you to enter without a proper bath."

Dorthia narrowed her eyes. "I'm as clean as you."

Mary frowned. "The mistresses didn't cut your hair."

At the mention of her hair, Dorthia's hand flew to her head to touch what was left of her once beautiful locks. "No, Mrs. Charlotte cut it."

"You are lucky. At least you still have some hair on your head. Everyone who comes in gets clipped nearly bald." Mary ran a hand through her own hair as if remembering.

"Your hair is long and beautiful. How long have you been here?"

"Too long."

Though curiosity begged for more, Mary's tone let it be known she did not wish to be besieged with questions. Instead, Dorthia nodded her understanding.

"Headmistress will not tolerate any improprieties."

"Is that the same thing as promiscuity?"

"In this case, yes."

"Okay, because I told the headmistress I wouldn't do that

since the boys wouldn't have the money to pay me," Dorthia said, casting a glance around the room.

Mary sucked in her breath. "You mean boys pay you for a kiss?"

Dorthia shrugged. "Among other things."

Another intake of air. "You're smiling. You did not hate such things?"

"Sometimes, I did. But mostly, it wasn't bad."

Mary lowered her eyes and rubbed her arms. When she spoke, her voice held a tremble. "I think it is all bad."

Once again, Dorthia nodded her understanding. "It was terrible for me at first as well. Perhaps one day you will not find it so bad."

Mary held her gaze as if judging her sincerity. Finally, she smiled the barest of smiles.

"Perhaps, one day." Mary grew quiet for a moment, then her smile brightened. "Come. I'll introduce you to my little group."

There was something about how she'd said it, as if the children belonged to her, but as Dorthia followed Mary across the room, she felt a sense of belonging that she'd not had since she'd lost her father.

*** 

Dorthia stood in line waiting to go upstairs to the girls' dorm. While some of the children whispered, Clara had been adamant that there was no talking in the halls, so she stared straight ahead, not wishing to do anything that would have her sent away from here. Though she'd only been in the asylum a few hours, she already considered the place her new home. The line started moving, and Dorthia followed. As she slid her hand along the smooth handrail, she recalled the two-story Boston apartment she'd shared with her father. It, too, had smooth handrails and long, beveled windows that allowed the light to filter in. It was dark now, and the hallway was filled with shadows, but come morning, the sun would fill the hallway with glorious beams. The girls filed into a hallway on the second floor and soon spread out in a large open space filled with metal beds.

Mary waved a hand to her. "This is your bed. I hope you don't mind sleeping near the window. It's nice in the summer, but it could get a bit chilly when winter sets in."

"It's perfect," she said and meant it. Having been sleeping outside, Dorthia wouldn't have cared if they'd given her a pallet on the floor. She started to tell Mary that, but decided not to, as she didn't want to remind anyone she didn't belong here.

Mary helped her place the sheets on the bed, then reached into the pillowcase and removed a cotton nightdress.

Tears sprang to her eyes as Mary handed the gown to her. While Dorthia could have easily stolen one from a line, nightclothes weren't a luxury allowed to someone sleeping on the streets. Having spent years sleeping in doorways, hallways, and against the sides of buildings, she never knew when she would need to run to protect herself. Dorthia ran her fingers across the soft cotton fabric, then batted at the tears. "I'm sorry. I don't mean to cry."

"It's okay to be scared. Almost everyone cries on their first day."

Dorthia was just about to tell her that she wasn't scared, that it had just been a long time since she'd had the good fortune of wearing a nightdress, when two girls began squabbling.

"I'm sorry," Mary said, glancing over her shoulder. "I need to see to that before one of the mistresses gets involved."

"Go. I'm good," Dorthia said, meaning it. She hurried to undress, slipped the nightdress over her head, and lay on the bed. While the nightdress was soft to the touch, the bed turned out to be hard, and the pillow offered little support. Still, they smelled of clean soap and were a welcome end to the day. She'd no sooner climbed into bed than the lights blinked. A moment later, they blinked once more and then gave way to darkness.

In the darkness, she heard someone sob. Comforting words came in quiet whispers, then a bed squeaked on its metal frame. As the room grew quiet once more, Dorthia shed her own tears.

***

"I didn't cry because I was scared," Dorthia said to Emily. "I cried because I was angry."

Emily lifted her pen. "Why were you mad? I thought you'd agreed to go to the asylum."

"I was angry because it was nothing like I'd been led to believe. I was clean, my sheets were clean, and I even had a clean nightdress to wear to bed. The last time I'd worn one of those was at the hotel before my father was killed. If I'd known it was going to be like that, I would have run straight to that asylum and never looked back. Granted, not all asylums were the same, but other than the food being redundant and never quite enough, I didn't complain."

"That was the first night. What about the rest of the time you were there?"

"Oh, it had its moments just like every place does. While some may have hated their stay there, I thrived. Mary helped me catch up on my schooling, and Dr. Todd kept his word by letting me help him in his clinic. I even went with him on occasion to help convince others to come in."

"So, you liked it at the asylum?"

"Maybe more than most."

"Did you refrain from scandalous behavior?"

Dorthia smiled a wicked grin. "I may have stolen a kiss or two."

"You stole them? Are you saying the boys didn't try to kiss you on their own?"

"The boys were closely watched and not as likely to be as brazen. I had a bit more freedom, so it was I who initiated the kiss. And that was all there ever was, as I was able to act my age for the first time in years."

"Were you sad when they made you go out on the train?"

"They didn't make me go out. I begged them to send me."

"I thought you liked it there, plus you were working for Dr. Todd…"

"It was Dr. Todd who implored me to go."

# Chapter Twenty-One

*1924*

Dorthia knew there was something on Dr. Todd's mind, as he'd been overly quiet since arriving at the asylum that day. He'd barely mumbled a morning greeting and not said more than a handful of words since. While she'd wanted to ask him about it, she decided to wait to see if he would unburden himself on his own. He finally came to her just after the noon meal and told her he had something to discuss. Something about the sadness in his eyes told her she was not going to be pleased with what he was going to say.

"I'm afraid I exhausted every means at my disposal in my attempt to locate your family. I've sent out letters and posted an advert. Nothing I've done has panned out. Perhaps one day, someone will invent a tool to better aid such a search, but I'm afraid we don't have time to wait. There's going to be a train going out and I've arranged for you to be on it." His words were quick, as if saying them that way would somehow make them less painful.

"A train?"

"Yes, taking children out west to find new homes."

Fear rippled through her. She knew of those trains, as they'd collected children from the asylum multiple times over the last few years, whisking them away to unknown parts, never to return. "But this is my home."

"You will reach your seventeenth year next month, yes?"

"Yes."

"Then you must go now."

"I don't understand."

"When you are eighteen, you will be discharged from the asylum."

She'd known that day was coming, but since her eighteenth birthday was so far away, she had not let the worry enter her mind. "Then I will go out next year."

"No, you'll be too old. The truth of the matter is you're too old now, but I convinced the headmistress to allow you this chance." Dr. Todd firmed his voice. "You've lived on the streets before. I don't have to tell you what is waiting for you on the streets of this city."

His words were true. She did know and did not care to return to that life. "But Mary and the others…"

"They have all been chosen to go out this time. That is why it's so important we get you on that train."

"Mary is leaving? She said her mother is coming back for her."

"Mary has been holding on to that story ever since her mother left her here. Her mother isn't coming for her. The woman stopped paying her tuition years ago. Mary knows it; she has just never been able to let go of the lie her mother told."

An image of Mary came to mind. Though she tried hard not to show her pain, Dorthia had often seen her staring at the gate in the play yard as if silently willing her mother to return. "Oh, how awful."

"Be that as it may, it is not your place to bring it up," Dr. Todd said firmly.

"No, of course not. I would never say anything to cause Mary pain," Dorthia assured him.

"Good. I had a difficult time getting the headmistress to agree to sending you out. I was finally able to convince her that you would be an asset on the trip."

"Me, an asset? How?"

"You know how to fix scrapes and soothe tummy aches. I told her you would help with the children."

"This train, it takes children away to find new families, does it not?"

"That is the goal."

"I am not a child. What kind of family would want me?"

Dr. Todd smiled. "I've sent word to a colleague of mine in Oklahoma and told him of you. I assured him you have the makings of a fine assistant should he find himself in need of one. I asked if he would sponsor you and offer you a place to stay until such time as you manage to find one of your own."

"What'd he say?"

"Nothing yet. I only sent word yesterday when I found out about the train. I told him this matter was of the utmost urgency, and I would like him to ring me with his response right away. I know this man and think it is safe to assume he will be able to find a place for you."

Though Dorthia wasn't keen on leaving the asylum, the thought of being sent back out into the streets was even more frightening. "Would your colleague pay me?"

"Excuse me?"

"If I were his assistant, would he pay me?"

Dr. Todd considered this for a moment. "I believe it is safe to assume that if you work for him, he will pay you a wage of some kind."

"What if he doesn't like me?"

"Of course he'll like you."

"But what if he doesn't?"

"Then I suppose you will be sent back here."

"But I would be here without my friends."

"That is correct."

Dorthia forced a smile. "Then I will have to make sure that he likes me."

Dr. Todd raised an eyebrow. "By being a good assistant, of course."

Dorthia giggled. "Of course."

The door opened, and a little blonde-haired child by the name of Charles entered. His hand to his chest, the boy's face was ghostly white with a blue tinge as he stumbled through the door, gasping for air.

Dorthia stood waiting for instructions as Dr. Todd lifted the boy onto the exam table.

"Dorthia, fetch some ice water from the icebox," he said, loosening the boy's shirt.

Dorthia hurried to the small icebox, retrieved the pitcher of water, and grabbed a towel on the way back. She handed the pitcher to the doctor and watched as he poured the liquid down the back of the boy's neck. Though the child sucked in his breath, it was clear he was still having trouble getting air.

"Dorthia," Dr. Todd said without looking, "get me a cigarette from the cabinet and light it for me."

Dorthia hurried to the cabinet and pulled out a pack of Lucky Strikes. Plucking a cigarette from the carton, she pulled a match from the metal wall box, then struck a match against the striker plate. While she wasn't overly fond of the taste of cigarettes, she loved the smell of a lit match. She inhaled the sulfur as she stuck the cigarette into her mouth, puffing to ignite the tobacco. The end grew red, showing it had caught flame. She puffed in once more to be sure, then coughed out the smoke as she handed it to Dr. Todd.

The door opened, and a thin, freckle-faced girl stuck her head inside. Eyes brimmed with red, she held her hand to the left side of her jaw. The girl saw the boy lying on the table, gasping for air, and froze in the doorway.

"Toothache?" Dr. Todd asked.

The girl nodded.

"Dorthia, get some of that camphor oil out of the cabinet and put some on a pad to place on the affected tooth."

Dorthia hurried to the cabinet, watching over her shoulder as Dr. Todd placed the cigarette into the boy's mouth. The boy must have received this treatment before, as he clamped his lips around the paper and sucked in the smoke.

"Hold it in," Dr. Todd encouraged. "One, two, three, four, five, six, seven, eight, nine, ten. Ready."

The boy nodded.

Dr. Todd removed the cigarette. "Okay, blow it out slowly."

Charles exhaled in a flurry of coughs.

"Good," Dr. Todd handed him the cigarette once more. "Now, let's do that again and try to hold it a little longer this time to allow the tobacco to open your airway."

Dorthia poured several drops of camphor onto a piece of gauze and turned her attention to the girl. "Which tooth hurts?"

The girl opened her mouth and pointed to a back tooth.

Dorthia nodded and carefully placed the gauze between the girl's tooth and gum. "There, that should make it feel better."

Dorthia looked to see that the color had returned to the boy's face. "It's working."

"The miracles of modern medicine," Dr. Todd agreed.

"What would you have done if the cigarette didn't work?"

"We would have tried one laced with Datura. That is dangerous and only used if you know the proper dose. And if that didn't work," he said, sensing her next question, "I would have given him an injection of ephedrine."

"What kind of injection?" she asked when the boy's eyes grew wide.

"Adrenaline." Dr. Todd smiled. "Charles here is looking much better, so we shan't have to do anything that drastic. Here, sit here and finish this. Remember, deep inhales and slow exhales," he said, handing the boy the cigarette.

The little girl wrinkled her nose. "Am I going to have to get an injection if this doesn't work?"

"Does it feel better?" Dr. Todd asked as he approached her table.

The little girl nodded.

"Then I suppose we won't have to worry about that today." Dr. Todd patted the girl on the head and then smiled at Dorthia. "You are an excellent assistant."

"I wish I could keep working for you," she said sincerely.

Dr. Todd sighed. "I have a full-time nurse at my office, and I'm not here enough to justify keeping you on. Besides, I think a smaller town would suit you better."

The comment took Dorthia by surprise. "Why would you say that? I've lived in cities all my life."

"That's precisely why I said it. Small town folks are most eager to help people out. Here in the city, you would get lost in the crowd and be forced into choices that would be detrimental to your health. That won't be the case in a small town. You are a most fetching young lady. I'm sure you'll find a husband to take care of you in no time. Then you can settle down and raise a family all of your own. A big family and you'll be right there to raise them," he said when she started to object.

The girl wrinkled her brow. "Are you going to have a baby?"

Dorthia laughed a carefree laugh. "I suppose I just might have a couple of them, someday."

***

Dorthia left Dr. Todd's office with a profound sense of accomplishment. Not only was the boy breathing easier, but she'd stopped the girl's toothache even before Dr. Todd got a chance to examine her. Dr. Todd was right; she was a good assistant. His colleague would see that as well. While she had not expected to go out on the train, now that Dr. Todd had broached the possibility, she felt practically giddy at the prospect. She paused her step, recalling Mrs. Harper's words, "Perhaps one day you'll ride one to a place that will make you happy." Dorthia sighed and, not for the first time, wondered what had happened to Mrs. Harper and the children. They went to Charleston to make a fresh new start. Dorthia told herself, *If they deserve to be happy, then so do I.* Her thoughts trailed to her father, wondering what he would think of her being sent out on the train. She was still pondering this when heavy footsteps jarred her from her thoughts. A second later, a boy came barreling toward her, running so fast, she had to dodge out of the way so he didn't plow into her headfirst. She lost her balance and landed on her backside. Irritated at having her good mood spoiled, she glared at him. "Why you!" Her mood softened when she saw it was Slim, an awkwardly shy boy with legs that never stopped.

The boy's face turned a brilliant shade of pink.

Dorthia softened her tone. "Slim, I didn't know it was you. Where are you off to in such a hurry?"

"I'm going to the infirmary to see Dr. Todd. It's time for my tea."

The tea in question was medicinal and seemed to help calm the boy's legs. It dawned on her that if he told Dr. Todd she'd yelled at him, the good doctor might rethink his assessment of her. *I could ask him not to. No, he wouldn't lie about that.* She touched his arm, hoping to make him forget her anger. "I just came from there. Dr. Todd is with a little girl with a terrible toothache, so I have no doubt he'll be another few minutes yet. Your face is all red." She skimmed his cheek, trying to think of something to say that would keep him from telling Dr. Todd she'd been short with him. "Are you feeling alright?"

"Yes." He gulped.

"Slim," she wrinkled her nose and trailed her fingers around to the back of his neck, "what's your real name?"

"Percival." The word came out in a squeak and she recalled how shy he was. While he might tell of her anger, he would never tell Dr. Todd she'd kissed him.

"Have you ever been kissed, Percival?"

"Only by my mom, but I don't think that counts." His voice squeaked once more.

She laughed a flirty laugh. "No, I'm talking about a real kiss."

He shook his head.

Dorthia leaned in and kissed him. Not a measly penny kiss, but one she'd get a whole shiny nickel for had she been back on the street. The second she let go, Slim bolted up the stairs like a kid who'd just got caught stealing a salami. She wiped off the kiss and stifled a giggle. She didn't know what story the boy would give for being in such a rush but felt confident he wouldn't mention her. Not to Dr. Todd anyway, though she wasn't as certain he wouldn't share the telling with one of his friends. As she descended the stairs, she decided it wouldn't hurt to be proactive and make it known it was he who had caught her unaware on the stairs and stolen the kiss.

# Chapter Twenty-Two

Dorthia rapped on the headmistress' door, then entered when the woman waved her inside. "You sent for me, Headmistress?"

The headmistress opened the drawer of her desk and retrieved a slip of paper. "Your sponsorship has come through."

Dorthia's heart skipped. "My sponsorship?"

"Allowing you to go out on the train with the others. Did Dr. Todd not tell you of his plan to send you out to his colleague?"

"Oh, that. Yes, ma'am, he did. I just didn't know the post would come through so soon."

"Dr. Todd received the telegraph this morning and sent word to me right away. Dr. Todd thinks mighty highly of you and put his good reputation on the line by vouching for you like he did. I trust you know how important it is that you live up to the praise that was uttered on your behalf."

"Yes, ma'am."

"Dorthia," the headmistress said firmly, "this is a most optimal placement. You should be hanging from the rafters, not looking like you are walking to the gallows. Out with it, child.

Why do you look so sad?"

"It's just that I like it here so much. I know you are allowing Anastasia to stay…"

Headmistress cut her off. "What does Anastasia have to do with this?"

"Nothing. I just thought maybe you could find a position for me as well."

"There are no other positions currently open. If you wish to stay, you will do so at your own peril. Come next year, you will likely end up on the streets. Not to worry about the good doctor; I am sure Dr. Todd would be happy to recommend one of the other girls." She gave Dorthia a long look. "One that would be inclined to show a bit more gratitude."

"No, please don't say anything to Dr. Todd. I'll go, and you shan't hear another word about it."

"Very well, then. Push the door around and have a seat."

Dorthia clicked the door shut and sat facing the headmistress.

"Now, I am sure you will understand my next request. You will not tell any of your friends that you already have a placement."

Dorthia blinked her confusion. "You don't want me to tell them I'm going out on the train?"

"Everyone who is chosen will know at the same time. You will go to the briefing classes and get your instructions with the rest of the children. Unlike them, you will not be looking for a family. You will travel with the group until you reach your stop in Oklahoma." She paused briefly. "The other children are not as fortunate as you and do not have anyone to speak for them. As such, they might be upset that you do."

Dorthia couldn't believe her ears. "You're saying they would be mad at me?"

"No, of course not. They just might feel worse about their own situation."

"I wouldn't want them to feel bad," Dorthia agreed.

"And that is why you will refrain from telling them about your good fortune."

"Won't they know when I'm not chosen?"

"Not everyone is chosen at the first stop. You will go on,

and by the time anyone figures it out, they will have found a family of their own, and you will not matter anymore."

Though Dorthia knew she did not mean the words how they sounded, the comment still stung. "I won't tell anyone."

"Good. In the interim, you will be attending the classes with those going out."

"Oh, I'm finished with my schooling," Dorthia reminded her.

"These are different classes to prepare you for riding the train."

Dorthia frowned. "I know how to ride a train. I've been on them many times with my father."

"These are classes to prepare children for their new homes. How to act and behave to help them settle in." The woman raised her hand to silence her. "I know you are not looking to be chosen, but I am sure there will be something of value to you."

"Yes, ma'am."

"Good. Dr. Todd said he will be speaking with Miss Agana to let her know of your circumstance."

"Miss Agana?"

"She is the head placing agent who will be traveling with you and the children. He promised to tell her you will be most helpful in caring for any illnesses along the way. You must have made a great impression on the man."

Dorthia smiled, but words were not forthcoming. If she'd truly made such an impression, he wouldn't be sending her away.

***

*DEPARTURE DAY*

Having left her suitcase with the others waiting to be loaded onto the train, Dorthia clutched a single battered leather bag in her hands, staring up at the massive locomotive. While the children surrounding her were abuzz with eager anticipation, she was filled with mixed emotions as, once again, she recalled the many trips she'd taken with her father. So much so, if not for the fact the bag she now held was mostly filled with medical supplies, she would be able to imagine herself clutching her overnight bag on the way to accompany her father on a business trip. She glanced to her right, half expecting to see her father.

He wasn't there.

Then again, if he were, they would be getting ready to board the first-class car, not the immigrant car, which she was now standing in front of.

She heard a sob and looked to see Ruthie, a six-year-old girl who'd spent her entire life in the asylum. A pleasant child who was a ball of sunshine and well-liked by everyone in Mary's little gang, Ruthie now stood trembling as silent tears streamed down her cheeks.

Dorthia shifted her bag to her left hand and reached for Ruthie's hand with her other. "There's no need for tears, Ruthie. You're going on a grand adventure."

Having her tears acknowledged, the child let out a heart-wrenching sob. "But I don't want to go. I want to stay in my home."

Dorthia had always felt somewhat of a kinship with the girl ever since learning that the girl's mother had died while giving her life. She knelt and looked the girl in the eyes. "I like the asylum too, but it's not a home."

"It is my home," Ruthie said, and let out a whole new wave of tears.

Dorthia saw one of the agents staring in their direction. She pulled a handkerchief from her pocket and handed it to the child. "You must stop your tears now or they might send you back."

"I want to go back."

"No, you don't. Mary and the others won't be there. If you go back, you'll be all alone, and there will be no one to protect you from Anastasia," she said, referring to an older girl in the asylum who made it her mission to make everyone's life miserable. "I know you're scared, but remember what they said in class. You aren't being punished; you are being rewarded. It is not every child who gets to go out on the trains to find a new family. Wouldn't you like to have a real home with parents who love you?"

Ruthie struggled to squelch her tears. "Aren't you scared?"

"Of course not. You heard what the headmistress said. They are sending us to homes where there will be plenty of food to eat. I'm not talking about mush, bread and the occasional piece of fruit like we've been eating at the asylum. I'm talking real food, like ham and beans and cakes and pies. Food so good, you'll wonder how you could have lived so long without it."

"Have you had those foods?" Ruthie sniffed.

"Many times," Dorthia said, remembering.

"Is it true that if I don't like it there, they will send me back?"

Dorthia considered her answer for a moment before answering. Finally, she nodded. "Yes, but we don't want to do anything that will purposely get us sent back, as that would make the headmistress very unhappy. You will try and remember that, won't you, Ruthie?"

Ruthie nodded. "I'll try."

"Good girl." Dorthia smiled and rose to her feet. "Come. They're boarding the train. Stay with me and I'll see that you get a window seat so you can see everything there is to see. Okay?"

The girl grabbed hold of Dorthia's hand and walked toward the train without a word.

***

It didn't take long for Ruthie to settle down. Having never been out of the asylum, everything was new and held her attention until darkness made it impossible to see. By then, she was so emotionally exhausted, she fell asleep after they'd eaten their evening meal of cheese and crackers. Dorthia, on the other hand, remained awake long after the rest of the train car grew quiet. While she wanted to be excited about the trip, so many things weighed on her mind. Would Dr. Todd's associate like her? What would it be like to live outside the asylum once more? While she enjoyed the safety of living in the asylum, she'd quickly made up her mind that no matter how things turned out with Dr. Todd's associate, she would not allow the placing agents to send her back. She'd start to work on a plan as soon as she arrived in Oklahoma and became familiar with her surroundings. Dorthia was still deep in thought when Miss Agana stopped beside her seat.

Tall and thin as the rail of the train, the placing agent held a small boy who looked to be well into his first year. The child was fast asleep, with his head lying on the woman's shoulder. Sporting dark circles under her eyes, she, too, looked much in need of rest. "It's not always this quiet. You should try to get some sleep while you can," she whispered.

"I tried," Dorthia admitted. "I've just got so much on my mind."

The woman shifted the boy to the other side. "Dr. Todd told me you are going to work for a colleague of his."

Though the woman had whispered, Dorthia looked about to see if any of her friends had overheard. "The headmistress told me I shouldn't tell anyone."

A frown creased the woman's brow. "Why not?"

"She thought my friends would treat me differently if they knew I already had a place to go."

Miss. Agana's face relaxed. "Soon they will all have a new place to call home. We are barely out of the station, and I've already had someone ask for one of the children."

"You have? Which one?"

"I believe she's one of the girls from your asylum. A little brown-haired girl named Mileta. A well-to-do couple from Chicago wishes to take her to their home."

Dorthia knew of the girl as she'd caused quite a stir when she first arrived at the asylum. Even she had been asked to keep an eye on her and help see that she was safe. If Mileta were going to a nice home, she now would have one less thing to worry about. "The others aren't sad that she is getting a home before them?"

"Why would they be sad? On this journey, we should all be happy when a child gets placed, as it means they will not be returning to the asylum."

Dorthia started to tell the woman of her decision not to return, then, not knowing if she could trust her to keep her secret, decided against it. "Are you happy when children get placed?"

Miss Agana smiled and peered into the face of the boy sleeping in her arms. "Of course. When you are in my charge, then you become my child. All a mother wants is for her children to be taken care of."

"Do you have children of your own?"

"Of my own, no. But I have taken a few children into my home over the years. You were good with her today."

It took a moment for Dorthia to realize Miss Agana was talking about Ruthie. "She was just scared. She's never been out of the asylum before."

"That is the way with most of the children, but not everyone has the patience to help a child's tears turn into smiles. You will make a good assistant to the doctor, but if it doesn't work out, you could consider coming to work at the agency. We could always use another good agent."

Dorthia blinked her surprise. "You're offering me a job?"

"That is not my call, but I could put in a good word for you, and that will go a long way. It's not for everyone, but from what I've seen, you'd be a good fit. Plus, it seems you are comfortable riding the train."

"I used to ride them with my father before he died."

"And your mother?"

"She died birthing me." As the words came out of her mouth, she thought of what Miss Agana had said about considering the children in her company to be hers. While she herself was afraid to have children of her own, she enjoyed being around them and thought this might be a way to fulfill that desire. Her heart swelled with the thought of having so many children in her care. "I think I might like to be a placing agent."

The woman considered this for a moment. "Are you sure you can't sleep?"

"No, ma'am. I'm not sleepy in the least."

"Would you like to practice being an agent to see if you'd like it?"

"Sure, what do I have to do?"

Miss Agana smiled and handed her the child she was holding.

# Chapter Twenty -Three

"You want me to watch the baby?" Dorthia said, cuddling the boy.

"I trust you've held a baby before?" Miss Agana replied.

"Of course I have. I helped out in the nursery on days Dr. Todd didn't need me. I just didn't expect to have a job on the train."

"A practice job," Miss Agana corrected. "Just to see if it is something you could see yourself doing. I can't afford to pay you, but I could give you and Louie my seat in the forward cabin."

"The forward cabin? Isn't that where the first-class passengers sit? Won't they be upset if the baby cries?"

"You'll be sitting in the family car. They will expect babies to cry."

"Can Ruthie go with me? She'll be upset if she wakes and I'm not here."

"No, you'll have enough to deal with when the baby wakes. Ruthie will stay here. I'm sure there is someone else she trusts."

"Mary. Everyone trusts Mary."

"Very well. I will sit with her until she wakes, then ask Mary to look after her beyond that. Unless you'd rather not…"

"No, I want to," Dorthia said, cutting her off. "I just wanted to make sure Ruthie will be okay."

"See, I knew I was right. You have empathy that will make you a good agent."

"Is that all I will need?"

"No, you'll also need to be firm. It is important that the children know not to backtalk you."

Dorthia's thoughts drifted to Anastasia, one of the girls who made trouble in the asylum. "You mean I need to make the kids scared of me?"

"If that's what it takes, then yes. There is a time for compassion and a time when they need to know you mean business. When you are traveling with this many children, you won't fare well with disobedience. One bad apple will spoil the whole lot. If a child gets out of hand, you need to make an example of him so that the others listen. As their agent, I will do what I can to protect them, even if it means making them a little afraid of me. You don't need to worry about that today. This is only a trial, and you are only in charge of one. Louie here won't give you any trouble."

Dorthia nodded, then felt her tension ease the moment Louie stretched, gave a soft whimper, and then settled once more.

"Your seat is in the next car. Halfway up, next to the window." Miss Agana pointed. "Do you want me to walk with you?"

"No, I can find it."

She handed Dorthia a bag. "Here are some cloths for his bottom, plus some crackers and a bottle for when he wakes. I'll send someone up to check on you both in the morning."

Dorthia cradled the baby in one arm, while she stooped and carefully retrieved both the medical bag Dr. Todd had gifted her with and the bag with Louie's things. She hooked the handles in the crook of her arm, firmed her grip on Louie and started toward the forward car. As she walked, her mind drifted back to the day in the train station when she'd nearly taken Mrs. Harper's baby. She'd known nothing about taking care of infants at the time, but much had changed since then. She'd often worked with the babies in the nursery, knew how to change them, feed them, and pat their backs to keep them from being in pain. She also knew the proper measurements of evaporated milk, water, and corn syrup to put in the baby's bottle to keep him fed. If not for the fact she was on a train, she would be able to keep walking with no worry of the baby starving while in her care. *Don't be silly*, she chided herself silently, *Miss Agana gave you the baby because she trusts you, not so that you could whisk him away.* While Dorthia knew this to be true, she continued to fight the nagging inner voice that told her, with so many children to watch over, if two went missing, no one would notice.

As she moved forward, she expected to be jolted awake from what she was sure was a dream. Or worse, that her mind had somehow broken and she'd finally succeeded in stealing a child. Only it didn't feel like a dream, and the child sleeping in her arms was most definitely real.

For the first time since leaving the asylum, Dorthia wasn't afraid. Not only did she have a job, but now she also had a fallback plan in case that job didn't pan out. A good job that would afford her travel and give her the ability to watch over children to see that they were well cared for until they found someone to take her place.

As she stepped through the door to the forward car, the wind woke the boy, who struggled to sit up as he pulled at the fabric of her dress. Dorthia shifted him to get a better grip and stared into the bluest eyes she'd ever seen. That, along with a bewildered stare that told her it wasn't a dream. The speed of the train kept her from leaping from the back porch of the train car and running off with her precious cargo in tow. Instead, she hurried inside the car and quickly found her seat as Louie tightened his grip on her dress. The baby's expression was guarded as he studied her face. Worried he was going to cry, Dorthia bounced him in her arms and played the game she'd often played in the nursery whenever there was no one close enough to hear. "It's okay, little one, Momma's here." Her words, soft and clear, were met with a cautious smile. Encouraged, Dorthia dipped her hand into the pouch Miss Agana had given her, retrieved a cracker, and offered it to

Louie. His fear forgotten, Louie loosened his grip on her dress and reached for it.

"How old is your son?"

Dorthia's gaze drifted to the older woman with grey-streaked hair and kind eyes sitting across from her. "Excuse me?"

"I was just inquiring as to how old your baby is."

Dorthia opened her mouth to tell her the baby wasn't hers. "Louie is seven months," she said instead. It wasn't a lie; she was just repeating what Miss Agana had told her. Plus, hadn't Miss Agana said she considered all the children in her care to be hers? She wanted her to practice being an agent. It wasn't a lie; she was merely practicing by pretending Louie was hers.

"That would have been my guess."

At first, Dorthia thought the woman had listened to the lie she'd just told herself, then she realized she was speaking to the baby's age.

"He looks just like you except for the blue eyes. He must get those from his father."

Unsure what to say, Dorthia held Louie close.

"I'm sorry, I didn't mean to upset you."

"It's okay. It's just that my husband was killed and I don't know what to say about it." Okay, so that went past pretending and on to an out-and-out lie.

"Oh, you poor thing. I'm so sorry."

Instead of fessing up, Dorthia continued with her lie. "My mother-in-law sent for us as my husband's brother has pledged to take care of us," she said, using the story Mrs. Harper had told her. As the half lie spiraled from her mouth, she wondered when she had become so good at telling untruths.

"His brother sounds like a good man."

"I hope so."

"You haven't met him?"

"No. We weren't married long, and his family lives so far away."

"Oh, my. You must be terrified."

Only of being caught in this terrible lie. Dorthia pushed that thought out of her mind. "I would do anything to protect my son," she said without looking at the woman.

"Of course you would. You're a mother. It's what we do."

"You're a mother?" Why that surprised her, Dorthia did not know. Perhaps it was just because the woman looked so old.

"I'm a mother, but my children are all grown. Now they've had children of their own, making me a grandmother as well. I'm on the way to visit my daughter in Chicago. She is with child and I promised to be there when the baby is born."

A lump formed in Dorthia's throat as she recalled her father telling how her grandmother had traveled to Boston when she was born. The woman had wanted to take her home with her, but her father hadn't allowed it. She stared at the woman sitting across from her, imagining how different her life could have been if only her father had agreed to let her go.

"You're crying," the woman said softly.

Dorthia hurried to wipe the tears. "You remind me of my grandmother. She lives in Chicago." The statement was mostly true, as the woman did live in Chicago. At least she had the last she knew. The problem was that she'd only met her grandmother a few times and could not, for the life of her, recall her grandmother's name or what she looked like. She did recall her being nice.

The woman sitting across from her frowned. "She did not ask you to come live with her when the baby's father ..." Her voice trailed off without finishing the sentence.

"She doesn't know." Dorthia blew out a breath to steady herself. "I lost contact with my family years ago when my father passed."

The lady clutched at her chest. "Oh, you poor sweet child. What an awful time you've had. I'm sure if your grandmother knew of your dilemma, she would send for you and help you with your child."

"I'm sure that is true," Dorthia said confidently. "She wanted to take me home when my mother died."

"Oh, my sweet dear. You have so much death in your life. If you don't mind, I will say an extra prayer for you and your son each night so the lord will keep you and your baby safe."

Dorthia couldn't recall the last time someone offered to pray for her. "I would like that very much."

"Tell me your name so the lord knows who I'm talking

about."

"Dorthia Jean Smith."

"And your baby? What's his name?"

"Louie." Dorthia realized she didn't know the rest of the baby's name. Searching her mind for another, an image of her father came to mind. "Louie John Smith. John was my father's name."

"That's a fine name for a boy. I'm sure your father is proud that you named your son after him."

"Oh, he knows."

The woman smiled and looked to the ceiling of the train. "Your father might be gone, but I'm sure he's watching over you."

Dorthia followed her gaze and wondered if it was true. She further wondered what he would think of her lies and how he would feel about her giving the baby his name. As if Louie could feel her inner turmoil, he began to fuss. "It's okay," she whispered so only he could hear. "You're mine for now."

***

As soon as they departed the train in Detroit, the company of children was ushered into a large room, then separated so they could get washed up and change into the new clothes they'd been given. While Dorthia had changed Louie, she still wore her traveling clothes. She was holding Louie and studying the structure of the building when she saw Miss Agana. To her surprise, the woman no longer wore the simple black traveling clothes but had changed into a dress with a fitted jacket that showed the woman's slender waistline.

Miss Agana looked up, saw her standing there, and frowned. "Dorthia, why haven't you changed out of your traveling clothes?"

"I'm not looking to be adopted, so I didn't feel the need to impress anyone."

Miss Agana sighed. "The folks coming to see us will be judging all of us, myself included. If we look like vagabonds, they will assume we are just peddlers trying to pawn off less-than-desirable children. It is essential that we look and act our best so that those in attendance will know these children are to be treated well. Now, give me Louie and go get changed."

Dorthia pulled the child closer. "You have so much to do. I can manage Louie while I change."

A smile followed a moment of indecision. "Yes, I suppose you can. You have done well with him this trip."

"It was easy. He has the most pleasant disposition."

Miss Agana tickled the baby under the chin, a motion that elicited an immediate giggle. "He's lucky; babies always fare well on our excursions, especially those who are jovial. I expect our boy here will be one of the first chosen."

"I wish to keep him." The words were out before she could stop them. "He already calls me Momma."

Miss Agana's eyes grew wide, then softened once more. "I'm afraid that isn't possible. You are but a child yourself."

"I am not a child! I haven't been one since I watched my father be murdered!" Startled by her outburst, Louie's lip puckered, and the baby looked ready to cry. Dorthia bounced him in her arms as she forced a smile. "My mother died while birthing me. I'm afraid to have a child of my own. Please, he needs a home. Let him come with me."

"Dorthia," Miss Agana said softly. "You know I can't allow Louie to go with you."

Struggling for words, Dorthia silently chided herself for becoming so attached to the child. She worked to keep the panic from her voice. "Why not?"

"Because you are but a child yourself."

"I'm not a child. I'm seventeen and well old enough to be married. Even the woman across from me on the train believed me to be his mother."

"That is because you are so good with him. And while you are old enough, you're not married, and he needs both a father and mother. Listen, I know I put a lot of responsibility on you during this trip, but you still need to see where your life will take you. What if you were to get to Oklahoma and find the arrangement is less than what you'd hoped? If it is just you, then you can sort things out and look for an alternative situation like the one I've already suggested. You will not have that option if you have a baby underfoot."

"I can find someone to look after him while I am on the trains." Even as she said it, she knew it wouldn't work. It was the same reason her father wasn't able to leave her behind when he'd been called away. It would hurt too much to leave him behind. She hugged Louie to her chest once more. "I'm not sure I can bear to let him go."

"It will be difficult, especially the first time. But in the end, you'll know you are doing what's best for the child. There are so many children out there who need our help. It's impossible to help them all, so some don't even try. When I feel my faith wavering, I tell myself that God put me here. I may not be able to help them all, but I can put a name to each child I've placed."

Dorthia blinked her surprise. "You can?"

The woman lifted a hand to Dorthia's cheek. When she spoke, her words came not from an unfeeling caretaker who merely carted children off to the unknown but spoke the heartbreak of a woman who lost a piece of herself with each journey on the train. "Of course I remember. A mother never forgets."

Dorthia leaned into the woman's touch. While she'd heard others in the group moan about the woman and deemed her cold and harsh, she'd witnessed a different side. Underneath her cold exterior was a person who cared more about others than she did herself. She also knew at that moment that life had stripped her of that compassion. She hadn't wished to keep Louie with her to nurture him; she'd wanted to keep him so she herself wouldn't have to face the world alone.

# Chapter Twenty-Four

Freshly washed and wearing a new dress, Dorthia sat with the rest of the children listening to Miss Agana speak to the crowd of strangers who'd come to the station in hopes of taking one of the children home. Only, instead of looking upon the children with hearts filled with joy, most in the crowd looked apprehensive. Could it be the prospective parents were as scared of taking in a child as the children were of going to homes where everything would be strange and new? Even though she knew she wouldn't be staying in Detroit, she hung on each word Miss Agana said.

"These children need homes, and each of you is in a position to help them. You do not need to adopt the child you choose, but we will expect you to properly care for them in sickness and in health."

"I don't aim to take in no sickly child," a man's voice rang out.

Dorthia looked to see who'd spoken, thinking to assure him that she had personally witnessed Dr. Todd examining each child in their company, and that if a child were ill, it was likely something they'd contracted on the trip. As if on cue, someone sneezed. Miss Agana quickly covered for the child, assuring the man that the child was merely sneezing because of the dust on the train. Cool and confident, she then fielded other comments from the crowd and was quick with her responses. Though some of her speech mirrored what the headmistress had told them before sending them on their way, Dorthia hung on each word, listening as Miss Agana spoke about the Placing Out Program. The inflection in the woman's voice was the firm, matter-of-fact, authoritative voice used when she wanted people to pay attention. If Miss Agana hadn't shown her softer side when suggesting she should consider becoming a placing agent, Dorthia would have been scared. As it was, the only thing she was frightened of was the thought of handing Louie over to complete strangers and knowing she would never see him again.

"The Children's Aid Society places thousands of children a year," Miss Agana continued. "The program has been in place for over seventy years, and we've learned a thing or two along the way. I assure you, if we were in the habit of placing out sickly children, the papers would have gotten word of it by now. No, I assure you all the children in this company are healthy, trustworthy, and on their way to becoming good citizens."

Dorthia looked at baby Louie. "Is that true, Louie? Are you on your way to becoming a good citizen?" she whispered. Louie giggled and buried his face in the bodice of her dress. She was still playing with the baby when the people in attendance started rushing toward them, not in an orderly way as she'd expected, but in a frenzy. Dorthia tightened her grip on Louie, knowing it wouldn't be long before her arms were relieved of his weight. Whether he felt her unease or only that the baby was frightened of the sudden murmur of excitement, Louie began to cry. A man who'd been heading toward them scowled and turned his attention to one of the other children. While Dorthia's initial instinct was to coddle the baby, she realized his crying might be in her favor. Instead of cuddling him close, she turned him, holding his back to her chest, a move that hastened his wails. She worked to keep from smiling as one after another bypassed them and instead set their sights on another of the children. While some went in search of older children, most gravitated toward the younger children in the company. One by one, she saw children being offered a home; she wondered how her life might have differed if she'd ridden one of the earlier trains. Louie twisted in her arms, regaining her focus. *He's not your baby; he needs a family who will love and care for him.* Instantly, she regretted her decision not to quiet his tears. "It's okay, Louie. We will find you a home."

A woman approached, her gaze locking on Louie, who had yet to settle down. "Please, may I try?"

Dorthia's heart clenched as she handed him over, the pain letting up as a man stepped up beside the woman. He was followed by four little girls, each wearing a matching dress. Seemingly content in the woman's arms, Louie's tears ebbed as he peered down at the girls.

The smallest of the girls tugged on the woman's dress. "Is that him, Mother? Is that the brother you told us of?"

The woman frowned. "No, I'm afraid not. As you can see, this baby already has a mother."

"I'm not his mother." The words were out of Dorthia's mouth before she could stop them. "I've just been asked to care for him until he finds a home."

The woman rewarded her with a timid smile as she looked to the man for confirmation. Her husband nodded his consent, and the woman's smile grew broad. "I have not been able to give my husband a son. While he cherishes our girls, he would like a son. My last birth was complicated, and the doctor told me there would be no more. When we learned of the train, we knew it to be God's way of granting our wish for a son."

While Dorthia wanted nothing more than to tell her there were other boys to choose from, she knew in her heart that the woman was right and that Louie had found himself a home. No, he'd found himself a family, and that was something she didn't have to offer the boy. She forced a smile. "Did you fill out an application?"

"I handed it to the committee several weeks past." The man pulled an envelope from the inside pocket of his jacket. "They've already verified our references."

Dorthia nodded. "You'll follow that hallway to the vetting room, where they will take down your information. Louie—

that's his name—has his information sewn into his gown."

While the others turned to leave, the woman hesitated. "Do you wish to say goodbye to him?"

Dorthia handed the woman Louie's bag and shook her head. "No, I've already said my goodbyes." It was a lie, but she was afraid that if she took him back, she would not be able to let him go. Dorthia tucked her hands in her pockets, knowing she wouldn't be able to resist if he reached for her. She needn't have bothered, as the baby never even whimpered when the woman carried him away.

Dorthia was still stinging from the rejection when screams filled the air. *Ruthie!* She wasn't sure how she knew, but was certain the screams belonged to the child. She scanned the crowd and saw the girl being dragged away by a tall, bearded man who looked to be much in need of a bath. Dorthia pushed her way through the bystanders and stood blocking the man's way. Ruthie's screams turned to sobs as Dorthia held out her hand to stop the man. "Leave her be."

She saw Miss Agana heading their way and hurried to control the situation. "May I please see your application?"

"This is none of your business," he said, ignoring her request.

Dorthia firmed her stance. "It is my business. If you wish to take a child, you need to show me your application."

"I don't have no blasted application."

Dorthia matched his step when he tried to skirt his way around her. "Then you cannot take her."

The man's lips curved. He released his hold on Ruthie, who fell to the marble floor and scrambled backwards in spiderlike fashion, her eyes wide with fear. Dorthia reached to help her, surprised when the man grabbed her by the arm and pulled her close. His breath smelled of alcohol, and he slurred his words through badly stained teeth. She struggled to get away.

"Then I'll take you instead," he sneered.

Ruthie's shrill screams filled the air. The man laughed and pulled out his pocket watch, checking the time.

Instantly reminded of the man who'd killed her father, Dorthia thrust her elbow into the man's gut and pulled herself free. She bent her fingers, thinking to claw his face, when Miss

Agana appeared next to her.

The intervention gave the man the opportunity to take hold of Dorthia once more. Ruthie shuffled to her feet and rushed to the woman.

Miss Agana placed a protective arm around the girl to silence her sobs. "What on earth is going on here?"

"The man hasn't filled out an application," Dorthia said, attempting to pull her arm free once more. "He tried to take Ruthie. I told him to let her go; now he's threatening to take me."

"She jabbed me in the gut." His words came out in a slur.

"Because you wouldn't let me go."

Several men stepped forward, but Miss Agana held up her hand to keep them from intervening. "You'll unhand her at once," she said firmly.

"The sign said you're looking for homes for the children. I aim to give her a home."

Mrs. Agana firmed her stance. "The notices said we are looking for good homes. You, sir, will not be taking any of our children."

"I'll fill out one of those applications."

"Which will be denied." Miss Agana's tone left no doubt that she spoke the truth.

"How much?"

"Excuse me?"

"I'll pay. Just tell me how much."

"I assure you our children are not for sale."

"Right," he said, shaking his head. "You're giving them away. I aim to take one."

"Dorthia is not a child. She is an agent with the Children's Aid Society. I suggest you release her before I summon the police." Though there was an edge to the woman's tone, her face lacked any sign of fear, even though the man towered over her by at least two feet.

"And who pray tell do I have the pleasure of speaking with?"

"I'll not give you the honor of having my good name in your mouth. You and I are finished with our conversation." Miss Agana was thin and pale, and for the most part looked as if a breeze would blow her away, but at that moment, she was the epitome of a mother prepared to do battle to protect her children.

Dorthia admired the woman's strength. The man must have been likewise impressed, as he loosened his grip. Dorthia pulled her arm free and moved to Miss Agana's side.

The woman nodded to the men who'd joined them. "See that he is escorted from the building."

A burly man stepped up and faced the man who had caused the uproar. "It's time for you to leave."

The man sized him up. "And if I don't?"

The rest of the men stepped forward. Two looped their arms through the man's arms and they escorted him away.

"That man was scary!" Dorthia said once they'd gone.

"I'm glad he didn't have an application," Ruthie agreed.

"I highly doubt that a man like that would have passed the vetting," Miss Agana said. "Our applications require references. The committee would have found him to be unsuitable."

"What if they didn't?" Ruthie's voice was just above a whisper.

"Then I would have found him unsuitable," Miss Agana said firmly. "Either today, or if he'd been on his best behavior, I would have found out when I came to do my visits. The program isn't perfect, but we do our best. As such, the Children's Aid Society has a good track record for ensuring our children go to good homes."

"You were amazing," Dorthia said, meaning it. "You didn't look at all scared."

"It is my job to appear in control. Truth be told, I was terrified."

"Then why not let the men deal with him in the first place?" Dorthia asked.

"Because it is my job to handle things. I knew the men had stepped up and that gave me the courage to continue. Men are used to fighting our battles. I believe it is important for them to see that we are capable of doing more than having babies, mending their clothes, and cooking their meals. You did well today."

"No, I was ready to claw his eyes out," Dorthia admitted.

"That's because you haven't had the training that I have. Courage comes with experience. The Children's Aid Society will train you, plus they never send women out alone. Have you considered my offer of becoming a placing agent? I'll vouch for you."

"Yes, ma'am. I have given it a great deal of consideration."

"And?"

"I do not think I would like to be a placing agent."

A frown creased Miss Agana's brow. "May I ask why not?"

"You said you consider all of these children yours. I only had to give up one, and my heart is already filled with so much sadness." Dorthia glanced at Ruthie, knowing it wouldn't be long before she had to say goodbye yet again. "I do not think it is good for a soul to endure all that pain."

Miss Agana's frown was replaced by a smile. "No, Dorthia, I don't think it is."

# Chapter Twenty-Five

Though Dorthia had expected to feel butterflies in her stomach when she arrived in Guymon, Oklahoma, the trip had worn her out so much that she was both physically and mentally exhausted. Instead of being giddy, she wanted nothing more than to go to the local hotel, check into her room, curl into a ball, and cry—something she'd not done when saying goodbye to Louie, Ruthie, or any of the friends she made while at the asylum. While they'd left New York City as a group, everyone she'd grown to care for had been plucked away one by one until she was the only one left.

Miss Agana had graciously offered to accompany her the rest of the way, but Dorthia had declined the offer, fearing the woman would eventually wear her down enough that she'd forgo traveling to Oklahoma altogether, opting instead to return to the city, finish out her time in the asylum, then become an agent for the Children's Aid Society. Though Miss Agana had promised her things would become easier, Dorthia knew in her heart she wouldn't be able to bear the thought of constantly saying goodbye to those she cared for. She wondered if that was the reason God had taken her mother from her when she was too young to recall the loss. Perhaps he knew she would one day lose her father and felt that was enough for one child to bear.

As Dorthia stepped from the train, she half expected Dr. Baxter to greet her. Though she had no clue what the man looked like, she was sure he wasn't there. Then again, why would he be, as he hadn't been given an exact date of her arrival. Hoisting her bag, she checked the address that Dr. Todd had given her and started toward Main Street. She walked two blocks then pulled the paper from the pocket of her dress once more. Though the address was correct, she was standing in front of a bank. She was still looking at the paper when she ran smack into someone.

Mortified, Dorthia covered her mouth with her hand. "I'm so sorry!"

"Don't be. It was just as much my fault as yours." The girl displayed the most brilliant red hair on an uncovered head and looked to be close to her in age. She laughed and held up a novel. "I'm just so engrossed in this. Have you read it?"

Dorthia scanned the title— *The Man in the Brown Suit*. "No, I haven't. Is it good?"

"So far, yes. It's by Agatha Christie. You've heard of her?"

Dorthia shook her head.

"No? Oh, well, do you like to read?"

"Yes, very much so."

The girl beamed her approval. "Oh, you would love her books. This one isn't even out in the States yet. It was sent to me from London by my mother's cousin. She works for the publishing house and sent me an advance copy for my birthday. Anyhow, this girl—the one in the book, not my mother's cousin—she's the orphaned daughter of Professor Beddingfield. Can you imagine being an orphan?"

Dorthia started to tell her that she actually could imagine it, when she continued.

"Anyway, she witnesses an accident and then the man dies, and well, now she's trying to solve this whole mystery. I just love Agatha Christie. Do you live here in town? If you do, I can let you read it when I'm done. Oh, my heavens, where did I leave my manners. I'm Becky, Becky Wilson."

"Dorthia Smith. I don't live here." Dorthia paused. "I guess I do now. I just came in on the train."

"Oh, how splendid. You'll have to give me your address."

Dorthia held up the paper.

The girl snatched it from her hand. "Why, this is Dr. Harvey's address."

Dorthia frowned. "Dr. Harvey? I thought his name was Baxter."

"It is. A lot of people call him Dr. Harvey on account of…" Becky took a step back when Dorthia sneezed. "Are you ill?"

"No, I'm not ill. I'm covered in dust from taking the train," Dorthia told her. "I came here to work for Dr. Baxter," she said, using the name she was given.

Becky's eyes grew wide then settled once more. "Oh."

"Is there a problem with me working for him?"

"No, not at all. I just find it odd he sent for someone when there are so many eligible girls here in town."

Eligible girls? Dorthia reached over and plucked the paper from Becky's hand. "I'm not here to marry the man!"

"Why not? He's a doctor. Every girl wants to marry a doctor."

Dorthia felt a blush creep up her cheeks at the thought of Dr. Todd. Though he was older, she would have gladly married him if he'd only asked. She wondered if his colleague would be more agreeable.

"Your smile tells me you're interested. Won't that just put the hometown girls in a tizzy?" Becky held up a hand to silence her. "You don't have to worry about me, mind you. I'm engaged to William Hanson. He's a dream, plus he's set to inherit his father's farm. Even if I weren't engaged to William, I don't want to be someone's second choice."

"Second choice?"

Becky shrugged. "Dr. Harvey being a widower and all."

"Oh."

"You didn't know?"

"No, we've never spoken."

Becky's eyes grew round once more. "You mean you haven't met him?"

"No, we've not met."

"Just written letters, I suppose?"

Growing increasingly tired of the questions, Dorthia decided to take her leave. "No, we haven't written letters either. I told you I'm just here to work."

"Probably a good thing since the marriage would come with children."

Dorthia felt her heart skip. "Children?"

Becky nodded. "Two. Little boys, Mark and Paul. Twins. Can you imagine birthing two at once? Anyway, they're not babies. They're six if memory serves. Julie—that was the wife's name—died last year, leaving Dr. Harvey to raise the boys alone. Everyone said he should send them to live with their grandmother, but Dr. Harvey wouldn't hear of it. Can you imagine a man raising those boys all by himself, and him being a doctor and so busy at that?"

"How'd she die?"

"Accident. She was on a ladder and fell. She hit her head and never woke up. Mark saw it happen and ran all the way into town to get his dad. Can you imagine seeing your mom die? And the poor kid was only five years old. That's got to be tough on a kid. He's going to need someone who understands what he went through."

Dorthia's mouth went dry. "Listen, I really must be going. If you can just point the way."

Becky giggled. "You're already here."

Dorthia looked at the building. "It's a bank."

"The doctor's office is upstairs in the rear of the building. I can show you if you want."

"No, I can find it," Dorthia insisted.

"Okay. Welcome to town. Now that I know where to find you, I'll drop the book off when I'm done with it."

"Thank you."

Becky smiled a brilliant smile. "Of course, what are friends for?"

Friends. She'd only been off the train for a moment, and she'd already made a friend. Dr. Todd told her there would be benefits to living in a small town; this must be one of them. As she walked to the back of the building, Dorthia wondered why the good doctor had not mentioned that Dr. Baxter was a widower or that he had two children. Especially since their situations drew parallels. As she started up the back steps, she wondered what it would be like to be married to a doctor, and further wondered what it would be like to be the mother of two little boys. A mother. After all these years of wishing it were true, the possibility of making it a reality grew with each step. By the time she'd reached the top, she had convinced herself she'd been sent here to marry Dr. Baxter. At the top step, she saw the door to the inner office and emitted a soft giggle. She was so excited that she didn't see the twist in the rug. As she turned the doorknob, her foot caught, pushing the door to his office with such force that it flew forward, slamming against the wall, leaving a doorknob-sized hole.

"What in tarnation?" a gruff voice called from within the room.

Dorthia cast a glance over her shoulder, wondering how long it would take her to run down the stairs.

Too late, as an elderly man moved into the doorway, craning his neck to inspect the damage. Tall, balding, and thin, except for his stomach, which protruded over his pants, making him look as if he had a watermelon stuffed inside his shirt, the man sighed. "Give me a moment to collect my bag, and you can take me to the emergency."

Dorthia frowned. "I don't have an emergency."

"You're telling me you simply make a habit of destroying private property? Why, that right there will cost me a day's pay."

Dorthia glanced at the wall. Though she hadn't personally done it, she'd seen those kinds of repairs dozens of times when visiting construction sites with her father. "Don't be silly. Anyone can easily fix that with a little plaster."

The man cocked an eyebrow. "You going to fix it?"

"I could, if you get me the materials."

"I'll not have no woman doing my work for me." He turned and walked to the other side of the room. "You got an appointment?"

Dorthia gulped. "You're Dr. Baxter?"

"Well, I'm not Teddy Roosevelt, if that's who you came to see."

"No, I came here to see you, I suppose." Obviously, Becky

was not a girl who could be trusted. Too bad, as she actually liked the idea of having a friend close to her own age in town.

"You suppose. Did you or didn't you?"

Dorthia worked to hide her disappointment. "I did. I'm Dorthia Smith."

"Is that name supposed to mean something?"

The previous moment of disappointment was now turning into full panic. "Yes, Dr. Todd spoke with you. He said you sponsored me to come and be your assistant."

Dr. Baxter lifted his hand, waving her away with a flip of the hand. "I don't know any Dr. Todd, and I don't need any assistant."

Dorthia fumbled to pull her train ticket from her pocket. "But you must, as you paid for my fare. Dr. Todd said so, and he wouldn't lie."

Dr. Baxter lifted an eyebrow. "But you're insinuating that I would."

She wanted to say no, but it was the only explanation. Turning without comment, she started down the back stairs. It didn't make sense, any of it. Becky seemed genuine, and even if she weren't, what reason would Dr. Todd have for lying to her? Maybe it was just his way of getting her out of the institution? But if so, why lie about it? If she'd known, she could have accepted Miss Agana's offer. No, she couldn't bear it; already, she was hurting over not being the mother to Dr. Baxter's boys. It dawned on her that that was why she was so upset. It wasn't because Dr. Baxter hadn't sent for her; it was because she'd already envisioned herself as being a mother. The door at the bottom of the stairs opened, flooding the stairwell with light. A man stepped inside and started up the stairs.

The door closed. Even though the man appeared to be young, he ascended the stairs slowly and smiled a weary smile when they passed. He opened his mouth as if he were going to say something, when an exaggerated yawn robbed him of his voice and he continued without speaking.

Dorthia couldn't help noticing that the man's clothes were disheveled, and he smelled as if he'd been sleeping in a barn. As she continued down the stairs, she wondered if the man was ill and if that was the reason he'd been made to sleep in the barn.

Though she'd helped Dr. Todd with the children in the asylum, she'd never actually treated an adult and certainly wouldn't know how to treat anything she couldn't see. By the time she pushed open the outer door, she'd nearly convinced herself that not working with Dr. Baxter was for the best. Not only was she ill-equipped to do the job, but the man seemed to be cantankerous and not at all enjoyable to work for. With that part settled, her new dilemma was to figure out what to do from here. She wasn't going to starve, not right away, at least, as she had the five dollars of emergency money Dr. Todd had given her. While it wouldn't pay for a ticket back to New York, it would keep her fed until someone could wire her enough money to purchase a ticket home.

Home.

Though she'd originally thought she would stay in Guymon even if things didn't work out with Dr. Baxter, she suddenly wasn't so sure she wanted to remain in a town where people told lies. A pity, as the town itself seemed to welcome her. Then again, perhaps it was simply because the buildings were so low that the wind was able to flow through the town unimpeded, allowing the air to smell clean and fresh.

As she walked along the street, she also noticed the noise. While the city was a constant hub of noise, here, it was easy to actually pinpoint each sound. The chug of a single motorcar, voices from two men chatting on the other side of the street, a horse-drawn wagon clopping along in front of Langston Hardware Store. She concentrated once more, her lips curving as she heard children laughing in the distance. Not having anywhere else to go, Dorthia walked toward the sound and then leaned against the wall of the building, watching the children play. It warmed her heart to see them running and chasing each other seemingly without care, and no fence to hold them in. It dawned on her that the children were not only free, but they were safe. A memory from what seemed like a lifetime ago, of when she, too, used to run and play with the neighborhood children while her father sat on the stoop talking to their neighbors, floated into her memory. Dorthia casually glanced about, half expecting to see her father, and sighed a heavy sigh at not finding him.

# Chapter Twenty-Six

Unsure of her next course of action, Dorthia spent the better part of the afternoon exploring the town. It wasn't until her stomach grumbled loudly enough to be heard that she decided to give in to her hunger and made her way back to a café that had caught her eye on the east side of Main Street. All heads turned as she entered Wilson Café, each person staring at her as if they knew all of her dark secrets. If not for the smell permeating the room, Dorthia would have bolted from the room. Instead, she forced her feet forward and took a seat at the first empty table. After an uneasy moment, conversations resumed at the nearby tables, and a low hum filled the air.

Dorthia casually glanced around the café, noting the clientele. While a couple of the men wore suits, most wore simple shirts and pants, and each had a dark hat sitting on the seat next to them. The women wore simple printed dresses and small, unadorned hats atop their heads.

A lady wearing a blue and white apron tied at the waist approached her table and set a glass of water in front of her. "The special of the day is pot roast and mashed potatoes. Comes with green beans, rolls, and a slice of pie. Unless you prefer to look at a menu."

At the mention of pot roast, Dorthia's mouth began to water. She hadn't had pot roast since leaving Boston. "Pot roast would be amazing."

"Always is unless it's late in the day. Then it gets a bit dry. It's early yet, so don't you go worrying about that."

Dorthia started to tell her she'd eat it even if it were dry, but the woman continued before she could.

"The special comes with milk. Unless you prefer water. Drinking water don't bring the price down none."

"I'd like milk, please." If it had brought the cost down, she might have passed on the milk. Since she didn't have a plan, Dorthia was reluctant to spend too much. While she was rusty, she wasn't opposed to dipping a pocket or two to help get her by until she figured out her next move.

"Traveling?"

"Excuse me?"

"Your accent. Plus, I haven't seen you around here before."

Dorthia noticed that the conversations around her had grown quiet. "Yes. I came in on the train just this morning."

"Where are you coming from?"

"New York."

"New York?" the waitress repeated loudly enough for all to hear. "You must have been on the train for days. I'd give anything to live in the city."

"I was just thinking the same about Guymon."

"You're planning on hanging around? Have you got family here?"

"No."

"Then what brought you here?"

Uncomfortable with all the questions, especially since she wasn't sure how to answer, Dorthia squirmed in her seat. "Is there a place I can freshen up before my meal comes?"

"There's a deep sink in the back hallway. Privy is out the back door. You can leave your bag at the table." She must have picked up on Dorthia's reluctance as she smiled and added, "No one's going to bother your things. It's a small town, and we watch each other's backs. The townsfolk don't cotton to stealing around here."

Dorthia wasn't sure if the waitress had somehow read her mind or if she figured everyone from the city was a thief. Matching the woman's smile, she pushed away from the table. "Good to know." As she walked to the back of the café, she felt all eyes watching.

Dorthia stepped outside and let the fresh air fill her lungs, then slowly blew it out to help calm her jitters as the woman's words repeated in her mind—the townsfolk don't cotton to stealing. Of course, they would be untrusting of those they didn't know; it was a small town, and small-town people looked out for one another. On one hand, the thought of living in such a community thrilled her. On the other, it terrified her. If she couldn't steal to pay her way, she only had one other skill to call upon, and that wasn't a skill she'd planned to revisit. A deep sadness touched her heart as she knew her odds of remaining in this town were dwindling.

Her food, along with a tall glass of cold milk, was waiting for her when she returned. Dorthia slid into her chair and tucked her napkin into her lap. The roast was so tender that it fell apart when her fork touched it. She took a bite and instantly thought of Sunday dinners with her father. Not wishing to bring further attention to herself, Dorthia dug her fingernails into her palm to stave off tears and took another bite.

***

When Dorthia went into Owl Drugs looking for headache powder, she never expected to come face-to-face with the skeletal remains of an Indian, but here she was. And, from what she could tell, the person who'd once laid claim to the bones could have used the headache powder more than she, as there was a hole in the upper portion of the skull. Then again, it was probably a bullet hole and most likely killed the man instantly. At least she hoped that was the case, as getting shot in the skull couldn't have felt good.

"There you are! I've been looking everywhere for you."

Dorthia turned to see a tall, thin man with a neatly trimmed beard hurrying in her direction. She glanced around to see who the man was speaking to, only to discover no one else in sight. "The man who works here is in the back." She left off telling he was getting her some headache powder as she didn't think it was any of his business.

Undeterred, the man stopped directly in front of her and took a small piece of paper from his pocket before retrieving a pencil from behind his ear. "Actually, I believe you are who I am looking for."

"Me?"

"Yes. You're the young lady from New York City, are you not?"

"I didn't steal anything. I was just looking at the bones."

"I'm not here to accuse you of anything." The man shoved the pencil back behind his ear and pulled out a handkerchief to wipe the sweat from his brow. "I just wanted to get your name for the paper."

"Paper?"

"Oh, my, I'm sorry. I really should introduce myself. I'm Robert Ness. I'm a reporter for the *Guymon Herald* and your name is?"

"Dorthia Smith. Why do you want to put me in the paper?"

"You're from New York City, are you not?" he asked, repeating his earlier question.

"I am."

"Wonderful," he said, plucking his pencil from his ear once more. "A stranger comes all the way from New York and that's big news around here."

"I don't understand."

"It's one thing to write that Mrs. Myrtle Davidson visited Sara Simms, but to say that Miss Dorthia Smith came to call on." The reporter stilled his pen. "Who did you say you were calling on?"

"I didn't."

"Yes, well, if you could just give me the name, I'll leave you to the bones."

Embarrassed to tell him she'd come all this way for nothing, Dorthia motioned to the sign that read *'Here lie the bones of a dead Indian found by Geo Foreman.'* "They are just bones. How do they know they belong to an Indian?"

Robert smiled and moved closer to the remains. "See that little bag? It's full of glass beads. There were hundreds. Some were in the bag, others were found around his legs. Since most white men don't wear beads, it is safe to assume it was an Indian."

"He was shot," Dorthia replied.

Robert bobbed his head. "Excellent guess."

Dorthia pointed to the skull. "The bullet hole kind of gave it away."

Robert moved closer and pointed. "You see how the skull is in better condition than the rest of the remains? A good thing, or Geo might not have found him. It was back in April after the spring thaw. Geo had just arrived home from church and decided to check on his property, when lo and behold, he saw something glistening in the sun. Since he'd never seen it before, it didn't sit well with him. So he got out to have a look-see. After a bit of digging, he discovered this here skull and a few more bones, which he brought to town. I told him there must be more, and so he and I went back to dig up the rest. He did the digging and I wrote an article about it in April. It was big news and got picked up by some big papers."

"Why do you think someone shot him?"

"My guess would be buffalo. Lots of bad blood when the white man came to drive the Indians from No Man's Land."

"No Man's Land?"

"The land didn't belong to anyone for years." Robert shrugged. "The name kind of stuck, though most folk around here call it God's Country."

Though she hadn't gone to church in many years, Dorthia liked the sound of that, which made her decision to leave even harder.

"Now, if you can give me the name of the person you came to visit," Robert said, pulling her from her thoughts.

"Why is that so important?"

Robert raised an eyebrow. "It's news. Why, the whole 'who did what with whom' section of the paper is one of the local favorites. Readers gobble it up. And a stranger in town, especially one as lovely as you, will have people talking. Wouldn't it be best to just tell them to avoid all the hearsay gossip?"

Dorthia realized the man wasn't going to leave without an answer. "If you must know, I came here to see him."

"Him who?" Robert arched an eyebrow. "The Indian?"

"Yes. I read about him in our newspaper."

Robert's jaw dropped. "In New York City?"

Dorthia bobbed her head and emitted a giggle. "I know it sounds silly, but I'd never seen an Indian before and I thought, *Dorthia, here's your chance.* So, I bought myself a ticket for the train and here I am. I guess that's too silly to put in your paper."

Robert beamed his delight. "On the contrary, it will make a splendid post. Imagine the local folk finding out that my article made it all the way to New York City. If you'll excuse me, I have a story to write."

The man's excitement almost made Dorthia regret her fib. Then again, was there really any harm in the telling? The only real untruth was telling the man she'd read his article in the newspaper. Had her situation been different in that she actually had enough money for leisurely travel, she just might have been inclined to travel all this way to lay eyes on a real-life Indian skeleton. That is, had she actually known of his existence. As if to fortify the lie, she lingered in front of the bones and even grew bold enough at one point to trace her finger along the jawline of the skull. As she pulled her hand back, she replayed the conversation with the reporter. He'd come into the drugstore looking for her and yet he'd not been in the cafe. She was sure of it, as she could recall the faces of everyone in the room as they turned to stare in her direction. That meant that someone in the room had to have told him she was there. It dawned on her that not only would people know if she picked pockets, but they would surely find out if she started taking money for favors. Would she want to live in a town where nothing was a secret? Then again, she'd heard it be said that if someone were down on their luck, the neighbors would pull together to help. Would they help her if they knew she was in dire straits?

Dorthia recalled the hole she'd put in Doctor Baxter's wall and started to panic. It wouldn't be long before the whole town learned of her destructive nature. People liked to think the worst of people, and here she'd already given them reason to dislike her. It didn't matter that she hadn't done it on purpose. The more she thought about the people of the town not liking her, the more upset she became.

"Here's your headache powder." The druggist sighed. "Sorry about the delay. I had to open a new bottle and had a devil of a time getting the lid off." The druggist sighed and studied his hands, which were gnarled with age. "Blasted fingers aren't what they used to be. That is no worry of yours. Is there anything else you'll be needing?"

Dorthia glanced around the store. "Do you have anything that would fix a hole in the wall?"

The druggist frowned. "What kind of hole? Wood or plaster?"

"Plaster."

"No, but one of the Jackson brothers will get you set with everything you need."

"Jackson brothers?"

The druggist pointed a crooked finger. "Over at the hardware. Probably fix the hole for you if you bat your eyes enough."

She smiled. "How much for the headache powder?"

"No charge. Now don't you go fretting," he said when she started to object. "It took me entirely too long to open that bottle. I'm lucky you didn't haul yourself over to the competition. I give you this sample for free, and perhaps next time, you'll come see me again."

Dorthia started to tell him she was leaving town and there wouldn't be a next time, but there was a kindness in his eyes that reminded her of her father, and she couldn't bring herself to voice the words out loud, especially since a large part of her didn't want to leave. "If I get another headache, I promise to come to see you."

"That's my girl." He pulled out his pocket watch and studied it for a moment. "Take some now and then again in about four hours if the pain hasn't subsided."

Dorthia's hand trembled as she wrapped her fingers around the envelope.

# Chapter Twenty-Seven

Dorthia stood outside the hardware store, admiring the white milk-glass hurricane lamp that hung in front of the window. It wasn't so much the rose-decorated globe light that held her attention, but the many crystals that hung from the brass rim. A similar lamp once hung in the music room of the apartment she lived in with her father. Her father had told her the music room had been a favorite of her mother and remained a silent memory of the woman she never knew. While neither she nor her father was musically inclined, they'd spent many hours each lost in their own thoughts while watching the sun dance off those crystals. She briefly wondered what had happened to that lamp as well as the rest of their belongings in the wake of their failure to return home. It was but one of the mysteries of which she knew she'd never have an answer.

Her eyes trailed to the ladies' gloves that hung in the lower section of the window, then at last to the assembly of men's pocket watches. As she stared at them, they evoked yet another memory of her father, this one was not nearly as pleasant as the one before. A shiver raced along her arms, and she wondered momentarily if she would ever be able to see a pocket watch without thinking of her father and recalling his final moments. Shaking off the memory, she continued inside the store. Stopping to admire the lamp once more, she kept her eyes trained upward to avoid looking at the watches.

"She's a beauty."

Dorthia turned to see a man coming up the aisle. Dressed in black pants with a matching vest, his hair was neatly cut and slicked into place.

He nodded toward the lamp. "Just got her in. She's all electric, but if you'd prefer oil, we've got more in the back."

She started to tell him that while she'd love to have it, she had neither the money for something so extravagant nor a house to hang it in. Instead, she smiled. "I'm not in the market for a lamp today, thank you. I have a hole in my wall that needs to be repaired. The druggist told me Mr. Jackson could help. Are you he?"

"One of them. My brothers are out and about right now, but I'm sure one of us could come by to look at it before the day is done."

"Oh, that won't be necessary. I caused it, so I intend to fix it myself."

"I see." He motioned for her to follow, stopping halfway down the aisle. "House or barn?"

Neither, but she didn't want to tell him the wall in question belonged to Dr. Baxter. "Does it matter?"

Jackson grinned and rocked back on his heels. "Only if you want the right supplies to fix it. I need to know if we are talking about plaster from a house or wood from a barn."

"House," she said with conviction.

"Do you know if the lath is intact?"

"I'm not sure," she replied without admitting that while she knew the wall to be plaster, she had no clue what a lath was.

"Is the wall merely dimpled or does the hole go all the way through?"

She pictured the hole she had made and resisted the urge to cringe. "All the way. It was the doorknob."

Jackson smiled. "Happens to the best of us. Done it myself a time or two. Crystal or brass?"

"What?"

"The doorknob, was it crystal or brass?"

Dorthia visualized the doorknob, which again was the same as what was in their Boston apartment. "Crystal."

He cupped his hand. "Hole about this size?"

She nodded.

The man smiled and pointed at some thin wood strips. "You'll need to use one piece of this lath. Clean up the area with a file and then nail this strip to the wall." He snapped the wood so that it was about ten inches long. "Trim it to the size you need, making sure to overlap the hole."

Dorthia frowned. While the lath was long enough, it wasn't nearly wide enough to cover the hole. "That won't be wide enough to cover the hole," she said, mirroring her thoughts.

"You're not trying to cover it. You'll want to leave a quarter-inch gap between the board and the wall. That way, when you apply the plaster, it will ooze through, and the keys will hold it in place."

"Keys?"

Jackson nodded. "As the plaster dries, it will grab hold of the other side of those strips. Those plaster fingers are called keys, which will harden, thus holding the hole together."

Understanding the process, Dorthia brightened. "So, then it will be fixed."

The man chuckled. "Not hardly. The hole will be covered; however, the process will take a good couple of days to fix."

"Days? But the hole is so small. I wouldn't think fixing it would take more than a few moments."

"Plaster is tricky that way. You see, first comes the sanding, then nailing the lath in place and applying the plaster, making sure it is smooth. After that, you'll have to wait for it to dry so you can sand it. Depending on the weather and humidity, this could take a day or two. Then you apply the second coat, then more waiting and sanding. I hope the hole is not too noticeable, as you're probably looking at a good week or so before you even get it to where you'll be able to paint it. Are you okay there, little Missy? You look a little pale. You know, I could fix it for you myself if you prefer."

Dorthia considered this for a moment. While it would just be easier to pay to have it done, she thought that perhaps if the doctor saw she was being responsible, he would allow her to stay until she'd finished the job. Perhaps even allow her to help out in the office for a day or two. If he found her useful, he might rethink his decision and allow her to stay. While she didn't look forward to working for a grump, it would be better than the alternatives and allow her to walk down the street with her head held high.

"No, I made the hole, I'll fix it." At least she'd start the process. If Dr. Baxter balked at allowing her to stay, she would have no choice but to let him finish the repair himself.

"Give me a minute to mix up the plaster. I'll just add the dry. You'll need to add water to the mix once you're done prepping the wall." He pulled several bags from the shelf and took them to the back counter.

Dorthia watched as he dipped powder from the bags marked "lime putty" and "sand" and poured the contents into a small bucket. He picked up a bag labeled "gypsum" and added a little to the mixture before adding something black.

He saw her watching. "Horse hair. It helps hold the plaster together, and the gypsum will help it dry quicker. You'll want to add water to this, just a bit at a time. Keep a close eye on it; you don't want it too thick or so thin it runs down the wall."

"Can't you add the water for me?"

"No, you'll have to prepare the wall first, and that'll take a little time. This will set up like a brick and be too hard to work with if I mix it now," he said, then went over all the instructions once more. "Any questions?"

Dorthia smiled her best smile. "Do you have any tools I can borrow?"

***

Armed with everything she needed to start the job, Dorthia stood just outside the building, trying to gather the nerve to go inside. It wasn't that she was frightened of the man, but more that she was afraid he wouldn't accept her offer to fix what she'd broken. Adjusting her bag and the newly gathered supplies to even out the weight, she pulled open the door and started up the stairs. When she reached the top, she opened the door, being extra mindful of her step this time.

The waiting room was empty.

She lowered the bucket and supplies, then placed her bag on a nearby chair before knocking on the door to the inner office. When no one answered, she hovered her fingers above the doorknob, debating. *What's the worst thing that could happen? He'll yell at you and send you on your way.* At least she'd know she had tried. She turned the knob and peeked around the door at a long hallway with four additional doors. All but one door was open. She tiptoed down the hall, silently peeking into each room. She stopped at the closed door, lifted her hand to knock, then decided to try the handle. Locked. She heard someone cough and placed her ear to the door. Not a cough, snoring. Dr. Baxter was asleep. The last thing she wanted was to further irritate the man by waking him, so she moved away from the door and returned to the lobby, closing the door to the inner hall without a sound.

She stood there for several moments debating her next move. If she woke Dr. Baxter, he would have every right to be angry with her. Then again, he was sleeping on the other side of the building, and there were two closed doors between them.

Surely it was enough.

Deciding it was, she stood surveying the damage she'd done as she mentally recalled the instructions Mr. Jackson had given her. Feeling oddly confident, she retrieved the file, knelt in front of the hole, and began smoothing the area. She'd nearly finished when she heard footsteps on the stairs. She started to move out of the way. Too late, as the door opened, sending the doorknob into the back of her head.

"Ow." She sat rubbing her head as a man entered the waiting room.

He reached a hand to help her up. "What on earth were you doing behind the door?"

Dorthia shrugged out of his grip. "I was fixing the hole I made."

He raised an eyebrow. "You made?"

"Yes, this morning, when I fell into the door."

He looked her up and down as if looking for proof of her fall. "And you came back to fix it?"

She pointed at the supplies she'd brought. "I have." Her tone was terse, as she could tell he didn't believe her.

He glanced at the bucket and smiled.

Dorthia sucked in her breath as she realized him to be the sickly looking man she'd passed earlier on the stairs. Only he didn't look sickly now. Nor did he smell like he'd been sleeping in a barn. In fact, with his dark, wavy hair and boyish grin, he looked rather handsome. "Looks like Dr. Baxter fixed you up pretty well," she said.

The man raised an eyebrow once more. "Dr. Baxter?"

"I saw you in the stairwell this morning when you were coming to see him." She felt herself blush. "To be honest, I wasn't sure how good a doctor he was since he had such a foul disposition, but it seems he did right by you."

The man sat in a chair against the far wall, crossed one knee over the other, and balanced his hat on top. "Are you ill?"

Dorthia rubbed the back of her head. "I have a little bump, but nothing serious."

He chuckled. "No, I mean earlier. You said you'd come to see Dr. Baxter. I thought perhaps you were ill."

"No, I'm not ill. I came to… it doesn't matter."

"Sure it does."

"Not anymore." Dorthia sighed as the enormity of her situation overtook her. "I told the reporter that I came out on the train to see the Indian, but that's not true. I came out because Dr. Todd told me that Dr. Baxter sent for me. Only, when I got here, I stumbled through the door and wrecked this wall. It must have made Dr. Baxter awfully mad because afterwards, he denied having sent for me. I guess Dr. Todd could've been lying, but I don't think so because, unlike Dr. Baxter, Dr. Todd is a kind and caring man."

The man's smile faded. "You don't think Dr. Baxter is a kind and caring man?"

Dorthia glanced at the inner door. "I suppose I could have caught him on a bad day."

"Or, you could have met the wrong Dr. Baxter." The words were spoken so softly that Dorthia wasn't sure she'd really heard them.

She tilted her head. "Excuse me?"

"I said I am Dr. Baxter. I'm sorry I wasn't here to greet you properly. I have been at the Bailey farm since mid-morning yesterday, assisting with the birth of a calf. I truly am sorry. I would have sent someone if I'd known when you were arriving."

"But when I asked where your office was, they pointed me here. And when I came, the man said he was Dr. Baxter. Why would everyone lie?"

"They didn't. The man is Dr. Baxter. He's my father. He's retired, and as you found out, his age has made him a bit terse. He knew I was busy with the calf, so he stopped by this morning to lend a hand. As for the others, the locals call me Dr. Harvey. It helps with the confusion. Again, I'm sorry. I should have told him I'd sent for you."

"You said you were helping birth a calf," she said, ignoring the apology. "Does that mean you're not a real doctor?"

"I'm bona fide. I have a medical degree and a shingle hanging over the door to prove it."

"And yet you treat animals?"

He chuckled. "Most doctors do."

"I don't recall Dr. Todd ever treating animals."

"I stand corrected. I meant to say, most country doctors do."

"Oh."

"Oh, as if you don't like animals, or oh, as if you don't like doctors who treat them?"

"Just oh. I've never really been around animals or known anyone who treats them, so I don't believe I have a preference either way."

"Does that mean you are okay with working for a doctor who treats both people and animals?"

Dorthia's heart skipped. "You mean you still want me to work for you?" The excitement in her voice was evident.

"I sent for you, didn't I?"

Dorthia wasn't sure why staying in this town seemed so important, but knowing she wouldn't have to leave made her extremely happy. Plus, staying meant she would have plenty of time to repair the hole. She worked to steady her voice. "Yes, Dr. Baxter, I would very much like to work for you."

"Call me Dr. Harvey. It will make things easier. What are you doing?" he asked when she bent to retrieve the file she'd dropped.

For a doctor, the man didn't seem too bright. "I'm going to finish fixing the hole."

"I'm afraid my father hasn't been at all kind to you."

Dorthia frowned. "What do you mean?"

"Because that hole has been there for years. We plug it up, and not too long after, someone plows right through the door and opens it up again."

While she wanted to lash out for being made to feel like such a buffoon, the truth was she was much too happy about being able to stay to care. "Well then," Dorthia said, moving to the wall. "I'd better make sure it gets fixed right this time."

***

Emily interrupted her. "So you stayed?"

"I did."

"You weren't put off by all the questions?"

Dorthia smiled. "On the contrary, that is what drew me to the town."

"I don't understand."

"It was the first time since losing my father that people cared."

"They were being nosy."

"My father used to say it was human nature for people to be inquisitive. He considered it a good thing, as it held people accountable. If there hadn't been so many questions, I might not have had any qualms about going back to my old ways, which could have gotten me thrown into jail or worse. I might not have gone back to my husband's office."

"So the orphan train was just a way to get you out of the asylum. Is it safe to say you were a mail-order bride?"

Dorthia waved off the accusation. "Not at all. It was strictly a working arrangement until it wasn't."

"Where did you live?"

"There was a boarding house in town. Dr. Harvey paid my board as part of my salary."

"What was your salary?"

"Five dollars a week, which was very generous considering I didn't have to worry about food or a place to live."

"How old was Dr. Harvey?"

"When I arrived in town?"

Emily nodded.

"Twenty-six."

"How long between the time you arrived," Emily checked her notes, "at the age of seventeen, until you were married."

"Nearly two years. We were married in April of '26. I was old enough to wed at seventeen if he'd have asked me. Contrary to what the townspeople thought, Harvey wasn't looking for a wife. Though I never went to school for it, I became his nurse. I looked after the boys, and we were comfortable."

"But you eventually got married. What changed?"

"I thought you said your readers were interested in the orphan trains. I've told you all I know about that."

"I think the readers would like to hear more." Emily lowered her pen. "Please, Grandma Dottie, won't you tell the rest of your story?"

# Chapter Twenty-Eight



*April 1926*

Dorthia looked at the clock just as it chimed. "I've got to go."

Becky rubbed at the small of her back. "Dr. Harvey can wait until you bring your pie out of the oven. Besides, he'll forgive you the moment he tastes it."

Dorthia suppressed a giggle. "Providing it tastes as good as it looks."

"Of course it will taste good. I watched the entire process and didn't have to correct you once. You've come a long way, Dorthia."

Dorthia was sure that no truer words had ever been spoken. At first, Becky laughed when she had asked her to teach her how to cook. Having grown up in a family where everyone chipped in, the woman couldn't believe Dorthia had never learned to cook. Becky had quickly seen that she was telling the truth when Dorthia stared at an egg and asked if the chicken was inside. Seeing Becky's face when her friend realized she was telling the truth, Dorthia had burst into tears, saying she would never land a husband if she couldn't cook. Becky had quickly taken pity on her and made it her mission to teach her everything she knew about cooking. Dorthia wiped her face with her sleeve. "That's because I have such a good teacher."

"Not good enough. You should be wiping your face with the bottom of your apron, not the sleeve of your dress." Becky gasped and placed a hand to her stomach, which was heavy with child.

Dorthia felt a pang of her own, only hers was from the guilt of having her friend up so early when she should be resting. She'd tried to beg off making the pie today, knowing that Becky would be giving birth soon, but her friend had insisted she was fine, especially since Dorthia would be doing most of the work. She frowned at seeing the worried crease in Becky's forehead. "Are you okay?"

"I think Mr. Hanson is ready to make his appearance," Becky said, keeping up her insistence that the baby she was carrying was a boy. When Dorthia had asked how she could be so certain, her friend had merely laughed and said, "A mother knows."

Dr. Harvey, on the other hand, had told Dorthia that Becky was only saying what most wives said, as they aimed to please their husbands by providing them with sons to carry on the family name. "How long have you been having contractions?"

"My back has been hurting for a couple of days, but I didn't think it was labor. Now, I'm not so sure."

"I shall go get Harvey… I mean Dr. Harvey."

Becky waved her off. "No, we have time yet. Take the pie out and sit with me for a minute."

Dorthia used the towel to remove the pie, then joined Becky at the table.

"It's obvious you care for Dr. Harvey and he for you. I've seen the way you dote on those boys, so why hasn't he asked you to marry him?"

Dorthia knew the reason. Everything had seemed to be moving in that direction, especially after Becky and William had announced they'd had the preacher marry them. Dorthia had been shocked by the announcement, as Becky had always talked about a church wedding surrounded by family and friends. The reason for the haste had made its appearance sooner than the couple had expected when Dr. Harvey had confirmed her pregnancy. That was the same day he'd caught Dorthia crying, and after some prodding, she'd then told him of her mother's fate and of her own concerns of dying in childbirth. It was also the day she'd told him she didn't wish to be a mother. He'd walked away and they'd never spoken of it again. Dorthia had never told any of this to her friend, as she hadn't wished to spoil her joy. Unlike her, Becky was thrilled with the thought of giving birth.

Dorthia searched her mind for an answer that would satisfy her friend. "I don't think he's ready for another wife."

"Of course he is." The sentence was followed by another contraction that had Becky gripping the table.

Dorthia watched as her friend's knuckles grew white.

As the pain eased, Becky released the table and used the hem of her dress to bat at the beads of sweat that had formed on her upper lip. "I guess the back pain wasn't just back pain after all. Have you ever delivered a baby?"

Though Dorthia detected a hint of fear in her eyes, Becky's voice was calm. Actually, aside from the occasional farm animal, Harvey had not asked her to be present during births. Dorthia shook her head. "Only livestock."

Becky smiled a trembling smile. "They all come out the same way."

Only they didn't. Dorthia recalled the time Harvey had had to stick his arm inside a cow to turn the calf. She took a step back. "I'll go get…"

"There's no time," Becky told her. "This baby is coming and I don't intend to bring him into the world alone."

Becky was right. She and William lived a mile from town and nearly half that from their closest neighbor. Given that she had walked here from town, there was no time to go for help. Dorthia swallowed her fear. "What do you want me to do? I've heard about boiling water. Do you want me to put some on the stove?"

"Boiling water is to keep the men busy. There's a basket in the closet with sheets and towels. There are scissors and twine for tying the cord. I've already boiled everything." Becky paused, waiting for another contraction to pass before continuing. "I didn't want to have him alone, but I thought it best to be prepared just in case."

"We should get you into bed."

Becky shook her head. "Not yet. Grab that shotgun from over in the corner."

Though Dorthia had never witnessed a birth, she was pretty sure there were no guns involved. "Why?"

Becky managed to laugh. "Relax. I'm not asking you to shoot anything. Take it out on the porch and aim it up in the air. With any luck, someone will hear it and come running."

Dorthia started for the corner.

"You're going to need to brace yourself before you pull that trigger," Becky told her. "She lands a wallop of a kick. If you're not ready, you'll end up on your keister."

Dorthia hurried to the corner and lifted the gun, the weight of it solid in her hands as she walked to the edge of the porch steps with purpose. Having never fired a gun, she relied on what she'd seen in the silent pictures and snugged it under her arm. The air was still, and even the birds had grown quiet as if the world was holding its breath. She placed her finger on the trigger, finding it solid and cool to the touch, and pulled.

"It won't work," she said when nothing happened.

"What won't?"

"The gun. My hands are too weak. I pulled the trigger, but nothing happened."

"Did you pull back the hammer?"

Dorthia lowered the gun as her gaze swept the porch. "I don't see a hammer."

"Not a hammer, the hammer on the shotgun. It sticks up in the back where your thumb should be. Pull it back with your thumb and pull the trigger." Becky's words were followed by an agonizing scream.

Spurred into action, Dorthia cocked the hammer, settled the shotgun under her arm, pointed it at the sky, and squeezed the trigger. A deafening blast filled the air as the shotgun ripped from her grasp, scooted across the porch, and clambered against the back of the house. Dorthia had once been kicked by a mule; she was pretty sure this was more in line with being shot from a cannon. She hurried to retrieve the shotgun and then went inside to tend to Becky. "It felt as if someone grabbed hold and yanked it from my hands," Dorthia exclaimed as she returned the gun to the corner.

"I told you she kicks," Becky said through gritted teeth, then bit the back of her knuckle and moaned as the pain grew.

"Come," Dorthia said when the pain subsided. "We need to get you into bed where you'll be more comfortable."

The moment Becky stood, a puddle formed on the floor. The woman sighed a heavy sigh. "I just scrubbed that floor yesterday morning."

"I'll clean it for you later." Dorthia stepped over the mess and ushered Becky from the room.

Halfway down the hall, Becky stiffened, her fingers digging into Dorthia's arm.

"Just breathe through the pain," Dorthia urged.

"Don't tell me what to do!" Becky snapped.

"I was talking to myself. You're killing my arm," Dorthia replied.

Becky eased her grip as the contraction waned. "I'm sorry."

"Don't be." Actually, Dorthia was glad Becky had hold of her, as the strength of the grip let her know she was strong.

"I've been after William to add an upstairs. I'm so glad he hasn't found the time. Can you imagine if I had to walk up those stairs to the bedroom?"

"I would carry you myself," Dorthia told her.

Becky laughed. "I'd not place a wager on that."

"I'm stronger than I look." Dorthia helped Becky remove her dress, then stripped the quilt and guided her into bed, placing a towel under her just as another contraction mounted.

"It won't be long now," Becky said when it subsided.

"I'll get the basket." Dorthia hurried to the closet and found the basket in plain view with a red bar of carbolic soap sitting on top. Dorthia smiled and took the soap to the sink to wash her hands before returning to the bedroom and lifting the basket just as another contraction mounted. She took hold of Becky's hand, noting that the contractions were getting closer. "I should probably take a look."

Becky nodded.

Dorthia caught her breath as she pulled back the sheet. Her heart skipped a beat as she forced a smile, then, turning to the basket, she retrieved a fresh towel. She took a breath to steady herself before turning back to her friend. "We've got a bit of a mess down there. Lift your buttocks so I can put another towel under you."

Just as she got the towel situated, Becky screamed.

Dorthia looked to see the baby's head crowning. The sight was both comforting and terrifying at the same time. She plucked a second towel from the basket. "It's time," she said, hoping she sounded more confident than she actually felt.

"Becky!" William's shouts filled the air. A moment later, he was in the room, kneeling at his wife's side. "I came as soon as I heard the gunshot. I sent Ray to fetch the doctor."

While Dorthia was glad William had the foresight to send the farmhand to fetch Harvey, she doubted he would arrive in time to assist with the birth. "The baby's not going to wait for the doctor."

William paled. "Can't she close her legs or something?"

"I do believe it's a bit late for that." Becky's words were followed by a scream.

Dorthia climbed onto the bed. "It's time to push."

"What's wrong? Is the baby okay? Have you delivered a baby before?" William opened his mouth to ask another question when Dorthia stopped him.

"William, I need your help."

William jumped to his feet. "What do you need?"

"Water. Find the biggest pan you can. Run to the well and fill it from the handpump. It will be faster," she said when he started to object. "The moment it's full, put it on the stove and wait for it to boil. Can you do that?"

William leaned in, kissing Becky on the head before racing from the room.

"The water will be so cold, it will take forever to heat," Becky said through gritted teeth.

"That's what I'm counting on," Dorthia said, holding the towel in place. "With any luck, we can get this baby out before William has a chance to think of any more questions. Now push!"

***

Dorthia stood at the kitchen sink replaying the events of the last few moments. As she scrubbed the blood from her hands, she made no move to stop the steady stream of tears that trickled down her cheeks. The engine of a motorcar rumbled in the distance, growing louder before sputtering to a stop. A door slammed, followed by quick footsteps on the porch. Dorthia looked up as Harvey approached. Even though he was no longer needed, she was comforted by the sight of him.

He opened the door and stepped inside. "Becky?"

Dorthia smiled. "Is just fine."

"And the baby?"

"A healthy baby boy."

Harvey frowned. "You're crying."

Dorthia sighed. "I can't seem to stop."

"It's understandable given your misgivings about becoming a mother. I'm sorry I wasn't here in time to help."

Dorthia smiled. "I'm glad you weren't."

His frown deepened. "You weren't scared?"

"I was terrified." Dorthia rinsed her hands a final time and reached for the towel.

"But you did it."

"Becky was in so much pain, and yet, the moment I placed the baby in her arms, it was like the pain didn't matter anymore." Dorthia closed her eyes briefly, remembering the moment, then opened them once more. "I'm not saying all the pain went away. I can tell she was still hurting. It just seemed that the love she had for the baby made it all worth it."

"That's what Julie told me," Harvey said, referencing his late wife. "She used to say that God took away the pain."

"So it wasn't holding the baby that took away the pain?"

"Who knows?" Harvey shrugged. "I guess it could have been. I just know something must take it away because, if not, women would not wish to go through it again. Not that they have much of a choice once the deed is done."

This was the opening Dorthia had been hoping for. "I love your boys. I don't think I could love them any more if they were my own."

Harvey frowned. "But?"

"I want more. I want to know the love a mother feels for the child she bears. I want to look into the child's eyes and know it is a part of me. I would like that child to be a part of you as well. If you're not willing to give me that, then I will look for someone who will."

"Not willing? I ache to share my love with you. I only distanced myself as I knew how you felt. I adore you, Dottie," he said, using the nickname he often used when speaking to her. "I knew if I'd asked you to marry me, you would have agreed. I didn't ask, because I didn't trust myself to abstain."

She blinked through a fresh set of tears. "Are you saying you wish to marry me?"

"I am. I'll get down on my knees right here and now and say it again, if you'd like."

Dorthia nodded to the pale pink stain on the floor beneath his feet that she'd yet to clean. "I think it's best you don't."

Harvey glanced at the mess on the floor and nodded his agreement. "If you have no objection, I would like to stop by the preacher man's house on the way home and ask him to marry us. That is, unless you have your heart set on a church wedding."

This was something Dorthia had given a lot of thought to since coming to town. Not having a family of her own or a great number of friends with whom she would share her excitement, she'd decided a church wedding was not something she wanted. Dorthia shook her head. "A church wedding is not needed."

Harvey's shoulders relaxed ever so slightly. "You'll wait for me?"

Dorthia smiled. "As long as it takes."

***

"You married the love of your life, had children of your own, and lived happily ever after," Emily said, pulling her back to the present. "I want a perfect marriage just like you and Granddad had."

Dorthia wagged a finger at her granddaughter. "There is no such thing as a perfect marriage, so get that out of your head right now."

"What do you mean? Even Mom says you and Granddad had a once-in-a-lifetime love. I've never heard you or Granddad speak ill of each other."

"Nor will you. I'm not talking about our love. There is no

denying that. I'm talking about what goes into a marriage. Being in love is not all sunshine and roses. Our lives were far from perfect; you'd best know that. So many young folk today wouldn't have lasted a minute in my shoes. I heard an interview once where this little girl was spending a fortune on her prom dress. When the interviewer asked why she didn't save the money for a wedding dress, the girl had the audacity to stand there and say, "A person can get married as many times as they want, but there is only one senior prom." Marriage is supposed to be sacred, not something to walk away from when times get hard. Had I had that point of view, I wouldn't have been married for but a few years. As it was, my strength was tested at every turn."

Emily leaned closer. "Tested how?"

"To see if I was strong enough."

"Strong enough to do what?"

"Endure," Dorthia replied. "Sometimes I think that was my lot in life… seeing just how much I could endure."

# Chapter Twenty-Nine

*1927*

Dorthia pulled the apple pie from the oven and noted the red marking the morning skies as she placed it on the windowsill to cool. "Skies red. That would be a bad omen if we were at sea."

"Could be one here too." Harvey stepped up behind her, wrapped his arms around her and caressed her round stomach. "You were up early."

Dorthia chuckled. "It's hard to get comfortable when you're as big as a barn."

Harvey dipped a finger in the pie where some of the filling had bubbled up and brought it to her lips. "You may be as big as a barn, but you are as sweet as this apple pie."

The chuckle turned into a full belly laugh as she turned to face him. "I know that was meant as a compliment, but it would have been nice if you'd have disagreed when I said I was as big as a barn."

"Yes, well, your size is what makes you even more attractive. It lets me know I can afford to feed you well."

"He likes to eat." While Dorthia kept insisting the child she was carrying was a boy, the truth was she couldn't tell either way. Unlike Becky, who'd been right in guessing the sex of each of her three children thus far, she herself had been wrong the first time and was not at all confident this time either. She only willed it to be a boy, as, according to Becky, men were happier when wives gave their husbands a son. "There's oatmeal on the stove."

"I'll be good until lunch," he said, then returned to the previous conversation. "You're carrying it the same as before, so I believe this one will be another girl. And you have yet to pick out a name."

"Why do I have to pick the name?"

"Because it is going to be a girl. That was our agreement; you pick the girls' names and I pick the boys'."

"Do you have a boy's name?"

"Nope."

"Why not?"

"Because you're having a girl."

Dorthia sighed. "Why's it so hard to think of a name?"

"You didn't have any trouble last time."

"That's because I named her after my mother." Even that hadn't been her choice, as Becky had told her that was how baby names were often chosen. She'd been worried about choosing the name, as she hadn't actually known her mother, but the moment she saw her daughter, she knew the name, Rebecca Sue, fit. "I'll find one that I like, but you need to do the same. I don't want our son coming into this world without a name."

"You're having a girl, and I'm going to be happy either way."

"Becky said men want sons."

"William is a farmer," Harvey said, cutting her off. "It's natural for him to want boys to help him work the farm. In case you haven't noticed, I'm not much of a farmer, and I already have two sons."

This time, Dorthia's laughter was genuine, as his words were true. They owned one cow, a calf, a handful of chickens, and an ornery rooster, all of which had come with the twenty-acre farm they'd bought at auction a year prior, when their family started to grow. The house wasn't much larger than the one Harvey had owned when she married him, but it had a loft for the boys. While the thought of milking a cow and collecting eggs seemed intriguing at the time of purchase, Dorthia had quickly learned it wasn't an easy task for a woman in her condition to manage. Luckily, Harvey's son, Mark, was happy to step in. At nine years old, the boy was more of a farmer than either of them combined. His twin brother, Paul, on the other hand, was more scholarly in nature and seemed more inclined to follow in his father's footsteps.

"Don't worry," Dorthia said. "He will have two brothers to show him the ropes. Paul will see that he washes his hands after he helps Mark on the farm."

"You do realize doctors do more than wash their hands, don't you, my dear?"

"I know all too well what your hands are capable of," Dorthia told him.

A pink blush crept up Harvey's face as he hurried to change the subject. "Mark told me he's saving the money from the extra eggs to buy himself a draft horse."

"Why would he want a draft horse when he has that nice Lulu?"

"To pull the plow. He's determined to plant a crop in the spring. A couple of the farmers have offered to let him help with the fall harvest so he can see how things are done."

"Meaning they are going to use him for free labor," Dorthia said heatedly.

"Easy, Momma bear. Since neither you nor I can offer any guidance, he'll have to learn somewhere else. I'll see to it he is treated fairly and make sure he gets a fair wage, even if I have to pay it myself."

Dorthia gave him a peck on the cheek. "You are a good man, Dr. Harvey Baxter. Just ask anyone in town."

"Yes, well, if I want to remain in the town's good graces, I need to tend to my patients. I can take the buggy if you'd prefer to drive the machine."

While she preferred the motorcar, she knew it was easier on Harvey if he didn't have to worry about the horse and buggy. While he could leave the horse at the livery, it wasn't practical to keep hitching the buggy every time he had to make a house call. That was the reason he'd purchased the machine in the first place, so he could get to his patients when they needed him.

Dorthia shook her head. "You go on ahead; Mark can help me with the buggy."

Harvey hesitated. "Do you want me to wake him before I leave?"

"No need. He's already in the barn milking the cow. Now quit your fretting and go before your father decides to start treating your patients." Dorthia had meant it as a joke, but they both knew it was a viable threat, as the man still lived in the spare room of the office, and though he was long retired, he often thought he was the doctor in charge. "I believe Mrs. Connely is your first patient."

Harvey's face paled. "Dear God, if I don't hurry, my father will have the poor woman disrobed and on the table before I get there."

"She's coming in so you can recheck her festered finger," Dorthia reminded him.

"When has that ever stopped the man?"

Harvey wasn't wrong. Only last week, Mrs. Randle fell asleep on the table. Dr. Baxter walked into the room, covered her with a sheet, and promptly pronounced her dead. The week prior, he'd tried to do an eye exam on a woman who'd come in for a boil on her toe. "You're right. Go. I'll get the children fed and be along directly."

Harvey hurried across the room and plucked his hat from the hook as he opened the door. He stood there for a moment, then stepped out of the way to allow Mark inside. The boy lowered the pail of milk he was carrying to remove his boots. "Good lad. Make sure to help Mother Dottie with your sister so you all can make it to town before they test the morning whistle. Unless you don't feel up to it," he said, peering at Dorthia.

"Of course I do," Dorthia replied. Actually, there hadn't been much she'd missed when it came to the new courthouse. She'd been there when they'd turned the first shovel of dirt. Had watched them set the first cornerstone and had insisted on accompanying Harvey to see his first patient when they started locking inmates in the new fourth-floor jail. It wasn't that she was obsessed with the new building, nor was she as shocked by the $150,000-plus price tag as some of the locals; it was just that she knew the new building was something her father would have approved of, and as such, made her feel closer to the man. "We'll be there in time." She waved, then went to the kitchen and lifted the lid to check the oatmeal. "Mark, I'll wake your brother up, and then he can look after your sister while we hitch up the buggy."

Mark grinned. "Already done."

Dorthia lowered the lid and glanced out the window to see Lulu already harnessed to the buggy and tied to the post. "You did that on your own?"

Mark bobbed his head. "You're getting too big to do it."

The boy wasn't wrong. Halfway through her pregnancy, she was already bigger than she had been on the day she'd given birth to Susie. "You're a good boy, Mark."

"This farm's going to be mine one day. And when it is, I aim to earn enough money to buy all the rest of the land around it." He grinned a missing-tooth grin, and for a moment, he reminded her of Vito, the boy who used to sell newspapers on the streets of New York. She wondered briefly what had become of him, and then gave thanks that Mark and the others would never know the horrors of having to fight for survival.

She matched his smile. "I know you will, Mark."

***

A small crowd gathered on the street in front of the courthouse, waiting for the morning whistle to announce its new location for all to hear. Mark stood next to Dorthia, while Paul hovered over Susie, who at eleven months had just learned to walk and was more content with toddling everywhere than being held.

"It's almost time. Paul, bring me your sister so I can cover her ears."

Paul scooped up the toddler, who squirmed for release. "It's going to be loud," he said, handing her to Dorthia.

"Loud," Susie repeated as she arched her back. "Down."

Dorthia tightened her hold on the child. "No down. The whistle is going to blow."

"Down!" Susie insisted.

Before Dorthia could answer, the whistle sounded. Susie stiffened, her dark brown eyes grew round, and her bottom lip began to quiver. Dorthia hurried to cover her ears. "It's okay, baby, it's just the whistle."

Susie blinked back tears. "Loud!"

"Yes, baby, it's loud," Dorthia said as the siren waned.

Susie gasped. "Loud all gone."

"Yes, the siren is all gone."

"Down!" Susie said, struggling to be released once more.

Dorthia obliged, her heart swelling as Mark took a turn following after his sister.

"How come you like this building so much?" Paul asked, misinterpreting her smile.

"Because she is beautiful," Dorthia told him.

Paul wrinkled his nose. "She?"

"Yes, she."

"How come?"

Dorthia suddenly wished her father were here to explain. "My father told me all buildings are ladies. I call her Charlotte."

Paul laughed.

"What's so funny?"

"Father said you haven't found a name for the baby. How is it you can find a name for a building, but you've yet to find a name for the baby?" That was the way with Paul, unlike his twin brother, who jumped in with both feet without considering the consequences. Paul was a thinker.

"Babies are more complicated."

"Complicated how?"

"When I name a building, I am just doing it for fun. If I decide later I don't like the name, I could change it and no one would care. But what if I were to give the baby the wrong name? Then he or she would be stuck with it for life."

"Dad said the baby is a girl."

"Your father is guessing."

"He's a doctor," Paul said, defending his dad.

"Yes, and a very good one. But doctors cannot see inside a woman's stomach, so his guess is as good as mine."

"I'm going to be an inventor. Maybe someday I will invent something that will allow doctors to see inside a woman's stomach."

Dorthia contemplated that for a moment. "Well, they have machines that can see the bones in the body, so why not? What would be the purpose of this machine of yours?"

"To help you decide on a name, of course. You can see if the baby is a boy or girl and then you'd know what to name it."

Dorthia started to tell him that it would take all the fun out of giving birth but decided against it. Why squash the boy's dreams by telling him there was no need for such a machine? Instead, she nodded her encouragement. "You know, Paul, if anyone could invent such a machine, it's probably you."

"Momma Dottie, I'm glad you married my dad. Mark is glad too; he just misses Momma too much to say it." The boy grew quiet for a moment. "Sometimes I feel bad for being glad you married my dad, as I miss Momma too."

Dorthia tried to stoop to his level, nearly lost her balance and gave up. She placed her hand alongside his cheek instead. "It's okay to miss your mom. I was younger than you when my father died, and I still miss him very much."

Paul swallowed. "You do?"

"Sure I do."

A frown creased his face. "Does that mean the pain will never go away?"

Dorthia sighed. "It will lessen with time, but there will be times when you'll see something or say something, and instantly, you will think of your mom. Sometimes I remember my father with tears, and sometimes the memory makes me smile. Like today."

"You thought about him today?"

Dorthia nodded. "That's why I'm here. Remember how I told you my dad was an engineer?"

"Yes, you said he built buildings."

"In a way. He helped design them so they don't fall down."

Paul's eyes grew wide as he scanned the courthouse. "It wouldn't be good if the building fell down."

"No, it wouldn't," Dorthia agreed. "I don't think there's any danger of that. They had someone just like my dad to help them design this courthouse. That is why I find the building so interesting. I know if my father was still alive, he would be here watching them build it and making sure it was all done right. Watching the progress makes me think of him and smile."

"You named Susie after your mom, right?"

Dorthia glanced at her daughter, who was now sitting on the courthouse lawn, pulling at blades of grass. "That's right. My mother was also named Rebecca Sue."

Paul pointed at Dorthia's stomach. "Maybe you could name the baby after my mom."

Dorthia rubbed a hand across her stomach, pondering her response. While she knew the boy was trying to help, it was the last name she would agree upon. She didn't have an issue with the name, but the child would grow up being a constant reminder of what they'd all lost. "You know, Paul, Julie is a fine name, but I think it would be best for you to save that name for your own little girl someday."

"I think I would like that." He nodded his agreement as another frown flittered across his face. "Then what will you name the baby?"

"Don't you worry, your father and I still have a couple of months to figure that out. We won't let the baby come into the world without a proper name," Dorthia said, sounding more confident than she felt.

# Chapter Thirty

"You look tired. Are you feeling okay?" Harvey asked as he entered the room.

"I am tired. Susie is into everything. She's napping, and if I thought I'd fit, I'd climb into the baby cage with her." Dorthia massaged her stomach. "You need to have a chat with your son and tell him to quit keeping me up at night."

"Her," Harvey corrected. "Or perhaps it's one of each."

Dorthia felt the color drain from her face. "We would already know if there were two, wouldn't we? And no jokes about how much weight I've gained, or you'll be spending the night here at the office."

"I wouldn't dream of mentioning your weight," Harvey said, then waggled his eyebrows. "And to your question, it's probably only one. Twins are a rare commodity, though not entirely out of the question, as you already know."

Though she didn't relish the thought of pushing out two babies, that wasn't the main reason for her concern. While Susie's birth had been uneventful, the child made for many sleepless nights since then. "I'm not sure I'm built for raising two babies at once."

"You'll be fine, and I'll be there to help," Harvey said, moving closer.

Dorthia held up her hand to stop him. "Your help is what got me into this mess in the first place."

"And I'll not apologize for it." Harvey winked, then stepped past her to look out the back window. "The consensus is it is going to rain."

Dorthia noted the sun coming through the window. "Consensus?"

"Three cases of rheumatoid, one case of gout, and Mrs. Winter's hip."

"Spoken like a true country doctor," Dorthia teased.

"A good country doctor," Harvey said, turning from the window, "knows a medical degree only goes so far. One gets that many cases of aches and pains in a single day, and he can be certain there's going to be a storm."

Dorthia giggled. "Who am I to argue with Mrs. Winter's hip?"

Harvey bobbed his head. "Exactly."

"Is that why you walked her down the stairs?"

"Partly. Plus, she wanted to pay me and needed help carrying it to the buggy."

Dorthia knew this meant the woman had not paid her bill with cash money. "Let me guess, another chicken?"

"Nope, today, she paid with three quarts of white bean soup and a batch of fresh cornbread. I put everything in the back of the buggy. Perhaps that would be sufficient for tonight's supper."

"Bless that woman."

"There are only a few more appointments. Why don't you go home early?"

"Are you sure?"

"Mama!" Susie called from the other room.

Dorthia sighed. "Miss Busy Bee is awake."

He followed her to the back room. "I'm sure. Put your feet up and read a little. Doctor's orders," he said before she could object.

Dr. Baxter sat in a chair, peering out the window. He looked up when they entered. "Bout time you come to spring her from that jail."

Dorthia bent and plucked Susie out of the wooden corral. While her father-in-law insisted it was a jail, she loved having someplace to keep Susie contained when she was needed to help Harvey with a procedure. The fact that Susie didn't seem to mind sitting in the baby cage playing with her toys was a bonus.

"Thanks for keeping her company, Pop," Harvey replied. "Dottie is going home. I'm going to help hitch the buggy. Do you want to walk with us?"

The man waved them off. "I haven't lost anything in town."

"Okay, Pop. I'll be back soon. Don't operate on anyone while I'm gone." Harvey hesitated as if waiting for him to answer, then followed her from the room when he did not. "School lets out in twenty minutes. Perhaps you could pick up the boys so they don't have to walk home."

It wasn't like Harvey to coddle the boys. Having been on their own until she joined their family, it was not uncommon for them to walk home from school, where they'd go right to work on their chores. Having lived on the street for most of her childhood, Dorthia relished the fact that not only did the boys attend a proper school, but they also had a home to return to at the end of the day and food to fill their bellies at night. "You're right, it wouldn't be good letting them walk home in all this sunshine."

"Oh, ye of little faith. I'm telling you, Mrs. Winter's hip never lies." He held out his arms to Susie, who eagerly accepted the invitation. "I've got a few minutes before my next appointment. I'll walk you to the livery."

Dorthia followed him from the office, grateful when he stopped at the top of the stairs so she could hook her arm through his. "You really should have a handrail. Not just for me but for your elderly patients who have to climb these stairs."

"I've been meaning to speak with you about just that thing," Harvey said as they descended the staircase.

Dorthia chuckled. "You don't need my permission to put up a handrail." Actually, as the man of the household, he didn't need her permission to do anything, but she liked that he seemed to value her input.

"I wasn't thinking about a handrail, I was thinking about a house."

"A house?"

"Yes, a big one that we can grow into."

A memory of her father floated to her mind. *Your husband will build you a castle and I'll buy you a crown as a wedding present.* Only he hadn't been there to fulfill that promise. She pushed the memory aside as she recalled their earlier conversation about Mark. It wasn't that she objected to having a larger house, as the one they were in seemed smaller by the day, but she knew how much Mark loved their little farm. "What about Mark? You know he wishes to own the property one day."

"And he shall. We have plenty of property. We will have the house built within sight of the one we have now."

"And what will we do with our current house?" Dorthia asked, being practical.

"That is the beauty of it. We will use our current house to see patients."

Dorthia's heart fluttered. "You mean they will come to us?"

"That's right. Of course, I suppose I will still make the occasional house call."

"What about the patients who live in town?"

Harvey grew quiet for a moment. "While I'd hate to see any of them go, there are three other doctors in town. I'm the only one who has an office on the second floor. In some ways, it would probably be easier for them to make the trek to our house than it would be to climb those back stairs with or without a handrail."

"And your father?"

"We will give him a choice. A ground-floor room in our house, or we could fix him up a room in the new office."

"You mean the house will have more than one floor?"

Harvey chuckled. "Yes, and I promise to give you your handrail."

Dorthia worked to contain her excitement. "Do you think he'll agree?"

"I'm fairly certain I could get him to see the advantages. He used to go for walks. Now all he does is stare out that window all day. I think if I told him he would have a rocking chair where he could sit on the porch and that he could have dinner with the family instead of us delivering his meals to his room, he would jump at the chance."

"I'm not so sure. He's kind of set in his ways," Dorthia said.

"You let me deal with my father. I'll get him to come around."

"If that doesn't work, set Paul to work on him. That boy can convince anyone of anything. You know what he told me today?"

"I can only imagine," Harvey replied.

"He said he was going to invent a machine that looks inside a woman's stomach so we would know if the baby was going to be a girl or a boy. Can you imagine that?" Dorthia laughed a hearty laugh.

"You laugh, but I think there would be a multitude of practical uses for a machine like that."

"Such as?"

Harvey grinned. "To see if there was more than one child. To see if there was anything wrong with the baby."

Dorthia knitted her brows together. "And if there was?"

"Then I would insist the mother deliver the child at a hospital instead of having it at home. I would think a machine like that would save many lives. Paul has a good head on his shoulders. To be honest, I'm disappointed I didn't think of it first."

"He's his father's son," Dorthia told him. "Besides, he merely wanted the machine to determine the sex; you are the one who made note of its practical uses."

"Yes, well, be that as it may, I don't foresee a machine like that being invented within the span of our lifetime and certainly not by a country doctor," he declared as they reached the livery.

Old Man Barnes came out of the livery barn leading Lulu. To their surprise, the man had already hooked her up to the buggy.

Dorthia looked at Harvey, who shook his head, then turned her question to Barnes. "How did you know I would be leaving early?"

Barnes smiled a toothy smile. "I done seen you two heading

this way. I figured you'd be wanting to get the young'un home before the storm's upon us."

Dorthia frowned. "How is it everyone in this town knows it's going to rain but me?"

Barnes slapped a hand on Lulu's neck to swat a fly. "There are signs if you know how to look for them."

"Like Mrs. Winter's hip?"

Barnes bobbed his head. "Yes'um, that'd be one of them. Me? I just look for the flies."

"Flies?"

"Yes'um, there are always flies, this here being a livery and all. But on days when it's going to come up a bad cloud, it seems as every fly in the county be coming and looking for a place to hang out until the rain passes. You keep an eye on the flies and you'll know." Barnes nodded his head. "Going to be a bad one."

Harvey looked to the sky. "It's awfully late in the year for anything too severe."

"I'd agree, if not for the flies. You get this many flies looking for shelter, and the rains are going to be coming down in buckets. Wouldn't be surprised to see a whirly spout."

Dorthia rubbed her arms. While she'd heard of tornadoes, she'd never seen one. "Really?"

"Not saying for sure, but my gut tells me there's more to it than a simple storm."

Harvey took the reins from Barnes and shot Dorthia a worried look. "Perhaps you should take the machine instead."

"Nonsense," Dorthia told him. "Look at the sky. We'll be home and settled before the rain starts."

Harvey checked the sky once more before nodding his agreement.

"You see the clouds turning green, you have Mark open the gate to the corral so that the mother cow and calf aren't blocked in there. This here mare too," Barnes told her.

"Turn them loose? Won't they run away?"

"That they will. That heifer won't let anything happen to that calf. Given the chance, she'll lead it away from the storm." Barnes waggled a finger toward Lulu. "That mare will likely follow."

Harvey nodded his agreement. "Mark knows how to follow

their tracks. He'll be able to find them once the storm has passed."

"Okay," Dorthia agreed. Though all this talk about tornadoes and turning the animals loose made her nervous, she tried not to show it. "Go, look after your patients. I'll see to the children."

Harvey wrapped his arm around her. Susie giggled at being included in the hug. "I'll be home as soon as I can." He offered Dorthia his hand.

Dorthia was grateful for the dropdown step as she heaved herself into the buggy and avoided Harvey's gaze when the carriage creaked as she sat. Harvey handed her Susie. Dorthia settled Susie on her lap as best she could, then tied the child in place with a long strip of leather she kept in the buggy for that purpose. The tethering method wasn't perfect, especially with Dorthia's ever-expanding girth, but it kept the inquisitive child from toppling out of the buggy.

Dorthia sighed. "If I get any bigger, I'm going to have to get a longer tether."

"Untie her when you get to the school and let Mark drive the buggy home," Harvey said.

"I'll manage just fine." Dorthia snapped the reins to get the horse moving. While she knew he was trying to help, that he actually thought she hadn't already thought of that irritated her. Halfway down the street, she realized she'd been on edge from earlier thoughts of her father and regretted her tone. She tugged on the left rein, thinking to go back and apologize.

Harvey wasn't in sight.

Not willing to trudge up the back stairs to give an apology that could wait until Harvey got home, she pulled the reins once again, and gave the horse its lead.

***

Not wishing to make Susie wait until Harvey got home, Dorthia fed her early. She'd just gotten her cleaned up when she heard the boys arguing. She lifted Susie to her hip and went in search of them, surprised to find them kneeling on her bed, looking at a book. "What's got you two so riled?"

"We're not arguing," Paul told her. "We just ain't seeing eye to eye."

"It sounded like arguing to me. What's that you're looking at?"

Paul showed her the book, which turned out to be a Sears and Roebuck House Catalog. Dorthia was well aware of the catalog as she'd thumbed through it more than once while at Becky's. The catalog offered a multitude of floor plans and guaranteed the price would include everything to build a completed house, from the lumber to the nails and paint. They even offered payment plans for those who wished to live beyond their means. Once purchased, the house would arrive by train and, if necessary, be hauled to your location via a horse or mule team.

While Becky had a perfectly suitable house, the woman always seemed to long for more. Dorthia didn't blame her, as she knew in her heart that she, too, would have been the same way if life hadn't intervened and shown her that family was more important than substance.

"There was a note that said pick one, so Mark and I were just trying to decide which one we liked," Paul told her.

"A note?"

"Yep." Paul held up a slip of paper. "See!"

Dorthia glanced at the note. "That is your father's handwriting. Where'd you get the book?"

"It was in the back of the buggy," Paul replied. "I found it when you asked me to bring in the beans. We thought someone was fooling us on account of we already have a house. Do you really think Dad wants us to pick one?"

Dorthia shifted Susie to the opposite hip. "He mentioned it today, but I wasn't sure he was serious."

Mark scowled as he slid from the bed.

"Mark, where are you going?" Dorthia said, noting the boy's sudden change in demeanor.

"I forgot to give Lulu fresh water." He left the room before she could stop him. A moment later, she heard the door slam shut.

Dorthia handed Susie to Paul. "Keep an eye on your sister while I have a word with your brother."

The moment she stepped outside, she noticed the air had a different feel. She looked to the sky, saw a ledge of dark clouds in the distance, and sent up a prayer that Harvey would make it home before the rain hit. "Rain's a coming. Don't either of you stray too far from the house," she said when Paul stepped outside holding Susie.

"I'm just going to show Susie the chickens," Paul replied.

"Stay within eyesight of the house," Dorthia said firmly.

Paul's shoulders slumped. "Yes, ma'am."

"I'm going to the barn. You tell me if the sky turns green."

Paul laughed at the prospect. "Green?"

"Just tell me," Dorthia glanced toward the well. Not seeing Mark, she cradled her stomach and hurried toward the barn. It was dark inside, the only light coming from the cracks between the wood. "Mark?"

There was no answer.

"Mark, if you're in here, answer me."

She heard a rustling sound and then breathed a sigh of relief when Mark peeked over the top of the loft. "I'd like to talk to you."

"So talk."

"I've had a long day and do not feel like shouting. So you either need to come down here or I'm coming up there."

"I've had a long day too. I think I'll just rest here a bit. You're too big to climb the ladder, so we'll talk when I come down," he said, calling her bluff.

Dorthia stomped the edge of the loft and gripped hold of the ladder rung. "We'll see who's too fat to climb a ladder."

Boyish giggles filled the air as Dorthia placed a foot on the bottom rung. Four steps later, Dorthia began to rethink her decision. She froze, unable to move.

"I told you that you're too big," Mark taunted.

"You're right." Dorthia's voice shook as she spoke. "I don't think this climbing is good for the baby."

The giggles stopped. Mark peeked over the side of the loft, his eyes round. "Is there something wrong with the baby?"

"No. The baby is fine. I just can't seem to move."

"Why not? Are you hurt?" There was a touch of panic in the boy's voice, which calmed her enough to realize he was recalling his mother's death. Instantly, she regretted her decision to climb the ladder.

"It's okay, Mark. I just can't bring myself to let go so I can climb back down."

"Sure you can. Just take your foot and lower it to the next rung," Mark urged.

While she wanted nothing more than to do as he said, her body wouldn't cooperate. "No, I can't. I'm too scared."

Mark turned and started down the ladder. When he got halfway down, he jumped.

"What are you doing?!"

"It's okay, I do it all the time," he said, brushing off his pants. He took hold of Dorthia's right foot.

Dorthia stiffened. "What are you doing?"

"Helping you down. Let me move your foot."

Dorthia allowed him to guide her foot to the lower rung. As soon as the foot was settled, Mark took hold of the other one, switching off until he'd safely guided her to the ground. She took a deep breath to calm her nerves. "Thank you."

The boy frowned. "Aren't you going to yell at me?"

"No, I think I feel more grateful to you for rescuing me than angry at you for making me climb up there. Your father, on the other hand, might not be as forgiving."

Mark's mouth dropped open. "You mean you're going to tell him?"

She nodded. "I'm afraid I'm going to have to."

"Why?"

"Because you didn't listen to me. What if the others had seen you disrespecting me like that and thought, *Well, if Mark can get away with it, then I can too*? There will soon be four of you. How would it be if you all were to act like that?"

Mark sighed. "I guess it wouldn't be good at all."

"No, it wouldn't." Dorthia softened her tone and messed his hair with her hand. "While I do have to tell him, I promise to make sure he knows that you saved me in the end."

"Mother!" Paul's voice was full of awe. "Come quick. The sky is green!"

# Chapter Thirty-One

Mark raced from the barn as Dorthia followed at a somewhat slower pace. Her breath caught upon seeing the sky, which was indeed an eerie shade of green.

Paul stood gaping at the sky, while Susie struggled to get down. "That's going to be some storm," he said as Dorthia reached for Susie.

While she didn't wish to alarm the boys, she didn't want to play down the danger. "Mr. Barnes said if the sky turned green, to watch for a tornado."

"Should we go to the root cellar?" Paul asked without taking his eyes off the sky.

Unlike some homes in the area, their root cellar was an add-on that butted up against the back of the house, with a set of wooden stairs hidden under the back porch steps. It was the size of a large closet with shelves along the walls. Built underground, the storage remained at a constant temperature and was the perfect place to store fruits, vegetables, and dry goods to maximize freshness. It was also a safe place for the family to ride out the storm.

"Not yet. We'll see it coming before it gets here," Mark said, then turned to Dorthia. "Get the kerosene lamp and matches ready."

"What are you going to do?"

"Paul and I are going to watch the sky. If we see a funnel, we'll let you know."

"Maybe you should open the gate to the corral," Dorthia suggested.

Mark shook his head. "Nah, not unless we see a funnel. I don't want to have to chase that momma cow unless I have to."

Having no experience with tornadoes, and chiding herself for not being proactive in learning what to do, Dorthia decided to let Mark take the lead. While she was ready to bite her nails, Mark seemed to have everything under control. She nodded her agreement, then hurried to the house. She put Susie on the rug and set to work gathering supplies, knowing she should have done so sooner. She'd been tired when she arrived home, her only thought to feed Susie before the child got cranky. Dorthia checked the lamp and was pleased to find it was full. She retrieved a small blanket and string with dried gourds that Susie liked to play with as well. She looked at the rug.

Susie was gone.

"Susie!" There was no answer, only an increasing panic at thinking the child had picked the worst possible moment to have wandered off. A quick search of the two adjoining rooms proved futile. Dorthia rushed back to the main room, saw that the door was still closed, and pushed back the panic. "Susie," she called with a voice that sounded much too calm for the situation.

Giggles filled the air as Susie peeked her head around a chair.

Dorthia scooped her up, holding her tight. "You scared Momma."

Susie placed her hands on Dorthia's shoulders and arched her back. "Momma, no. Down."

Dorthia settled the child on her hip and handed her the string of gourds. As she did, the wind pushed through the cracks of the house in a most eerie tune. Okay, enough of this; it was time to get to the root cellar. She placed the matches and striker box into her pocket and plucked the kerosene lamp from the table.

She opened the front door to an eerie darkness, and though the air was dry, she could smell the rain. "Oh, God, please keep my family safe," she said as the first raindrop hit her face.

"Boys! We've waited long enough." Her voice was firm so as not to leave room for argument. "Paul, help me with the steps. We are all going to the cellar."

She half expected Mark to argue. Instead, he nodded his head and took off running toward the corral.

"I'm going to open the gate," he called over his shoulder.

Dorthia started to tell him there wasn't any time, but the wind was so loud, she didn't think he would hear her. "He'll be okay," she said to calm herself as well as Paul, who looked ready to run off after the boy. "Please, Paul, I need your help."

Paul gave his brother one last long look, then hurried toward the back of the house. Once there, he pulled up the stairs to expose the hidden staircase.

Dorthia handed him the lamp, then motioned him into the cellar. "Hurry, and I'll hand you Susie."

"No." Paul reached for his sister as the sprinkles turned to large drops. "You first. Hurry."

Arguing was futile as the boy was right; her stomach was too big to bend that far. Reluctantly, she handed over Susie, then picked her way down the steep stairs as fast as she dared, as the steep steps were obviously not built with a pregnant woman in mind. Once at the bottom, she reached for Susie, set the child on the dirt ground, then took the lamp from Paul.

She lit it and hung it on the hook, then looked up, expecting to see Paul.

He wasn't there!

"Paul!" Dorthia held her breath, her panic rising.

Susie pulled on the hem of her dress. "Up!"

"Just a minute, baby." Dorthia peered toward the opening as the rain splattered against her face.

"UP!" Susie insisted.

Tears welled in Dorthia's eyes as she continued to peer out at the opening, mindless of the rain. The boys were gone, and it was all her fault. She should have insisted on the four of them going to the cellar sooner. Mark had been so insistent that it never dawned on her to question whether or not he knew what he was doing. Just because she'd lived on the streets as a child didn't mean the boys were as adept at judging danger.

Susie's cries pulled her back to what she could control. Dorthia stooped to pick up the child and hugged her close. Susie continued to sob, but didn't try to turn away.

She heard shouting and looked to see Paul running down the steep steps like only a boy could. Before she could ask him where he'd gone, Mark followed, carrying a heavy quilt.

Mark tossed the quilt to Paul and climbed the ladder once more to close the opening.

Then all was quiet.

Dorthia covered her mouth with a trembling hand. "I thought the storm had carried you both away," she said at last.

Paul grinned. "I couldn't see Mark, so I went to find him."

"I didn't need any help. I just went to get a blanket because I didn't want you catching a cold. You being with baby and all."

"Mark brought the blanket, and I brought this!" Paul grinned and pulled the Sears catalog from the waist of his pants.

Dorthia was incredulous. "You risked your life for a magazine?"

"Naw. I went to find Mark and saw this book. I figured it would keep our minds off the funnel cloud. I was going to bring the apple pie, but it wouldn't fit in my pants, and I didn't have time to figure out how to cover it."

Dorthia wanted to scream at them both to let them know how worried she'd been, but there would be time for that later. "Did you see a funnel?"

Both boys bobbed their heads and a chill raced up her arms.

Paul looked to the ceiling. "Do you think Papa's okay?"

"I think your father has the good sense to get in out of the weather at the first sign of the storm," Dorthia said, hoping it were true. She felt Susie shiver then realized she, too, was cold. The boys were soaked. It wouldn't be long before they also caught a chill. While she was angry at Mark for not coming straight to the cellar as promised, she was grateful the boy had the foresight to grab the quilt. She lifted the lamp from the nail and used it to find the best spot to wait out the storm. There was a pallet in the corner with several baskets of potatoes. "Boys, do you think you're strong enough to move those potatoes?"

Mark and Paul each strained to lift a basket.

"No, one at a time, both take an end."

"It worked." While still heavy, their combined strength was enough to lift the baskets off the pallet. They continued until they'd succeeded in moving three more baskets of potatoes, two bushels of apples and a basket of squash off the pallets.

Dorthia smiled. While tight, it would be enough room for them all. She handed Paul the small blanket she'd brought. "Spread it out and we'll all sit on it."

"Do you think you can get down there?" Paul asked, being practical.

Dorthia chuckled. "Getting down there will be easier than getting up." Oh well, she'd deal with that problem when the time came. She hung the lamp on the closest hook and handed Susie to Paul before clumsily lowering onto the pallet.

Mark snickered.

"What's so funny?"

"You remind me of the cow when she was heavy with calf," he replied then cringed as if waiting to be scolded.

Ignoring the remark, she reached for Susie.

The boys exchanged a glance. "You're not mad?" Paul asked.

"No sense getting mad at something that's true. Now both of you get down here before you catch your death of cold and bring that quilt."

Though the outside had gotten wet, the inside of the quilt was still dry. Paul and Mark sat on either side of her and helped pull the quilt up around them. Susie seemed content to sit under the quilt, playing with the string of gourds.

"What about the book?" Paul started to get up, and Dorthia stopped him.

"How about we keep our arms under the quilt for a bit."

"Good. I don't want to look at no houses anyhow," Mark agreed.

Dorthia realized this would be a good chance for a discussion, as the boy would not be able to run off. "You ran off before we could talk about things," she said, echoing her thoughts.

"What's to discuss? We ain't selling the farm," Mark

replied.

"You're right, your father isn't selling."

"You mean he was joshing about the new house?" Mark asked.

"I don't believe that!" Paul said heatedly. "Papa wouldn't joke like that."

"Your father wasn't joking. Nor are we selling the farm. Your father plans to have the house built within sight of this house."

"He does?" Mark's voice was lighter.

"Yes, he plans to work from home and use our current house as his medical practice."

"Does that mean if I become a doctor, I get to have the farm?" Paul asked.

"No," Dorthia said before Mark could pivot out of control. "I suppose we will have to find a solution."

"What solution?" Mark asked.

"One that makes everyone happy," Dorthia told him.

"I'll be happy to inherit the farm," Mark said.

"And I want to inherit Papa's practice."

"When I was your age, it never occurred to me to think about what I would want if my father died. After he was gone," Dorthia said softly, "I would have been happy to have my father alive."

The boys grew quiet.

"You know, there is a solution," Dorthia said after a moment.

"What?" both boys said at once.

"Your father said he wants a large house with enough bedrooms to grow into. If you were to share the property, then you could share the house."

"What if our wives don't want to share a house?" Paul asked.

"You could split the house," Dorthia told them.

Mark wrinkled his nose. "You can't cut a house in two."

"No, but you could separate it. I saw a house like that before. It looked like a single house on the outside, except it had two front doors. There was a wall right down the middle so that even though it was a single house, there were two families living inside. If you did that here, then you could both share the work on the farm."

"I don't really want to work on the farm," Paul told her.

"Then don't. Once you grow up and become a doctor, then you will have the money to pay Mark to do your share."

"You mean he would do all the work and I would get to eat what he grows?"

"Sure, as long as you two set rules you both can agree with."

"Then it's settled," Mark's voice was cheerful once more. "I'll grow the food and you can pay me to eat it."

"Deal," Paul said.

Mark spat in his hand, and both boys shook on it. "The wind has died down. Can we open the door?"

"Not just yet. I would feel better if we wait here for your father to rescue us." Dorthia's response was two-fold. Not only did she want to wait for Harvey, she also knew she would not be able to rise from the pallet without Harvey's help.

"Do you think Papa is okay?" Paul asked after a moment.

"I do."

"Will you still take care of us if he's not?"

"Of course I will. That is what family does," Dorthia promised.

"Why didn't your family take care of you after your father died?" Paul asked.

While she'd told them bits about her past, she had spared them most of the details. "I was seven." Even though the boys were nine, Dorthia's heart clenched at the thought of them being sent out into the world without a soul to help them. While she thought Mark would somehow find his way, she wasn't so sure about Paul, who seemed a bit more sensitive. "We were in Germany, and I didn't know how to contact them."

"Germany? You were in the war?" Mark's voice was full of wonder.

"No, I managed to leave before it started."

"How did you leave?"

"I met a family there who let me travel with them when they came to America," Dorthia said, sparing them the details.

"That was nice of them," Paul said.

"If they were so nice, why didn't you stay with them?" Mark

asked.

Dorthia struggled with how much to tell them. While she didn't mind telling them of her story, she wanted them to be old enough to know she didn't have a choice in what she had to do to survive. She decided to say just enough to satisfy their curiosity. "While the mother and her daughters were kind, the father was not, so I chose not to stay with them."

"I wish he had been nice to you so you could have had a family," Paul told her.

Mark nodded his agreement.

"So do I," Dorthia said softly.

"But if you had, you might not have come here," Paul said.

"You're right," Dorthia agreed.

"I'm glad you're our new mother." It was Paul who spoke. "Only I don't like calling you Mother Dottie."

"The kids make fun of us for calling you that," Mark agreed.

"Would you like me or your father to talk to them and explain?"

The boys exchanged a glance.

"What is it?" Dorthia pressed.

Mark glanced at Paul, who nodded his agreement. "Paul and I would like to call you Mom on account of you're our new mom. But we don't want our old mom to get mad."

"I don't think she can get mad on account of she's dead," Paul interjected. "Mark's not so sure."

Dorthia was glad for the dimness of the room, as the boys wouldn't be distracted by her tears. When she spoke, she worked to keep her voice steady. "I've thought about this a lot, as I've spent a great deal of my life wishing someone would adopt me. When I lived in the children's home, people would sometimes come through looking for a child. I often found myself looking at them and wondering what it would be like if they were my parents. I don't think my father would have been upset. Actually, I think the opposite would have been true, as I truly believe he would have been happy to know I had someone who loved me."

"Does that mean you love us?" Mark asked.

Dorthia nodded. "I love you both very much."

"But it's not the same as how you love Susie," Paul said.

"I think it may seem as though I love her more because she needs the most care. That will change when the baby comes, as then he will need the most care." Dorthia took a moment to gather her thoughts. "I think all love is different. For instance, I know your father loves me, but it's not the same as the love he felt for your mother. She was his first love, and there is a special place in his heart for her. It is the same with both you and Mark."

Dorthia wrapped an arm around each of the boys. "No matter how many children I have, I loved both of you first, and you will always have a special place in my heart."

"Mom," Mark said, using the new title for the first time. "Was the children's home scary?"

"Some thought so."

"Not you?"

"No. I rather liked the place." Dorthia thought back to her first day at the asylum. "Mary, she was one of the girls there, was surprised I didn't cry. She said it was rare that kids didn't cry on their first night. She didn't know it, but I did cry. Only they were happy tears because I felt safe."

"Was Mary your friend?"

"Mary was everyone's friend." Dorthia wondered, not for the first time, what had become of the girl who was more like a mother to most of the girls in the asylum than a friend.

"Mary's a nice name," Paul said.

"It is," Dorthia agreed.

"Did you have any…" Mark's words were interrupted when the door to the cellar opened.

"Dorthia? Are you down there?"

A tremendous weight lifted from Dorthia's shoulders the minute she heard Harvey's voice.

"Papa!" Paul and Mark said, scrambling out from under the quilt.

"Papa!" Susie repeated, pushing at the quilt.

Dorthia removed the quilt and handed Susie to Paul.

Harvey gave the child a hug, then handed her back to her brother as he turned his attention to Dorthia.

She soaked in his image. "I sure was worried about you."

"I'm here!" he said, offering her both hands.

"The tornado?" she asked as she struggled to get up.

"A little damage, nothing too severe."

"Any issues here I should know about?"

Mark's face went slack.

"No, the boys were perfect angels," Dorthia told him.

Mark's jaw dropped. "Mom, I thought you were going to tell him…"

"That's right. The boys have decided they want a house with two front doors." Dorthia looked to Mark. "You'd better go see about the livestock before they go too far."

Mark shot her a grateful look as he stooped to pick up the Sears catalog, and plucked the lantern from the hook. "Thanks, Mom," he said, then ran up the stairs.

"Mom?" Harvey studied at Dorthia as if to gauge her reaction.

"We had a breakthrough."

"Good," Harvey said, bobbing his head. "Now what's this nonsense about a house with two front doors?"

"I'll explain later," Dorthia told him. "But while we're talking about houses, I've added a basement with an indoor cellar to my wish list."

"Done," Harvey agreed.

"And," Dorthia said, placing her hands on her stomach. "If the baby is a girl, I'd like to name her Mary."

"Mary, it is," Harvey said, pulling her into his arms.

# Chapter Thirty-Two

Emily practically floated into the room, brandishing a slender box. "Grandma, I have something for you."

Dorthia eyed the box. "Well, it must be something, the way you're waving it around."

"It's a DNA test."

"What's it for?"

"To help us find your family."

"I know where my family is. Let's see, it's Monday. Paul is in California, probably getting ready to operate on someone as we speak. Susie is working the dayshift at the hospital. Mathew and Mary are both teaching at the high school. Mark is where he always is, married to the farm. Your granddad, God rest his soul, has been buried in the family plot down at the cemetery since 2010." Dorthia looked to the ceiling. "And Jed is somewhere up there testing his wings."

Emily laughed. "Stop sounding so morbid. Just because you don't like dad being a pilot doesn't mean he's not good at it. Besides, I'm talking about your other family. Grandpa Smith's family."

Dorthia waved her off. "I gave up looking for them ages

ago. Besides, I've given enough blood."

"This isn't a blood test; it is a saliva test," Emily said, peeling open the box. She pulled out a little tube and offered it to Dorthia. "Please, Grandma, do it for me. All you have to do is spit in this, and I'll do the rest."

Dorthia worked up some saliva and spit it into the tube. "There."

Emily peered at the container. "We'll need more. You have to get the liquid up to that little line."

Dorthia worked her jaw, repeating the process several more times before filling up the tube. "Now what? Do you put that in a computer or something?"

"Sort of." Emily replaced the lid and shook the tube. "I will put it in this mailer and then send it back. When the lab is done processing, the results will be uploaded to Ancestry dot com."

"How long does that take?"

"Most of the time, it takes six to eight weeks, but it could take longer if they are busy."

"Oh, for heaven's sake, don't waste your time sending it in. I'll be dead and in the ground by that time."

"Don't say that."

"I'm not saying anything the doctor hasn't said. Besides, it'll be good to see your granddad again. Course I'm not sure Julie will be happy to have me there ruining their reunion."

Emily snickered.

"You laugh, but I'm serious. She's had him long enough. I'm going to boot her off the cloud and take my rightful place beside him."

"I have no doubt of that." Emily placed the tube in the envelope and set it aside. "I'm sending this in. It's not just for you, Grandma. Don't you see, I've been writing down everything you've told me. If you're not here, I'll be able to tell them your story, and even if I never find your family, I can share your story with my children, and they can share it with theirs."

"Okay," Dorthia relented. "I guess there's no harm trying. Are we finished with your interview now?"

"Yes, I think so. I brought you some pears. Do you want one?"

"I suppose." Dorthia took a bite and wrinkled her nose at

the gritty texture.

"What's the matter, Grandma? I thought you liked pears."

"It's gritty." She handed the pear to Emily. "I guess it's just all this talk about the past. I feel as though I'm eating dirt."

Emily turned it to the other side and took a bite. "There's nothing earthy about them. They are super sweet. How could they remind you of dirt?"

"Just an old woman remembering things better left forgotten."

"I'd like to hear your story if you don't mind."

"You've heard of the Dust Bowl?"

Emily nodded. "Of course, everyone has. I read that a lot of people left town because of it. How come you and Gramps never left?"

"Partly because there was nowhere to go and mostly because we were needed here, and ultimately, because while we knew Paul, Susie, the twins and Jed would someday leave the farm, we knew Mark would never leave the land. The Depression didn't touch us at first, but then things trickled down, and the price of wheat made it so farmers couldn't afford to grow crops. Friends, many of whom were your grandfather's patients, were losing their farms by the droves. First, the Depression hit, driving wheat prices down. Then the rain stopped. We hadn't had more than a few drops of rain in going on four years when that storm hit. Black Sunday, they called it. I don't know if it was as much because the sky was so dark or because the storm was the final nail in the coffin for so many."

***

*April 14, 1935*

"Are you sure you don't want a ride home?" Harvey asked when they exited the church.

"You go and check on Mrs. Winters," she said, speaking of the woman who had not found her way to church that day. "I promised the kids we would stay for the picnic."

Harvey planted a kiss on her cheek. "Mark's going to ride with me so he can tend to his livestock. I'll drop him off on my way."

"Okay. Susie, Mary, Mathew and Jed can walk home with

me. I suppose Paul will be staying as well," Dorthia said and gave a nod to where Paul was standing, talking to Sara, an orphan girl who'd moved in with Becky and William after her parents died of influenza. Becky had never had a daughter of her own, and though there were only thirteen years between them, Sara had quickly filled that void. Becky wasn't the only heart the girl had captured, as Paul couldn't stop talking about her.

Harvey sighed. "I've seen that look before. Better keep an eye on those two."

Dorthia laughed. "From the way Paul talks, I would expect him to ask her to marry him soon." Though Dorthia knew Harvey wanted Paul to wait until after he went to medical school, she knew Paul enough to know he would not be able to hold out that long. The boy had eyes and knew a medical diploma wouldn't change anything for a country doctor. The boy was right. Aside from Harvey's patients who worked in the drilling fields, times were so tough that most didn't pay with paper money these days. Instead, the majority of his patients paid with whatever they had. For some, it was eggs, milk, cheese, and preserves. Occasionally, they would receive gold, by the way of whatever vegetables could be coaxed up from the brittle soil.

Those were welcomed luxuries, as it was a constant battle to keep the jackrabbits from getting to them first. While she'd been fascinated by the long-eared creatures at first, she'd seen firsthand what damage they could do and knew their ferocious appetites had caused way too many people to lose their farms when the animals had hopped in in droves and stripped the land of every last blade of grass. It was getting so bad that farmers had taken to organizing huge drives in which hundreds of men, women, and children would force the hares into makeshift enclosures and do away with them. Dorthia had witnessed one such roundup, and even though she didn't care for them, it had traumatized her so that she'd woken in the middle of the night hearing the rabbits' screams. As such, she declared that while she wanted them gone, she never wished to witness that again.

"He should wait until after he finishes medical school. At least then he'll have a way to support her," Harvey said, pulling her from her musings.

"Don't worry, if they get too cozy, I'll send Jed over," she said, speaking of her and Harvey's precocious three-year-old son, a headstrong child who had a knack for getting himself into trouble.

Harvey glanced at Jed, who was currently sitting just at the edge of the quilt, eating a cake of dirt. "I think it would suffice to merely threaten to send the boy over."

Dorthia laughed. "You're probably right."

"Mark," Harvey called as he started for the motorcar. "Time to go."

***

Dorthia spent the next couple of hours reading and stopping for the occasional peek at the young love birds and to fuss at Jed for one thing or another. His latest escapade was chasing after a jackrabbit that had raced onto the quilt. Dorthia was surprised to see it so close to people, then realized there were others hopping around as if in a panic. Odd, but then again, they were jackrabbits, and nothing they did made sense. It was close to two when Jed pointed to the sky and uttered the sentence that made her blood run cold. "Look, Momma, the sky is red."

The shelf cloud was massive, but it could be seen from a far distance and this one looked to be quite a ways away. "Paul, get the kids. We've got a dust storm heading this way."

They'd been in enough dust storms that Paul knew the urgency of the matter. He was up and running in an instant, gathering his siblings and warning everyone of the incoming storm.

Dorthia peered at the sky, trying to gauge the distance of the cloud.

"I think we have time to get home," Paul said, coming up beside her. "Besides, if Mark sees it, he'll meet us with the buggy."

Paul was right. Mark would come looking for them. It would be best if he found them because he wouldn't seek shelter for himself until he did. "Okay, we're going home. But we stay on the road. No shortcuts, or we could miss both Mark and your father if he decides to come looking for us," Dorthia told them.

Paul bent and started wadding the quilt. "Take the quilt or

leave it? It's heavy and might slow us down."

"It could also save our lives if we've misjudged how fast the storm's moving. Where's Sara?"

"She's letting the preacher know she's coming with us in case Becky calls. He asked if we wanted to go to his house, but I told him we needed to get home." Paul shrugged. "I'm worried about Mark. The preacher lives a mile in the opposite direction of our house."

Dorthia saw Sara running toward them and reached for the quilt.

"I've got it," Paul told her.

"No, you carry Jed. It will be quicker."

Mathew took the quilt from her. "I've got this." Unlike his twin sister Mary, Mathew was small for his age, and though he'd try, Dorthia doubted he'd make it all the way home without needing a break from the heavy quilt.

Dorthia nodded her agreement. "We'll switch off. Everyone, let's go."

Susie and Mary started running.

"Girls, stay with us. I don't want to have to go searching for you if things get ugly."

They were halfway home when the wind picked up, and Dorthia instantly regretted her decision. There was no turning back, so they kept pushing forward. They'd gone another quarter of a mile when Mark appeared through the cloud of dust with Grace attached to the wagon he used for hauling in wheat.

Mark pulled the reins, slowing to a stop. "It's coming, and it's a bad one." He jumped down, and placed a pillowcase with tiny slats for holes over Grace's head.

Dorthia had seen him do that before during storms, but not when the horse was hooked to a wagon. "Do you think it will work?"

"She's used to wearing it to keep away the flies. She won't mind it now," Mark said, petting the sturdy horse to calm her while Paul helped everyone into the back of the wagon.

Dorthia spread the quilt to cover them.

"You get under too," Paul insisted.

"No, I'll help Mark watch the road," Dorthia told him.

"I'll help Mark. You get in there; the kids need you."

"The horse knows the way. All I have to do is give Grace her lead, she'll head to the barn."

Dorthia looked at them in turn. "Are you sure?"

"We're not going to find out if we stand here arguing about it." Mark's voice held an edge. "Please, Mom, let me do my job."

Dorthia nodded her agreement and climbed over the buckboard to the back of the wagon. As she was ducking under the quilt, she saw Mark hand Paul a pillowcase before slipping one over his own head. A second later, the wagon was in motion.

Several times along the way, the wagon came to a halt, then after a moment or two of bouncing, it started to move once again. The wind roared around them, threatening to pull the quilt free. It reminded her of the time they spent the evening in the cellar waiting out the tornado. There had been other trips to the cellar over the years, but that one was the most memorable, as it was when the boys officially accepted her as their mother.

Dorthia tucked the quilt under her knees and wrapped her arms around Jed. She sent Sara and the girls a look which she hoped assured them everything would be okay and sent up a prayer asking to help them make it home and to keep Harvey safe.

The wagon stopped. A moment later, Paul tugged on the quilt. "We're home."

Dorthia lifted the quilt and was surprised to find the horse had guided them into the barn. She looked at Sara. "Keep the kids under the quilt until it's time to go inside."

"I left the doors open to save time," Mark said. As he jumped down from the wagon, his feet disappeared into a mound of red dirt.

That the storm hadn't passed surprised her even more and she wondered what kind of mess she would find inside the house. She thought of Harvey and was glad he had taken the motorcar, as she wouldn't be able to stand it if she knew he was in the buggy. She pushed aside her panic. Harvey could take care of himself; she needed to get the kids inside. "We need to get everyone in the house."

"You go ahead. I need to see to Grace," Mark said, patting the work horse, who glistened with sweat even though the wind had cooled significantly since they'd left town.

He was right, but she didn't welcome the thought of splitting up when the dust storm didn't show any sign of stopping. "I don't like you being out here all alone."

"I'll be okay. I put the guide rope up before I left. I strung one to Pop's office as well." Mark said, speaking of the thick ropes they often used in the winter to allow safe passage from the house to the barn. Since they were also used when the dust hit, Harvey had insisted hooks were in place so they could be stretched in place at a moment's notice. As Mark ran to the back of the barn, Dorthia silently commended the boy for thinking to put them in place before leaving.

Paul drew her attention. "Sara will help you get the kids inside. I'll stay and help Mark."

Dorthia gave Paul a suffering look. "Okay, but please don't let him take too long."

A look passed between the boys. "It's okay, Mom, we know what we're doing."

Mark returned with a fist full of empty feed sacks. "Quit worrying; there are enough for everyone," he said, handing them to her.

As Mark turned his attention to the horse, Paul went to the back of the wagon and lifted the quilt. "Okay, everyone out. It's time for an adventure." He helped Sara from the wagon, holding her hands for a few extra seconds before releasing her and helping Mary and Susie down. Mathew jumped down on his own as Paul lifted Jed from the wagon.

Jed blinked in the swirling dust. He rubbed at his eyes and began to cry. "It hurts."

Dorthia slipped the feed sack over the boy's head. "Try not to rub your eyes. I'll rinse them when we get inside."

Paul helped the others cover their head then stooped to tie a thick rope around Jed's waist. He tied the other end to Dorthia's wrist. "You won't be able to carry him in this wind. He can use the guide rope, but this will keep him close if he lets go."

"Thank you." She grabbed Paul's hand, held it for a moment, then released him once more. "Okay, kids, it's time to go inside."

Mathew hesitated. "I want to stay and help Paul and Mark."

"No!" Dorthia said and shot Mark a pleading look.

Mark gave him a look very much like the one Harvey used when he meant business. Then, relaxing his face, he placed his hands on the boy's shoulders. "Paul is going to help me cool the horse, so I need you to step up and be the man for a bit. Even with the rope, it's dangerous out there. I need you to make sure everyone gets to the house safely. Can you do that for me?"

Mathew nodded his agreement.

"Good. Once you have everyone inside, there will be lots to do to keep the dirt out. I want you to listen to Mom and do exactly what she tells you. Okay?"

"I will," Mathew promised.

"Okay, now put this sack over your head."

Mathew frowned. "How can I make sure everyone is okay if I can't see them?"

"It's dark out. You'll not be able to see them either way. Just hold on to the rope and you'll know if anyone isn't following you."

Sara peeked out the window. "It looks like the black of night. I've never known them to last this long."

"The cloud was huge, but it should be letting up soon." Mark gave Dorthia a stern look. "It's time to go."

Dorthia blew out a ragged breath. "Okay, children, we are off to the house. Mathew will be leading the way."

"I'll help you get to the guide rope. Hold hands with the person next to you," Mark said, then walked to each one, took their feed sack and covered their head.

When Mark stopped in front of her, Dorthia gave him a fierce hug. "Promise you won't be gone long."

"Only as long as it takes." He kissed her on the cheek.

Paul stepped forward and met her gaze before wrapping his arms around her. He released her and covered her head. Seconds later, tiny pebbles of dirt blasted her arms as the wind threatened to rip the feed sack from her head. She felt a tug on the rope and knew Mark was leading Jed to the rope. She followed the pull and breathed a sigh of relief when a hand guided hers to the rope. She walked slowly, allowing her hand to inch along the rope. She'd visited the beach once with her father and took great pleasure when walking through the hot sand. Though trudging through the mounds of dirt brought back that memory, there was no joy in the day. No, this was a day filled with foreboding. Dorthia inched her way forward, all the while praying she and her family would live to see another day.

The lead rope connected to Jed went taut and Dorthia knew the boy had fallen. Gripping the rope with her right hand she groped for the boy, found his arm and pulled him back to the rope as they began walking once more.

Moments later, Mathew's words cut through the wind. "We made it to the house!"

Several more steps, and Dorthia was inside. Even before she closed the door, she counted heads to make sure they'd not lost anyone.

They had not.

She hurried to pull the door too, then bent to untie the tether from Jed's waist. After untying it, she wiped the tears from his face with her thumbs, then pulled him into her arms. While she wanted to tell him to stop crying, she knew the tears would help cleanse his eyes. She continued to comfort the boy for another moment before releasing him. Getting to the house was only the beginning; there was still much work to do. "Susie, run to all the rooms and make sure all the windows are closed. Mary, show Sara where we keep the towels and extra linens. Grab everything you can find. We need to cover the windows to keep the dirt from getting in."

"What about me?" Mathew asked.

Dorthia turned to the boy. "You have the most important job of all. Run and get four flashlights from the cupboard. Make sure the batteries work and put one in the window of each side of the house. Put them under the curtains near the glass so they shine through the glass. Keep checking them to make sure they are burning. I want anyone who's out there to be able to see the light from the house."

"What about me?" Jed asked between sobs.

Dorthia pulled a chair around. "I want you to sit here in the chair and don't move."

"But I want a job," Jed wailed.

Dorthia picked him up and sat him in the chair facing the door. She knelt in front of him. "Yours is the most important job."

"You said Mathew had the most important job," Jed reminded her.

Dorthia lowered her voice in a conspiratorial whisper. "Shh, we don't want to upset your brother. Mathew's job is important, but not as important as yours. I want you to watch that door and yell for me the instant Mark, Paul, or your father comes home. Can you do that for me?"

"Sure, I can," Jed said, bobbing his head.

"Good. I'm counting on you. You mustn't leave that chair."

"I won't."

"Don't open the door," Dorthia warned.

Jed gripped the bottom of the chair with his fingers as if to hold himself in place. "I won't."

Dorthia scooped up a feed sack

"Where are you going?" Sara's voice was incredulous.

Dorthia moved away from Jed and lowered her voice. "I'm going to Harvey's office to get some supplies."

"What kind of supplies?"

"Everyone is going to need their eyes washed. We have some jars of distilled water in the office."

"They're on the counter in the kitchen," Sara offered a smile. "There's a note."

Dorthia followed Sara into the kitchen. Sure enough, there was a crate of mason jars filled with water. Sitting next to it was a small box of assorted medical supplies, all of which looked as if they'd been tossed inside in a hurry. She picked up the note and instantly recognized Mark's handwriting.

*Dear Mom, I saw the cloud, and I'm coming to get you and the kids. If by chance I don't find you, please don't come looking for me. I will find my way home. P.S. I closed all the windows and brought in some supplies, so you don't need to go outside. Your loving son, Mark Harvey Baxter.*

Dorthia's hands shook as she folded the note and stuffed it into the pocket of her dress.

"It's not just words. The boys love you." Sara continued before Dorthia could respond. "Paul told me so. It was shortly after I came to live with Becky and William. I was sad on account of I was missing my own mother and father, and Paul must have sensed it because he came up and told me about you. He told me he and Mark were uncertain about you at first."

"Oh?"

"It wasn't that they didn't like you. They were scared you'd go away like their mom did."

"I know that feeling all too well." Dorthia started to tell her that she was still scared of losing her family, and not having the boys and Harvey in the house right now was terrifying. Knowing how much the girl cared for Paul, she decided not to add to her worries. "It's normal to worry about those you care about."

"I feel like I'm going to go mad worrying about Paul," Sara said, wringing her hands. "I don't know why they haven't come in yet."

Dorthia had her own thoughts about why the boys hadn't returned. She knew in her heart they'd gone in search of their father. Though she hadn't voiced her thoughts aloud, she'd seen it in their eyes and knew it was why Paul stayed with Mark instead of seeing Sara safely to the house. The thing was, she didn't blame them, because if not for the children, it was exactly what she would have done.

# Chapter Thirty-Three

"Momma! They're here," Jed called.

Dorthia hurried to where she'd left the boy, expecting to find him in the chair. Instead, Mark and Paul stood in the entryway covered in red dirt. The boys grinned and stepped aside. Also covered with dirt, but standing on his own two feet with Jed clinging to his leg, Harvey managed a weary smile.

Tears of relief sprang to Dorthia's eyes as she hurried to embrace her husband. "Oh, Harvey, I was so worried about you. All of you." She released Harvey and gave Mark and Paul a pointed look.

Footsteps raced down the stairs. "Daddy!" Mathew, Susie, and Mary called in unison.

Sara ran into the room, nearly knocking Paul off his feet, kissing and hugging him mindless of the giggles from the children.

Mark shook his head as he watched Sara making a fuss over Paul. "I've got to get me one of those."

"Where have you been?" Sara scolded. "You've had us all worried sick."

"Or, maybe not." Mark chuckled.

Dorthia hugged herself to stop the trembling waves of excitement at having her family home safe. "What were you boys thinking going out in that storm like that? I don't know whether to hug you or thrash you both for scaring me like that."

"I'd prefer a hug given the choice," Mark told her. "And something to eat."

"There's a stew on the stove. The girls made pies. Kick off your boots and try to leave as much dirt at the door as possible, though I'm not sure it matters since the whole house is full of it. I don't understand how it got in, as we had the windows covered and shoved towels under the doors. Girls, go see to that stew and, for what it's worth, wipe that table again." Dorthia watched Sara and the girls head to the kitchen and offered a shrug. "I've cleaned it twice myself. I walked in after a few moments and could write my name on the thing."

Mathew pulled back the blanket to peek out the window. "I didn't hear you drive up. Where's the Nash?"

"Buried." Harvey smiled at his older sons. "If not for your brothers, I never would have found my way home."

"We couldn't have done it without Grace," Mark said.

"That horse deserves some extra oats," Dorthia told them. "After all she's done for our family this day, we should change her name to Saving Grace."

Harvey wiggled a finger at Mark. "After you eat, you find yourself a rag and clear that dirt from that horse's nose. I'd imagine you'll need to do the same with the cows too. Not just today; it'll take some time for this dust to settle."

"Yes, sir," Mark agreed.

As if just thinking about the dust made him do so, Harvey coughed. "We should probably check our supplies. I imagine we are going to be seeing a lot of patients with lung issues."

"You won't be seeing anyone today," Dorthia said when Harvey swayed and coughed once more. She moved closer to lend him her shoulder. "You can wash up in the deep sink. I don't want you on those stairs or anywhere near your office until after you get some food in your stomach and have a chance to rest."

Harvey reached a hand to hers. "That's pretty good advice. You should think about getting your medical degree."

"I don't need a medical degree to cure what ails you," Dorthia replied. "We've got ice in the icebox and tobacco in case we need to clear your airway. Until this afternoon, I would have said we have clean sheets on the bed, but I think it will be some time before I can make that promise."

Harvey grinned. "You hear that, boys? Your ma's going to have me fixed up good as new in no time."

Dorthia's gaze trailed to the dusty footsteps that trailed off toward the kitchen. "Fixing you is going to be easy. Getting ahead of this dust is going to be another matter altogether."

***

*August 1936*

Dorthia heard the rumble of an automobile and peered through the suds to see a sedan turning into their long driveway. Piled high with what was probably everything they owned, the car left a rooster tail of dust, coating the two vehicles that trailed behind it. She wiped the suds from the window she was washing and dropped the rag into the bucket. "Mary," she called to her daughter. "Run to the house and let your father know someone's coming."

A splash, followed by a giggle, let her know Jed was playing in the water bucket. Dorthia turned to see him whirling the rag around in the sudsy water. "Jed, leave that water alone. You spill it and I'm going to lay my hand alongside your backside."

Knowing the threat wouldn't dissuade the boy once whoever was coming had arrived, she motioned to Mary. "Take your brother with you and keep an eye on him. I swear, left to his own devices, that boy won't reach the age of five."

Most of their patients were in the habit of calling ahead. That it was after hours, and no one had called ahead, let her know it could be an emergency. Then again, since the automobile was loaded to its breaking point, the bigger assumption was that it was someone coming to settle their bill before heading out of town. Some offered them whatever belongings wouldn't fit on the automobile, a few left with the promise of sending money as soon as they found work, and a handful just disappeared into the night without a word of where they were headed or if they expected to return.

"Looks like we're losing another one," Harvey said, coming up behind her.

Dorthia jumped. "Harvey Baxter, between that son of yours and you sneaking up on me, you're going to scare the wits out of me."

Harvey laughed. "Mary told Mathew you said it was his turn to watch the boy."

"Mary is telling tales. I told her to watch him. Either way, one of them better do it on account of that boy can't be left to his own devices. This morning, I caught him poking at a hornet's nest with a stick. The hornets were flying all around madder than all get out when I pulled him away."

"We got lucky with that one."

Dorthia nodded her agreement, knowing he was speaking about the boy being of a single birth. "Mary and Mathew combined were better than that one."

"Yes, well, my mother always said God won't give you more than you can handle."

Dorthia snorted. "She said that because she never had a child like Jed."

"You're probably right." Harvey nodded toward the driveway. "Must be the day for leaving; there are two more right behind this one."

Dorthia followed him outside, her heart sinking when she saw her friend Becky get out of the second car. The woman had been her first real friend and confidante, and that she'd expected her to leave didn't ease the pain of seeing her standing beside the car. "Oh, Harvey, that's Becky and William."

"It was inevitable," Harvey said softly. "Try to be strong, dear. You know this can't be easy on either of them."

Easy for him to say. He was only losing a patient; she was losing her dearest friend who'd become something of a sister to her. The sedan's rear door opened, and the children began filing out. Dorthia's heart sank for a second time when she saw Sara.

The girl pushed the hair from her face. Even from a distance, it was easy to see the girl had been crying, as her eyes were red-rimmed and swollen.

Dorthia sucked in breath. Could it be that the girl was ill and that was why they'd come?

"She's been crying," Harvey said, as if reading her mind.

"Paul's going to be devastated," Dorthia whispered in return.

Harvey stiffened. "Maybe not."

Dorthia gasped as Paul came into view, carrying a large satchel. "Oh, Harvey, no."

"The boy's eighteen. He's old enough to make his own decisions."

"I'm not letting her go without me," Paul said firmly.

Harvey squeezed her hand, then stepped off the porch, following his son to where William was standing next to Sara and the others.

Dorthia stayed in place and narrowed her eyes at her friend. "Why didn't you warn me?"

"I didn't know until today," Becky replied.

Dorthia nodded toward the trailer, which was hitched to the back of the sedan and filled with all their belongings. "You have your whole house in there; don't tell me you didn't know until today."

"I knew we were leaving," Becky corrected. "I didn't know about Sara and Paul. She told us that if you don't let him go, she will stay."

Dorthia stayed firm. "Then let her stay. We have the room."

Tears welled in Becky's eyes. "She's sixteen."

"Exactly. She's old enough to make her own decisions."

"I've already lost two children; please don't make me say goodbye to another?"

Becky's words cut like a knife. Becky's oldest son, William Jr., was killed when he got his arm caught in a thresher machine, and no one was with him at the time. Her second son, Jamie, succumbed to pneumonia a year later. It was the same year Harvey's father had passed, and Dorthia had given birth to a child that did not live to see the light of day. She'd been so caught up in her own sorrow that she hadn't noticed when Becky began taking sips of laudanum to help dull the pain. It had been an ugly two years, but when Sara went to live with them, Becky had found her way out of the darkness.

That same year, Jed made his way into the world. Within

seconds of arriving, the boy was screaming, making it clear to all he was healthy and strong enough to survive whatever life threw at him.

"Oh, Becky." Dorthia's words came out in sobs.

Becky closed the distance and gathered her in her arms. "I promise to take care of him."

"I know you will." Dorthia closed her eyes to squelch the tears. When she opened them, she saw Harvey heading toward Mark, who'd just come out of the barn.

She felt herself begin to tremble, as the boy had seen his share of defeats. It seemed to be a never-ending battle to keep both his farm and animals alive. That didn't stop her from sending up a prayer: *Please don't take them both.*

As if he'd heard her plea, Mark looked in her direction and shook his head. As he disappeared into the barn, she took comfort in the knowledge that she and Harvey would only be losing one son that day.

Paul started in her direction.

"I'll miss you," Becky said, giving her another hug. "I'll let you say your goodbyes."

"It's only temporary," Paul promised.

Dorthia wasn't sure whether either one of them believed it, as while Mark belonged on the farm, Paul always seemed out of place. She forced a smile. "You were meant to see the world."

He blew out a sigh. "I knew you'd understand."

She nodded. "I do, but it doesn't make it hurt any less."

He hugged her, then kissed her on the cheek. "I love you, my mother."

This time, her smile was genuine. "I love you, my son."

Sara joined them. "I'm sorry." The words came out in a whisper.

"Don't be. Just promise you'll be good to him."

"I promise." Sara gave Dorthia a hug, and her shoulders shook as Paul led her away.

Unable to move, Dorthia was still standing in the same spot when Harvey joined her. "I saw you talking to Mark. For a moment, I was afraid he was going to leave with them."

"I wouldn't have stopped him if he'd wanted to go."

"Were you worried he would?"

"Not even for a moment," Harvey told her. "I know you're tired of all of this dirt, but to that boy, this is God's Country."

# Chapter Thirty-Four

Emily crossed out the number and dialed the next.

"Hello?"

"Is this Harold Smith?" While she was certain that was the right name, she was less certain it was the right person, as she'd already spoken with seven Harold Smiths in the last week.

"It is, but I'm not buying anything."

"Please don't hang up. I think we may be related."

"Related how?"

"I'm not sure, actually. But my grandmother's DNA test showed a strong match to your grandmother's. I tracked her down using social media, but she never answered my email, so that's why I'm calling you. Before you ask, I paid a site to get your number. Actually, I've paid for a lot of numbers; yours was the next in a very long line. There are a lot of Harold Smiths in the world."

"Tell me about it." His voice sounded a bit more relaxed now. "What's your grandmother's name?"

"Dottie Baxter."

"Never heard of her. Sorry, lady, you said it yourself, there are a lot of Smiths in the world. Tell your grandmother she's got the wrong one."

"I can't," Emily told him. "My grandmother passed away a couple weeks ago."

"Sorry, lady." His voice sounded more sincere this time.

"Yeah, me too. Thanks anyway," Emily said, disconnecting the phone. She lowered the pen to cross off the name when the phone rang, showing the number she'd just disconnected. "Hello?"

"It's me again," the man said without giving his name. "This grandmother of yours, her given name wouldn't happen to be Dorthia, would it?"

Emily palmed her forehead for not using her grandmother's birth name. "Yes, Dorthia Jean Smith."

"Well, kid, this is your lucky day. My mother lives with us and wanted to know who called. Hang on, she wants to talk to you. She's a bit hard of hearing, so you'll need to speak up."

"Dorthia?"

"No, I'm her granddaughter. My grandmother is dead. My name's Emily."

"Dead. What a pity. When'd she die?"

"A couple weeks ago."

"Weeks? Oh, what a shame. This number, where's it from?"

"Guymon, Oklahoma. Hello," Emily said when the lady didn't comment.

"I'm here. You're saying your grandmother lived in Oklahoma?"

"Yes, ma'am."

"Our Oklahoma, here in the United States?"

"Yes, ma'am."

"We thought she was still in Germany. How long did she live there?"

Any doubts Emily had were gone. "She arrived in 1924 and just passed away a couple weeks ago."

"What a pity," the woman said for the second time. "My mother said they looked for her. She even called the hotel in Germany trying to find them. They would have sent someone, but with the war, it was unsafe. She said the hotel told her their room was paid through the end of the month, but they hadn't returned after the first day."

"My grandmother said someone went back and claimed her things. Did they not call your mother?"

"No, I don't think they did, or my mother would have told me. My mother always wondered what happened to them. She kept a lot of your great-grandfather's things in a trunk. I still have what she kept, including the pocket watch he always carried and a locket with their picture. I think I recall her saying he used to leave the watch at home when he traveled, as he didn't want anything to happen to it. It belonged to his father. I guess it belongs to you now. I wish she were alive so I could tell her."

"Me too," Emily agreed.

"So, what happened? Something had to. The family often speculated they knew the war was coming, so they went into hiding."

"No, Grandma's father was killed right after they arrived. Grandma Dottie saw it happen and ran," Emily said, leaving out the other details.

"Oh, that poor child. How'd she get to Oklahoma?"

"She came to Oklahoma on an orphan train."

"An orphan. But she had family."

"She was only seven with a last name of Smith," Emily reminded her.

The line grew silent for a moment. "How'd she find her way out of Germany?"

"It's a long story."

"I'd love to hear it if you have time."

Emily settled in the chair and opened her notebook. "The year was 1914. Dorthia and her father had just arrived in Germany on a grand adventure…"

# A Note from the Author

I hope you enjoyed *Dorthia's Story*. I got the idea for her storyline from a reader who commented that her great-grandmother came over from Germany as a governess for another family. While the family returned to Germany, her grandmother stayed and was sent west on an Orphan Train.

The storyline seemed fitting for Dorthia. Although Endurance is a standalone book, anyone who has read the previous books in the saga knows Dorthia to have been promiscuous. I felt her story was the perfect way to showcase what young girls had to do to survive living on the streets.

The mention of the fourteen-year-old girl rescued after being locked in a house of ill repute was drawn from a newspaper clipping from the time. The child had been there for years before her rescue.

If you enjoyed this story, I would ask that you tell your friends on help me spread the word on social media. A review—even a few short words—would be most appreciated.

Please follow me on Amazon for alerts on new releases and visit my website to sign up for my newsletter or inquire about bringing me in for a lecture on The History of the Orphan Trains. www.sherryaburton.com

Thanks for taking this journey with me,

~ Sherry

# About the Author

Sherry A. Burton writes in multiple genres and has won numerous awards for her books. Sherry's awards include the coveted Charles Loring Brace Award, for historical accuracy within her historical fiction series, The Orphan Train Saga. Sherry is a member of the National Orphan Train Society, presents lectures on the history of the orphan trains, and is listed on the NOTC Speaker's Bureau as an approved speaker.

Originally from Kentucky, Sherry and her Retired Navy Husband now call Michigan home. Sherry enjoys traveling and spending time with her husband of more than forty-five years.